ROOM MATE

KATIE ASHLEY

CHAPTER ONE

THERE ARE some days you never expect to ruin your life, days where you want to throw your head back and scream to the sky, "Why?!!" Okay, maybe *ruin* is a little extreme of a description. It wasn't like I was in Scarlett O'Hara, "As God is my witness, I'll never be hungry again" ruination territory. It was way less dramatic than all that, but here's the thing: when you've planned everything to go a certain way and outside forces decide to shoot that perfect plan all to hell, it feels a little desperate.

Another reason the situation seemed so dire was because it seemingly came out of nowhere. For twenty-three years, I'd lived a somewhat uneventful life in Virginia. As the youngest of my family and the only daughter, it was safe to assume I was slightly spoiled. Considering my father was a US senator and former CEO of a Fortune 500 company, I could have been one of those trust-fund twats. But, thankfully, my parents ensured that never happened by instilling a strong sense of values in my siblings and myself.

My upbringing had inevitably influenced me when it came to my major. I'd chosen international relations so I could have a career that helped others not just here, but across the globe. I would be taking over at Read 4 Life, the literacy non-profit my mother had started back when she was a senator's wife. I was leaving for Charleston, West Virginia, on Monday to start my new career.

Before I left, I was slated to attend a wonderful going away dinner with my family at my parents' house, which happened to have one of the most famous addresses in the world—the White House. What I hadn't expected was to have the rug unceremoniously jerked out from under me. I found out every aspect of my life was about to drastically change. My loved ones sat me down for a family meeting, but it wasn't to discuss substance abuse or spending habits; I'm way too straight-laced for all of that.

Nope, it was to inform me that I was about to inherit a roommate—a *male* roommate . . . a six foot four, built like a brick shithouse, swoony British accent-speaking, Chris Hemsworth-looking male roommate.

I can imagine what you're thinking: who in their right mind would protest sharing their apartment with eye candy like that? Seriously, if it were anyone else, I'd be requesting to stay over on a daily basis to fully ogle all that perfection, but it wasn't anyone else. It was me. It was my plans and my life that were getting shit on. It could've been some Shrek-looking dude moving in with me, and the end game would have been the same.

Why?

Apparently, someone I've never met or even laid eyes on is obsessed with me. He only knows me because I'm six degrees of separation famous—my dad is the president of the United States. Instead of going to the beach or taking a trip this summer, he spent his days sending me creepy letters. My psych minor allowed me to know I was using humor to deflect from the crushing fear I was experiencing. *Because this shit was scary.*

But, before I get any more ahead of myself, let me flashback to earlier that day, a time of innocence when I was blissfully unaware of the creeping danger surrounding me, before I became aware of all the gloom and doom, before the sweetness of the apple dumpling served in honor of my soon-to-be new home in West Virginia soured completely.

I'd spent my last day in DC out on the town. I'd done lunch with some friends, gotten my hair and nails done at my favorite salon, and then hit the mall. Now I was fighting gridlock to get back to the White House.

After flicking a nervous gaze at the clock on the dashboard, I cringed. "We're late," my Secret Service agent, Stuart, announced from the passenger seat.

"I'm well aware of that, *Mom*. You've been telling me for the last half hour." I swear, having a Secret Service agent was like having my mother shadowing me twenty-four seven. It was the one thing I truly loathed about Dad being president—that and hearing negative things said about him.

Stuart grumbled something under his breath. He hated when I called him *Mom*. Since he was a six-five, two-hundred-and-fifty-pound hulking man, he didn't appreciate the analogy that he was a nagging mother. He also hated that I insisted on driving myself, but when Dad had been elected president, I'd vowed I wasn't going to let my life change. There were many times when I had to be driven to an event by an agent, but this wasn't one of those times. I felt like your normal twenty-something when I was behind the wheel—well, apart from the extensive sweep of the car before I unlocked the door. Nothing screamed subtle when a man in a dark suit and sunglasses combed your car for devices in the mall parking lot.

Turning to Stuart, I batted my eyelashes. "Don't you have some sort of siren in your briefcase we could use?"

"We're not abusing the office."

"You're such a hard ass, Stuart," I muttered.

After glancing at his phone, he said, "We can save five minutes if you take 17th Street."

Flipping on my blinker, I replied, "I'm on it."

I wasn't completely a stranger to having a family bodyguard. With Dad in the Senate, he often hired people to watch after my mom, brothers, and me while he was away in Washington. It was one thing to have someone assigned to the family, but it was a completely different ball game having someone—or a team of four someones—following your every move.

I'd been finishing up my graduate degree in internal relations at Oxford when Dad received the nomination for president. That's when Stuart and his team were introduced into my life. When Dad had been elected, my team had grown to six agents. Thankfully, they weren't all protecting me at once. Usually, it was just one agent at a time.

Although they never said it, I couldn't imagine protecting me was an exciting job. Sure, they had been able to experience life in jolly old England while occasionally getting to dress in plain clothes to attend a party or have a pint at the pub. Most of the time, though, they were sitting through my lectures or watching me work on schoolwork in the library. Thrilling stuff.

With Stuart's direction help, I finally turned into the White House gates and eased my Range Rover up to the security stand. "Good evening, Caroline," Terrence, the gate attendant, said.

With a smile, I replied, "Good evening, Terrence. How are you doing today?"

"Good, thanks. You?"

"I'm just fine. Thank you."

Terrence smiled. "We're going to miss you around here when you leave on Monday."

"Thanks. I'm going to miss you guys, too."

"You be sure to take good care of yourself."

"I will. Same to you."

Once Terrence waved us through the gate, I drove along the pathway over to the VIP entrance. That's where the family, along with VIP guests like foreign dignitaries, entered the White House. After I parked, I reached over for my purse and then tossed my key fob inside.

Stuart was already out of the car and around to my side before I could even open the door. Even though I was fully capable of doing it myself, he insisted he help me enter and exit the car every time we went somewhere. I was sure in his mind he envisioned some masked marauder grabbing me if he wasn't there to stop it.

After opening the Rover's hatch, I started weighing down my arms with bags.

"Would you please let me help you?" he asked exasperatedly.

"I've got it."

"You make me look bad."

"Stuart, while it might be your job to open doors for me and escort me to and from the car, it's not your job to carry my shit."

"While that's true, it is my job to ensure you don't face-plant on the marble floor before you get to the elevator."

Before I could argue with him that I wasn't that klutzy, he dipped his head and pressed his finger to his earpiece. "The family just headed into the dining room."

Shit. I really was late if everyone was already going into the dining room. "Just let me drop this off in my room then I'll be there."

He gave me a pointed look. "Or you could let me take them and you go on and meet your father."

Since it was fruitless to argue, I sighed. "Fine."

After handing over the mountain of bags, I chose to use the stairs so he could have the elevator. "Don't be snooping in my things," I called to him over my shoulder.

"I'll try hard not to."

"You know you secretly covet my shoe collection."

"Oh yes, the high heels are to die for."

I laughed as I bounded up the carpeted stairs. The last thing Stuart would ever do would be to pilfer through my underwear drawer or snoop in my closet. I knew without a doubt he would unceremoniously drop the shopping bags in the middle of the floor and then hightail it out of the room while grumbling about me being a shopaholic.

Normally, I wasn't a big shopper, but I was starting my first real adult career. In my understanding, when one starts a new career, a wardrobe is vitally important. Of course, I hadn't purchased the usual power suits since I wasn't going into the corporate world. While I might've purchased two or three nice dresses, I wanted to look approachable to my clients, which were going to be school-aged kids.

As I walked down the carpeted halls of the residence, I couldn't help feeling a pang of sadness at leaving. Since I'd spent the summer there, I'd grown to love every facet of the house. I loved peeking over the railings at the families on the guided tours as they came through. I'd spent days perusing the shelves of the library and eyeing the intricate patterns of the china in the China Room.

Call me spoiled, but one of my favorite parts was having a cook. There was something to be said for someone who prepared meals to my liking versus what I would have found in the dining hall back at Oxford. Of course, I'd felt slightly guilty that my agents had been subjected to the dining hall meals as well. I was sure they were glad to be back stateside for that reason as well.

Most of all, I was going to miss being with my parents. Even though they were both extremely busy in their own different ways, we still somehow managed to sit down to breakfast or dinner at least a few times a week. After being away from home for the last year, I'd forgotten how wonderful it was spending time with them. I'd certainly lucked out in the parent department.

When I entered the dining room, I found everyone milling around the bar, snacking on some hors d'oeuvres. Although we were eating in the formal family dining room, everyone was dressed casually. For Dad that meant a button-down shirt without a jacket and tie, while for Mom it meant ditching her usual pantsuits and skirts for a sundress.

I held up my hands. "I'm so sorry, guys. Traffic was insane today," I apologized.

"Are we using the traffic excuse again?" Dad mused with a grin.

"It's not an excuse if it's the truth," I countered.

With a wink, he said, "Perhaps it was more like you got caught up shopping and forgot the time."

I rolled my eyes. "Yet another reason why having a Secret Service agent sucks. They're always ratting me out."

A funny look flashed on Dad's face before he quickly turned back to the overflowing plate of stuffed mushrooms. "You better get over here before we eat all your favorites."

Mom set her wineglass down. "Don't worry, sweetheart. We never really expect you to be on time. You've been late since before you were born."

"Not that story again," I groaned.

She grinned as she hugged me. "Just wait until you're two weeks overdue. Then you'll appreciate me telling those stories."

My gaze bobbed from hers over to my older brothers, Thorn and Barrett. "Thanks for coming to see me off, guys."

"I wouldn't have missed it for the world, little sis," Thorn replied before drawing me into his arms for a bear hug. He'd always been the most amazing older brother. While he'd partaken in the usual teasing and torture all older siblings do, he'd also nurtured and cajoled me. With our blond hair and blue eyes, we took after our mother as well as looking the most alike.

Squeezing him tight, I remembered how close I'd come to losing him a year ago. After his convoy had been hit in Afghanistan, he'd been wounded and flown out to Landstuhl hospital in Germany. The moment I got the news, I left class. I'd walked aimlessly around the streets of Oxford while I waited for the necessary travel arrangements to be made so I could see him. I didn't feel like myself again until I was able to wrap my arms around him. It was like I couldn't process the fact that he was actually okay until I saw and touched him.

While I had been briefed on the extent of his physical injuries, what I hadn't been prepared for was the lifelessness in his eyes. I'd never expected such agony in his gaze. My heart had ached for such a long time, and it wasn't until he met his girl that life came back into his expression. Love looked very good on Thorn.

After Dad had been elected, Thorn had been forced to leave the Army and his men because of being a target to the enemy. He now lived in New York and worked for the corporation my great-grandfather had started. It was there he had met his fiancée, Isabel.

Once Thorn released me, I kissed his cheek and then moved to hug Isabel. As the newest member of the family, she remained somewhat skittish around us. Actually, it was more that she was skittish around the White House as well as the press. Unlike my siblings, she wasn't used to the cameras and attention that came with being a Callahan. As a ball-busting career woman, it was unusual seeing her unraveled. She also worked at the Callahan Corporation with Thorn.

After hugging her, I turned to my brother, Barrett. With an impish grin burning in his blue eyes, he said, "I have just one thing to say to you."

"Uh-oh," I mused. While Thorn was my straight-and-narrow brother, Barrett was the life of the party. I never knew what to expect from him.

With a wink at Addison, the two started singing. "*Country roads, take me home, to the place, I belong—*"

"Seriously? You're serenading me with John Denver?" I asked.

"*West Virginia, mountain Mama! Take me home, country roads,*" they finished.

I couldn't help applauding my goofball of a brother. "Very nice. I'm sure I'll have it stuck in my head the rest of the night, if not the whole weekend."

"At least you'll be thinking about us," Barrett said as he opened his arms to hug me.

"Of course I will be." I pulled back to grin at him. "I'll be thinking about how I'd like to secretly choke you for getting that song in my head." Turning to Isabel, I winked. "I'll also be grateful that at least one of you has professional singing training."

While Barrett and Addison laughed, Dad held up a hand. "Hey now, don't be knocking the Denver," he protested. It was because of him that I'd heard the song to start with. He was a connoisseur of oldies music. From the time we were kids, he always had Motown or the Beatles blaring in the car.

"Whatever, Dad," I mused.

It was then I noticed Ty Fraser, Thorn's Secret Service agent, was also among the group. Since Ty didn't warrant a hug, I extended a hand to him. "Uh, hello. It's nice seeing you again."

He smiled. "Thank you."

Although the etiquette I'd been taught told me not to question him personally on what he was doing at our family going away dinner, I couldn't help throwing a *WTF* look at my mother. After all, I'd been instructed it was *just family*, and that I shouldn't include my boyfriend, Perry. Instead, he'd been invited to brunch on Sunday. At the time, I hadn't stopped to argue why, but that was before Ty was about to sit down with the family.

When she gave me a pointed look, I didn't press it. I hoped it wasn't because Thorn was struggling with PTSD again and needed Ty's presence. I would *never* deny him that. Even with Isabel, he wasn't back to the Thorn I'd known as a kid.

Waving her hand, Mom instructed, "Come on, let's eat."

I took a seat next to her at the gigantic table. While it was half the size of the mammoth one in the state dining room, it was still insane.

"Tonight, I asked the chef to prepare delicacies of Appalachia in honor of your new home," Mom said with a smile.

"Oh goody. Bring on the coon and possum?" Barrett teased.

With a roll of my eyes, I replied, "Way to stereotype an entire group of people, B, especially one that lives next door to where we grew up."

"We actually had some coon when we were on the campaign trail, didn't we, dear?" Dad said.

Mom wrinkled her nose. "Yes, we did."

"Does it taste like chicken?" Barrett inquired.

"Not exactly."

While we didn't have any coon or possum, we did have chicken and dumplings and a plethora of vegetables, which were mostly fried. I had the feeling if I didn't watch myself with the fattening cuisine, I would end up looking like the Stay Puft Marshmallow man. Of course, those fears didn't stop me from partaking in the apple dumplings and ice cream.

As the dessert dishes were being cleared, Mom somewhat abruptly rose out of her seat. After throwing a nervous glance at my father, she cleared her throat. "Addison and Isabel, could you two please come on up to the residence with me? I'd like your input on the official White House Christmas ornament."

"Of course," Isabel replied while Addison nodded.

"Want me to come take a look too?" I asked.

Mom fidgeted with the sleeve on her pantsuit. "That's okay. I think there's something your father wants to talk to you about."

I expected Barrett, Thorn, and Ty to rise out of their chairs and head on up to the residence as well, but they remained seated. Once the last of the dining room staff had left, the air in the room grew tense, and I regretted eating all of my apple dumplings. "So, what is it you wanted to talk to me about?"

A pained expression came over Dad's face, which only caused my anxiety to spike. Hundreds of gloom-and-doom scenarios ran through my mind as I waited for him to speak. After pushing his chair back from the table, he drew in a labored breath.

"When I entered politics, I knew there was a chance my family could become targets. After becoming president, I knew the threat would only intensify." He gave me a pointed look. "Unfortunately, it has landed on you."

"It has?" Shaking my head in confusion, I asked, "But how?"

"For most of the summer, you've been receiving threatening letters."

"You must be mistaken. The only threatening letters I've ever received have been credit card bills."

"This is serious, Caroline."

I held up my hands. "I'm sorry, but I was just stating facts. You say I've been receiving letters, yet I haven't seen any."

Ty spoke up from across the table. "Stuart and your team have been going through your mail."

My eyes bulged. "Excuse me?"

"It's all part of the security process. It ensures you don't open any bombs or chemical envelopes," he answered.

I turned to Dad. "Is that true?"

"Yes, it is."

"But that's an invasion of my privacy."

"It's a necessary evil to keep you safe."

I shifted in my chair and tried processing the news. It made perfect sense that people went through my mail. I could understand that cerebrally, but someone was threatening me? *Me?* I'm not anyone significant in this family . . . *Shit.* "What do the notes say?"

Dad's expression paled slightly. "The specific content is irrelevant. However, it is very evident this person wishes you physical harm."

Swallowing down the lump in my throat, I took in the very serious face of my father. He wasn't supposed to look scared, not my father. "They want . . . want me . . . dead?"

"Yes."

A shudder rippled through me. While I was no stranger to bullying, I certainly had never had anyone threaten my life. Over the years, I'd grown accustomed to the hate speech of political life, especially when Dad ran for president. People seemed to love nothing more than to hurl insults. Usually, they said bad things about him, but they also occasionally turned their venom on me.

"It's not just someone playing around?" I questioned softly.

Dad shook his head. "We have reason to believe whoever is behind the letters is very serious."

My mind whirled with out-of-control thoughts. Having minored in psychology, I couldn't help focusing in on Dad's last statement. There had to be something truly heinous within the letters for them to be taking them so seriously. Statistically, it made more sense for the person to be male. "Are they romantic in nature?" I whispered.

Agony overcame Dad's face. "Yes. It appears in the man's mind, you have rejected him and his overtures. He wants you punished."

Another shudder went through me, and I gripped the arms on the chair to steady me as I felt like I was coming apart. Even though I was in the safest and most secure residence in the country, a feeling of absolute vulnerability came over me like I'd been exposed down to the bone.

"I know this is a lot to process," Dad interrupted the silence.

"You can say that again."

Dad reached out to squeeze my hand. "You don't have to be afraid, CC. I'm ensuring the best form of protection possible for you."

When I glanced up at Thorn and Barrett, I found their expressions were surprisingly calm. In fact, they didn't appear shocked or outraged by the news of the letters. Then it hit me like a ton of bricks. "Wait a minute—you two knew about this, didn't you?" When they bobbed their heads, anger replaced the fear within me. It was apparent Mom had used the White House ornament ruse as a way to get Addison and

Isabel out of the room. I had been reduced to being a little girl again. "I can't believe this."

"Come on, CC. It's nothing to get pissed about," Barrett said.

"How can you expect me not to be angry? Everyone I love has been going behind my back and affecting my life, yet no one thought I needed to be made aware until tonight."

"I didn't want to tell you until it was absolutely necessary," Dad argued.

I jabbed my finger at my brothers. "But you could tell them?"

"I sought their counsel, and it also affected them. Well, it affected Thorn since he would be losing his agent."

Furrowing my brows, I glanced from Dad over to Ty. His expression told me everything I needed to know. "You're going to be my agent?"

"Yes, and more."

"I don't understand."

Dad placed a hand on my shoulder. "We think it's in the best interest for your safety to have an agent with you at all times."

"How is that any different than what I have now?"

"There are too many scenarios that could occur when an agent is next door or across the hall. To ensure absolute security, we want an agent living with you." Dad nodded at Ty. "More specifically, I want Ty to live with you."

As wild thoughts whirled though my head, it felt like my mind might short-circuit at any moment. Ty was moving in with me. Surely I was experiencing a horrific nightmare or had stumbled into some alternate universe. How else could I explain the insanity transpiring before me?

"Ty is going to live with me in West Virginia?"

"Yes. He'll be going with you on Monday. The rest of your team will stay the same with their living quarters next door."

It was then that it hit me: I already had a roommate, my best friend, Selah, who I'd met in undergrad. Not only was she a friend, she was working as my right-hand woman AKA assistant at the foundation.

I held up my pointer finger. "Slight problem with your genius plan."

"And what would that be?" Dad questioned.

"I already have a roommate." I narrowed my eyes at Ty. "Are you planning on sleeping on the couch for the next few months?"

"No. I'll be taking the spare bedroom."

"That's Selah's room," I countered.

Dad stepped between Ty and me. "We've obtained another apartment for her in the same building." When I opened my mouth to argue that unlike us, Selah didn't have the money for her own apartment, Dad said, "We've covered her rent for the year for the inconvenience."

"How kind."

"Caroline, please," Dad said exasperatedly.

"Fine. It was nice of you to cover Selah's rent, but I'm sure she'll want to pay you back. She's just that kind of person."

"If she wishes to do that, we'll be happy to accept," Dad replied in a diplomatic tone.

"Apparently, you've thought of everything. Tell me, how does Perry factor into all this?"

"It isn't up to him," Thorn muttered.

I widened my eyes. "You can't be serious."

Thorn crossed his arms over his chest. "He's not a member of this family, CC. He doesn't get a say."

"But he's my boyfriend, and we're in a committed relationship. I think he has a say about whether he likes the fact that I'm living with a strange man."

"Considering he's met Ty numerous times, I'd hardly call him a stranger," Dad countered.

"He's basically a stranger to both of us." I knew Perry was going to go through the roof when I told him. He was already upset I'd taken a job in West Virginia. He'd not only wanted me to take a position closer to DC, he'd wanted us to move in together. Now I was going to be living in another state with another man.

"I think it's safe to say he's not going to be a big fan of the scenario."

"He should be grateful your life is being protected."

"I'm sure he will appreciate how thoroughly I'm being protected, but it doesn't mean he has to like the fact that some man is living with me—not to mention it's not some middle-aged father figure like the rest of the men on my team." I motioned wildly at Ty. "What single guy in their right mind would want their girlfriend living with someone who looks like he does?"

Regret instantly filled me at referencing Ty's good looks, and my embarrassment had my brothers chuckling. Thankfully, Dad had the good sense to remain straight-faced, though knowing him, he was probably laughing inwardly.

After clearing his throat, Ty stepped forward. "While I appreciate the compliment, I can assure both you and Perry that your safety will be my *only* concern."

"But can't you at least see what I'm saying?"

"Any man who isn't insecure in his relationship shouldn't be worried."

I gasped. "There is *nothing* wrong with our relationship."

"I didn't say there was."

"You alluded to it, which is just as bad." I turned to Barrett and Thorn. "Would you two have wanted Ty living alone with Addison or Isabel?"

"Come on, CC," Barrett replied.

"It's a reasonable question."

"But it's not the same playing field. Ty was my friend and body-guard long before I met Addison. Considering I can trust him with my life, there'd be no question I could trust him with my girlfriend."

Thorn nodded. "I would agree."

I shook my head as I processed their responses. "You're right, it's not the same thing, but I really wish you could try to put yourself in Perry's shoes for a minute." I stared pointedly at Thorn. "Even if you don't like him."

He held up his hands. "I didn't say anything."

"You don't have to."

Thorn sighed. "Bottom line is I just need to know you're safe, CC. That's why we ask Ty."

As an emotional shit-storm rained down on me, I hated myself for fighting the urge to cry. I was a grown-ass woman who had lived on her own on another continent, for goodness' sake. If I could handle that, I could handle anything, right? Even the prospect of some psycho stalker wanting to kill me.

Okay, maybe not.

With the walls of the dining room closing in on me, I had to get out of there. I couldn't stand being in the same room as the overbearing male members of my family. I had to get out before I lost it and started screaming or crying hysterically.

I slid my chair back. "If you'll excuse me, I think I've had enough of this conversation for tonight." Rising out of my chair, I quickly moved away from the table. I didn't want to give Dad or my brothers any time to object.

After I sprinted out of the dining room, I didn't want to go upstairs to the residence yet. I couldn't face Mom or the others. More than anything, I needed fresh air. So, I scurried across the hallway and over to the door leading out to the South Portico. The agent guarding the door didn't say anything to me as I slipped outside.

Leaning against the rail, I stared up into the sky encrusted with twinkling stars. It was a beautiful night that certainly didn't match my current mood.

"May I join you?" a voice questioned behind me.

I didn't have to turn around to know it was Ty. There was no privacy in the White House. I was sure he'd been alerted I was outside by the agent stationed at the door.

Whirling around, I spread my hands wide. "Sure. I mean, it's a free country—unless you have a psycho stalker," I mumbled. Part of me hated how childish I was acting. In the vast scheme of things, I should've been grateful he was willing to put his life on the line for me to the extent of cohabitating. Furthermore, I should have been grateful Thorn was at a place where he felt emotional stable enough to be okay without Ty. He hadn't been exaggerating about how much he trusted the man in front of me. Jesus, I had to get myself together. But man, I felt so . . . derailed. Worst of all, I felt controlled.

"I'm sorry for what I said about you and Perry."

I jerked my gaze over to him. Upon seeing the sincerity in his eyes, I nodded. "Thank you."

Silence blanketed the portico. The only sounds were of the bustling city in the distance, the honking of horns and the whooshing of public transit.

Finally, Ty broke the silence. "Come on now, you're starting to give me a complex." When I swiveled my gaze to stare at him, he smiled. "Am I really that bad?"

"It's not you. I would loathe and despise the idea regardless of who the agent was."

"That's understandable. Truth be told, I wasn't thrilled at the prospect myself."

"You weren't?"

Ty shook his head. "I've never been a fan of change. I think it's one reason the Army appealed to me. I like the discipline and routine. I've fallen into a familiar rhythm with Thorn."

"I don't doubt that considering how Type A Thorn is."

With a chuckle, Ty replied, "I suppose he is, but I like my life with him. After the bright lights of New York, West Virginia is a hell of a demotion."

"I agree." With a sigh, I added, "While it's going to be a change for me from Oxford and DC, I willingly made the choice." I shook my head at him. "But you didn't."

"No. I made my choice." At what must've been my look of surprise, he said, "I could have stood my ground and told your father no because of one reason or another, but in the end, it was about more than just my personal comfort." An intense look came over his face. "It was about your safety."

I merely nodded in reply. I was too overwhelmed by his words and the situation I currently found myself in. It isn't every day you have a man willing to put his life on hold to protect you from a viable threat. It also showed me how highly he regarded our family. My safety meant something to him. It was somewhat humbling, if I was honest, yet right then, I would still have gladly traded lives with anyone else to just have my old life back.

I rubbed my shoulders against the growing chill I was experiencing. "Can I ask one thing of you? Well, you know, besides keeping me alive."

He eyed me warily. "I suppose."

"Will you always be completely honest and transparent with me about the stalker? I know Dad is sparing me from the details because he thinks he's protecting me, but in reality, he's not. I need to know just how severe the situation is."

Once again, I was overwhelmed with the intensity of Ty's stare. I knew he was reading my emotions to try to gauge if I was being truthful or bullshitting him. "Ignorance can be bliss," he argued.

With a shake of my head, I replied, "Not when it's my life at stake."

Ty released his grip on the railing to move closer to me. "Your father and brothers will have my ass if they find out I told you this."

"Trust me, after they've been going behind my back, they're the *last* people I would tell."

He threw a tentative glance over his shoulder before zeroing his gaze in on mine. "He sent in a clipping of your hair."

Oh. God. My hand flew to my mouth to catch the rising vomit. He had been so close to me. He'd touched my hair.

In that moment, it couldn't have been plainer to me how sometimes it was one thing to say something and then it was a completely different thing to actually mean it. I realized I'd been terribly wrong about wanting to know the specific details. Receiving threatening letters was a thousand times more benign than being physically assaulted.

"I knew I shouldn't have told you," Ty muttered regretfully through gritted teeth.

Closing my eyes, I took a few deep breaths to fight against my body's physical reaction. After a few moments passed and the nausea subsided, I stared up at Ty. "He was able to get close enough to cut my hair?" I questioned breathlessly.

When Ty nodded, I swallowed hard. Now I got it. Now I knew why my father had instigated such a severe setup as Ty moving in with me. If the man could get that close to me in a crowd with my agents around, what else could he do? It wasn't too far-fetched to imagine him breaking into my apartment and . . .

I shuddered. "No. You were right to tell me."

"Bullshit. Your face is the same fucking color as the marble pillars."

"Well, duh. You just told me some freak cut my hair and sent it to me in the mail. It'd be completely understandable if I was running around the portico screaming my head off." I stared at him pointedly. "But I'm not. I'm keeping my shit together."

A look of respectful awe flashed in Ty's eyes. "Your ability to compartmentalize your emotions does you credit."

"Thank you, but don't get too crazy with the praise. I'm a nutcase on the inside, but in a way, I need that."

Ty creased his brows. "Why do you say that?"

"If you hadn't told me about the hair, I still wouldn't be taking the threat seriously. I would probably have pulled some immature and potentially dangerous shit like trying to ditch you to do my own things." With a nod, I added, "You did the right thing."

Ty seemed to appreciate my words. A shadow of a smile played on his lips. "You know, you're already leagues above Thorn."

"I am?"

"When I first started as his agent, he tried to ditch me all the time."

I widened my eyes at the thought of straight-laced Thorn being a rule-breaker. "He did?"

"Oh yeah, but just like I will with you, I learned how to outsmart him."

"You seem awfully sure of yourself."

He nodded. "I am, and for good reason. It's part of what they teach us. We always have to be one step ahead of any perpetrator, so in turn, we need to be one step ahead of our targets."

"That makes sense."

We momentarily fell into silence. As we both stared out onto the lawn, I supposed we were both lost in our own thoughts about our changing futures. I knew I was.

After a few moments passed, Ty turned to me, his jaw set and his body rigid. "You don't have to be afraid, Caroline. As long as I have a breath within me, I won't let that fucker lay one hand on you, least of all hurt you."

Tears stung my eyes at both his words and the determination on Ty's face. I still loathed and despised the idea of him living with me. I already felt suffocated by his protection, and we had yet to even begin, but in the end, I knew it was a necessary evil, one that would ensure my utmost safety until my stalker could be found and brought to justice.

"Saying thank you seems entirely too little for the sacrifice you're making, but I am thankful." A small smile played on my lips. "Even if I won't always act that way."

Ty laughed. "You're welcome. And hey, if you think it'll help matters with Perry, you can tell him I have a girlfriend."

My stomach twisted slightly at his proclamation. In my mind, I tried picturing what she looked like. She was probably some willowy model who woke up without morning breath or bedhead. "I didn't know you were dating someone," I casually replied.

He shook his head. "I'm not."

When relief surged within me, I couldn't help feeling surprised at the emotion. I shouldn't have cared at all if Ty had a girlfriend. "Then why would I tell him you did?"

"To make him fell less threatened about having me in the house with you."

I wrinkled my nose at his suggestion. "I don't think I could lie to him."

Ty shrugged. "It's not exactly lying. It's just stretching the truth for the better good of someone you love."

"Although it would probably help, I don't feel comfortable"—I made air quotes—"stretching the truth. I always like shooting straight."

"I understand. I was just offering."

"Thanks. I appreciate it."

"You think we should go inside and put them out of their misery?" he suggested.

"What do you mean?"

"Your dad and brothers. Apparently, they're wearing out the antique rugs in the dining room, as well as draining scotch.

I laughed at the visual that came to mind. "We could let them suffer a little longer."

He gave me a low whistle. "Man, you're cold."

"Oh, just wait," I mused before turning to go back inside.

CHAPTER TWO

A STEADY RAIN drummed against my umbrella with the presidential seal as I bounded up the stairs of the Callahan jet. The dismal weather did little to lift the bleakness of my mood. Inwardly, I told myself to stop being such a pussy. After all, from the time I was eighteen and joined the British Army, I'd fulfilled the orders given to me without argument or complaint. This was just another order, but this time, it had come from the highest level in the chain of command, the Commander in Chief himself, President James Callahan.

After shaking out the umbrella, I deposited it in the closet before heading to find a seat. Over the last few years as a bodyguard, I'd grown accustomed to flying on private jets. In the four years I'd been working for the Callahan family, I'd grown especially accustomed to this particular jet. It certainly was a different world for a kid from the East End of London. I'd never even been on a commercial airliner until I joined the Army.

As I started down the aisle, I sought out my target. Caroline had been ushered from the car to the jet while I ensured all the luggage made it on board. It wasn't just the First Daughter who was embarking on a new life in West Virginia; I was moving there as well. Unlike the other members of Caroline's protection team, I wouldn't be shuttling back and forth to DC on my off days. For the foreseeable future, I would be a native of Charleston.

With her blonde hair swept back into a ponytail, Caroline stared out the window, expressionless. The open book on her lap went unread. Focusing on her emotional grid, I noted the sadness of leaving DC and her parents. At the same time, there was excitement bubbling beneath the surface. Those were the two emotions she allowed herself to experience. If I dug deeper, I could make out the murky fear she was so desperately trying to bury.

It was understandable that she would be scared shitless. A psychopath's obsession was so severe he wanted to end her life, not to mention her life had been upended in the pursuit of protection. However, I could see Thorn in her, in her quiet, determined strength. She was possibly wise beyond her years.

I took the seat in the aisle across from her. Behind me, Issacson had his head buried in a mound of paperwork. I didn't have to ask him to brief me on anything; I'd gone through all the documents backward and forward. I knew the layout of the apartment we'd be living in along with all the entrances and exits. I knew it took approximately ten minutes to get from the apartment to Caroline's new job. Depending on traffic, it could be less or more. I'd read the FBI files on each and every one of the residents of the apartment building where we'd be living. Not only had I done the groundwork from DC, I'd flown out last week to canvas the neighborhood. When I was assigned a target, I didn't leave any stone unturned.

I'd spent the last year with Thorn Callahan, Caroline's older brother. As a fellow military man, his personality type wasn't entirely unknown to me. I'd easily fallen into a precise rhythm with him in the corporate world of New York City. Even him becoming engaged to a co-worker, Isabel, did little to disrupt things. Before becoming Thorn's lead Secret Service agent, I'd spent three years with his brother, Barrett. Before I'd experienced the frantic pace of life on the campaign trail with him, we'd spent our time in New York City along with some of the most exotic vacation spots in the world. It had been a hell of a gig.

With Caroline, I was entering completely new territory. I'd never served as a bodyguard or lead agent for a female before. Although I had yet to try, I couldn't imagine getting into Caroline's mindset the way I could with her brothers. It wasn't just the fact that she was a woman or that she was seven years younger than me. From the observations from her family along with what I'd read about her, Caroline was a strong and resilient twenty-first century woman who was bound and determined to change the world for the better.

Basically, she was an enigma to me.

Sure, I was the son of a strong-willed working mother, and I'd dated my fair share of ball-busting career women, but there was something very different about Caroline. I just couldn't quite put my finger on it.

As the jet took off, I couldn't help thinking about the night I'd learned my life was about to change. It felt like a lifetime ago.

Two weeks earlier

As Roy Orbison's *Pretty Woman* echoed through the East Room, President Callahan twirled the first lady around the dance floor. It was certainly a change from the classical music the Marine Corp band had been playing, but it was President Callahan's birthday. Since he was a huge fan of the oldies, he had insisted on a change of tunes. When you're the leader of the free world, you pretty much get your way on those things.

Although I was at the White House as a guest and not in an official capacity, it was damn near impossible to unwind. Something about being on the sacred ground made me unable to completely let my guard down. Maybe it was also the fact that I wasn't a huge fan of crowds. I was much more at ease when shadowing my target in quieter situations.

After sidling up to the bar, I requested a scotch. While I was waiting for the bartender to oblige me, a tingle worked its way down my scalp to the base of my neck. The prickling was my body's way of alerting me my target was nearby.

I didn't even have to turn around to know Thorn Callahan, the president's oldest son, was coming in for a refill. "Two white wine spritzers," he requested.

I cut my eyes over to him. "What kind of pussy drinks a white wine spritzer?" I teased.

Thorn chuckled. "Fuck off. They're for Isabel and Addison."

"Ah, yes, the Callahan men's balls and chains."

"Easy now. Isabel and I haven't tied the knot."

"*Yet.*" I winked at him. "But you will."

With a grin, Thorn said, "And then it'll be your turn." I nearly spat my drink right into Thorn's face. *Fuck, I can't even relax here, in what is theoretically the safest room on the planet, let alone consider finding a missus.* Not in this job, anyway.

"I seriously doubt that." After taking the scotch from the bartender, I pointed the glass at Thorn's sister, Caroline, dancing with her boyfriend, Perry. "I think someone else will beat me to it."

Thorn grimaced. "Bite your fucking tongue." His eyes narrowed on Caroline and Perry as he muttered, "I hate that wanker."

I snorted a laugh. "Since when do you say 'wanker'?"

"Since I've had you on my ass twenty-four seven."

"You just wish you were a Cockney boy."

Smirking, Thorn replied, "Dream on."

After leaning back against the bar, I eyed Caroline and Perry again. "So, what makes ol' Perry a wanker?" Considering I'd barely interacted with the guy, I had very little to go on. Sure, he had one of those swaggers that usually meant a mate wasn't totally carrying in the manhood department. While I would never admit it to Thorn, he reminded me of a wankier version of Scott Disick. Mainly, I didn't want to admit it because I didn't want him to know I watched the Kardashians.

"Everything," Thorn replied.

"While he has some issues, is it really about him, or is it more the fact that in your eyes, no one would be good enough for your little sister?"

Thorn responded by snatching my scotch away and downing a long sip. He then shoved the glass back at me. "First off, CC is leagues above him, not to mention he's everything vile and loathsome about trust-fund kids."

"Wait, aren't you a trust-fund kid?" I teased.

He scowled at me. "Yes, smartass, I was born with a trust fund. However, my parents ensured we were never treated like special snowflakes. They made us actually work and earn things. We never had a silver spoon in our mouths. Perry, on the other hand, is the worst kind of spoiled twat."

I gave Thorn a reassuring pat on the back. "I know, mate. I was only giving you a hard time. You and I both know I wouldn't put my ass on the line if you acted like privileged wankers." And that was the truth. I'd never been a sellout who could place themselves in harm's way for the almighty dollar—or pound when I was back home. One thing the Callahan men had in common was strong values along with a killer work ethic. Even though I didn't know Caroline as well, I was certain the same could be said for her.

At the sound of a throat clearing behind us, Thorn and I turned around. It was President Callahan's lead agent, Henry Darby. "Your father wishes to see you in the Oval Office."

"Uh-oh, sounds like somebody's in trouble," I mused into the mouth of my scotch glass.

Darby's gaze swiveled from Thorn over to me. "He's requested your presence as well."

I jerked my lips away from the amber liquid. "He has?"

Darby's response came in the form of curt nod. *I've got a bad feeling about this.* The *Star Wars* fan in me couldn't help but flash the classic Han Solo line in my mind. "Yes, sir," I replied. After quickly depositing my scotch glass on the bar, I looked at Thorn. "I guess we better get going."

Thorn held up his hands, which were now filled with the wine spritzers. "Give me two seconds to deliver these."

"Meet you outside."

As Thorn disappeared into the crowd, I made my way out of the East Room. I stood outside in the Center Hall and waited on him. When he appeared a few minutes later, his facial features were darkened with worry. I couldn't blame him since I was experiencing the same emotions.

We hurried along the West Colonnade walkway in silence. Occasionally I would bob my head at one of the agents stationed at the different posts. Normally, there weren't so many agents working the evening shift, but social events, like the president's birthday party, understandably called for more men.

When we entered the Oval Office, President Callahan was already inside. The jovial expression he'd worn earlier in the evening was gone. He appeared grim, like he was about to address the nation about some sort of tragedy. "I'm sorry to tear you two away from the festivities, but this matter can't wait."

Thorn shook his head. "I don't think it's us you need to be concerned about. Don't you think you're going to be missed at your own birthday party?"

"Your mother is making the necessary apologies for my unscheduled absence. Hopefully, as long as the drinks keep flowing and the band keeps playing, no one will really miss me."

With a champagne flute still in his hand, Barrett strode into the room. I couldn't help thinking the plot had just thickened with his appearance since the meeting wasn't only about Thorn and me. Using his free hand, Barrett began loosening the tie on his tux. "Okay, what is so hellfire important that you dragged us all the way to the West Wing to say it?" he demanded, echoing the sentiment running through my mind.

President Callahan leaned back against the Resolute desk. He appeared to be having a hard time finding the right words.

After the seconds ticked by, Barrett let out an exasperated sigh. "Jesus, Dad, don't hold us in suspense."

Thorn nodded. "What are we looking at? ISIS, North Korea?"

"No. This is more of a domestic issue." He glanced between his sons. "A *family* issue."

While Barrett and Thorn appeared momentarily relieved we weren't on the cusp of World War III—which, in hindsight, was highly unlikely given it was us in the room, not the Cabinet—their bodies remained tense. Considering how close I was to them, I knew the wheels in their mind were spinning wild theories. At the same time, I was having a hard time getting my own thoughts under control. I tried to imagine what family issue could possibly warrant a meeting at a time like this.

Narrowing his eyes at Barrett, Thorn questioned, "What exactly have you done this time, B?"

Barrett's mouth gaped open. "Me? Why do you automatically assume a family issue has to do with me?"

Thorn shrugged. "Perhaps it's because you're usually the one in hot water."

Jabbing a finger in his brother's shoulder, Barrett replied, "While that might have been true two years ago, I'm a married man now and living a G-rated life." His expression momentarily lightened. "Well, G-rated in public."

"Spare me," Thorn muttered.

President Callahan cleared his throat. "Oh, for fuck's sake. It's not about either of you two egomaniacs."

"It's not?" Barrett asked.

"No."

Thorn groaned. "Please tell me Perry didn't ask you if he could marry Caroline."

"No, he didn't, but the news is about Caroline."

"And?" Barrett prompted, his brows lined in concern.

"Earlier this morning, Issacson briefed me about an ongoing situation involving your sister."

A jolt went through me at the mention of Stuart Issacson, the lead agent on Caroline's team. There was only one reason he would be briefing the president, and it sure as hell wasn't a good one.

"What's going on?" Thorn questioned, his worried gaze bouncing over to me. When I gave a quick shake of my head to convey that I wasn't in the loop, he turned his gaze to his father.

"A few weeks ago, Stuart made me aware that after she returned from England, Caroline was receiving threatening letters. At first, they weren't anything out of the ordinary realm, but then this afternoon, he received this."

Turning around, President Callahan retrieved an envelope off the desk. After delving inside, he held up what appeared to be a lock of hair. "Holy shit," I muttered as I got a better look at the blonde strands.

"The lab confirmed it's Caroline's," President Callahan added.

"How the fuck was some sicko able to get that close to her?" Barrett demanded.

"His letter states he passed her in a crowd."

"Obviously, she needs a new service detail," Thorn stated.

Barrett nodded. "She sure as hell does."

President Callahan shook his head. "I wish it were that simple. Issacson and his men are some of most well-trained in the agency. She's truly been in the best hands."

"What about hiring from a private agency to supplement what the Secret Service is doing?" Thorn suggested.

"A logistical fucking nightmare," I muttered. With the stares of all the Callahan men on me, I ducked my head. "Just my opinion."

"Why do you say that?" President Callahan asked curiously.

"Because of protocol. It would be a constant question of who is on lead protection. It's damn near impossible to have two alpha teams when you're talking about security."

"But you and the agents managed just fine when you were protecting me during the campaign," Barrett countered.

"That's because it was *just* the campaign. You were just a candidate's son—not the *president's*. There also weren't any threats against you." Crossing my arms over my chest, I added, "As soon as your father got the nomination, I always deferred to the Secret Service when it came to your protection."

"It still worked," Barrett muttered.

"Maybe it worked because of *your* abilities, Ty," President

Callahan said. Pushing off the desk, he crossed the room to me. "There's a reason I asked you here along with my sons."

"I assumed you wanted to get my opinion as an agent."

President Callahan shook his head. "No. I wanted to ask you to protect my daughter."

I blinked in disbelief. "I'm sorry, sir, but what did you say?"

"I want you to become the lead of Caroline's team, and more importantly, I want you with her at all times. I even want you to cohabitate with her."

Insanity.

That was the only word to describe it. His request was pure and simple insanity. Becoming the lead on Caroline's team was preposterous in itself, but live with her? Obviously, the stress of worrying about his daughter's welfare had temporarily made President Callahan unable to process proper thoughts or make sound decisions. Why else would he possibly be making such a suggestion?

I drew in a calming breath to temper my response. "With all due respect, sir, you can't be serious," I choked out.

"I've never been more serious or more certain of a decision."

"Mr. President, I implore you to reconsider what you're asking of me. Perhaps consult with your advisors on a better course of action."

President Callahan's gaze narrowed into a steely glare. "I don't need to call a meeting of my cabinet. I'm fully capable of making decisions about the welfare of my family. After speaking with the other Secret Service team leaders, we all agreed this would be the best scenario."

"While that is incredibly flattering, I can't in good conscience agree with you or them that I'm the man for this job."

Barrett smacked me on the back. When I glanced over at him, he was visibly shaken at the news of Caroline's stalker. It was rare to see him so affected. "Dad's right, Ty. You're the best, and we need the best. Most of all, *Caroline* needs the best."

"I'm not some fucking toy to be passed around between the three of you! Did you even stop to fucking consider what I want?" I thundered. My anger, which inwardly had been stretched like a rubber band, had just snapped. I always prided myself on being able to contain my emotions, but in that moment, I hulked out into full-on beast mode.

Fuuuuck. I'd just gone psycho in front of one of the most powerful men on the planet.

After taking a deep breath, I took a step back from the wide-eyed, open-mouthed Callahan men. "Forgive me. I should have never spoken to you in that way, Mr. President."

Although he had been momentarily shell-shocked, President Callahan shook his head. "No. It's all right, Ty. You're more a member of the family than you are an employee. I want you to speak your piece." He winked at me. "Maybe just a little more peacefully next time."

"Once again, I apologize for the tone and delivery of my words. More than anything, I'm honored you both think so highly of my abilities, especially considering I came to my position in the Service somewhat differently than most."

I bit my tongue to prevent myself from reminding them that as foreign national, I'd been expected to renounce my British citizenship in order to become a member of the Secret Service. "While it's been a privilege to serve both Barrett and Thorn, I would once again have to respectfully disagree with the idea that I am the man to protect Caroline."

"I'm sorry if it seemed we were treating you like a toy, Ty. You've come to represent a lifeline to our family. We can never repay you for what you've meant to Thorn," President Callahan said.

At the mention of my current target, I turned to him. "I've voiced my thoughts about all this, but what about you?"

"I agree with the others. You're the right man for the job."

"But you always said *I* was the only agent you'd allow to protect you."

Thorn nodded. "I did say that, and I meant it wholeheartedly, but I was also in an entirely different place in my life." A small smile played on his lips. "I'm at peace now."

I knew the reason for his peace was enjoying the party in the East Room. Isabel had helped tame the PTSD demons he'd wrestled with so desperately. He'd also been helped by his therapy dog, Conan, who was enjoying a steak dinner tonight in his kennel in one of the guestrooms. Although Thorn didn't require Conan's presence daily anymore, he still always brought him along when he was traveling.

"Does that mean you're fine with me leaving?" I winced when my voice cracked slightly, but I couldn't hide the emotions coursing through me. Because of my background in the Army, I'd bonded to Thorn more than any of my former targets, which was saying something considering my friendship with Barrett. I couldn't quite explain it, but there was something about protecting a fellow brother.

"Fuck no. I'm mad as hell about you being taken off my detail for the foreseeable future," Thorn joked with a smile.

I chuckled. "Always putting yourself before others—the Thorn Callahan way of life."

He playfully punched my shoulder. "Last time I checked, Ty Fraser did the same thing."

Biting my tongue, I didn't remind him that I hadn't accepted the job. Bitterness twisted its way through my chest at the apparent fact that he and the others assumed I would automatically agree. Sure, I might protest a little, but in the end, dependable ol' Ty would never put his wants and needs above anyone else's. How could I sleep at night if I told the president of the United States to fuck off as well as his young, innocent daughter? No, no. A man of honor could never do that, and if Stuart believed this warranted tighter control and protection . . .

In that moment, I didn't want to be a man of honor. I wanted to be a selfish prick, but I couldn't do that. Not only did my president need me, there was Caroline to consider. She was an innocent in all this. She didn't deserve to be harmed because of some psycho's obsession. If I had any power within me to stop it, I had to do it.

"You aren't going to let me sleep on this or anything, are you?" I asked with a wry grin.

President Callahan smiled. "I would prefer to have your answer now. Caroline leaves for West Virginia in two weeks. We need to work fast."

"West Virginia?" I questioned.

"Yes, Charleston. She's taking over as CEO of Jane's non-profit."

Although I hadn't thought it was possible for my mood to tank even further, the news that I wouldn't be stationed in DC certainly did it. Inwardly, I tried talking myself out of it. *Come on, man. It's not forever. You're talking about a family with the best resources in the land. This jerkoff will be caught, and you can go back to your normal life with Thorn.*

Content in knowing I was doing the right thing, I nodded at the others. "Let's get started."

CHAPTER THREE

AFTER WE LANDED IN CHARLESTON, a chauffeur-driven SUV was waiting for us on the runway. The usual sunglasses-outfitted, earpiece-wearing Secret Service agent sat behind the wheel. I'd long since given up using Uber or Lyft after Dad was elected president. The Secret Service never allowed someone unknown to them to drive.

The agent exited the car and started helping Stuart and Ty load the luggage. Once they finished, we got into the SUV and headed to my apartment—well, I supposed I should say *our* apartment. Considering all the furniture was mine, it wasn't going to feel much like his apartment, but hopefully it wouldn't be for long.

Instead of fielding work emails, I turned my attention out the window to get used to my new home. Considering I'd spent the last year in Oxford, I knew I was in for somewhat of a culture shock. At the same time, I loved the idea of a living in a city that was a mixture of small-town life and urban culture.

When we pulled up to the entrance of the building, I glanced over at Ty. He didn't seem to be casing the place. It was almost as if he was familiar with it. Then it hit me. "You came out here last week, didn't you?"

"Yes. I flew out on Wednesday to do preliminaries of the apartment as well as your office building."

Man, my brothers were right—he really was always one step ahead. "What did you think?"

"Overall, I was pleased to find the building was gated with a code, and there is monitoring on the property. I wish the same could be said for your office building."

I should have known he would only be reflective about the security aspect. "I meant, do you think you'll be happy there?"

Ty chuckled. "This is about you and your safety. My happiness really isn't under consideration."

"But it should be. You won't be going back to DC to unwind on your breaks like the other agents." I shook my head. "I can't abide the thought of you being miserable on my account."

"Caroline, it's fine."

Although I didn't feel convinced, I bobbed my head in agreement. Stuart had gone through the security gate and weaved the SUV on up to my building. After Ty helped me out of the car, he started to head inside. "Wait, shouldn't we get the boxes?"

"I want to check the apartment first."

"Of course you do," I muttered with a roll of my eyes.

"I'll grab some on my way up," Stuart offered.

"Thank you," I murmured as I entered the code to get into the building. Once the door swung open, we headed to the elevator. After getting off on the second floor, we walked in silence down the carpeted hallway. Reaching in my purse, I grabbed my key fob that opened the door. At Ty's huff of breath, I threw a glance at him over my shoulder. "What?"

"I'm just not a fan of the lock. They can be easily cloned or disarmed."

"The same thing can happen with a key," I protested.

"It takes more effort to have a key made. Anyone who is tech savvy could silently hack that lock within seconds."

He really did think of everything, which was both annoying and comforting. When I stepped inside the apartment, I felt a tug in my chest. It was my first real place completely of my own. I'd lived in student housing during college, and even during my graduate time in the UK.

Besides a few last-minute things, everything was unpacked and ready to roll. When the growling of my stomach echoed through the hallway, I realized there was one thing I'd forgotten. "I—uh, I mean, *we* need groceries."

Ty didn't respond. Instead, his teal blue eyes kept flickering around the room like he expected a knife-wielding maniac to burst out of the hall closet. I couldn't help noticing how tight the muscle in his jaw was or how tense his shoulders were. He was in full fighter stance in the middle of the foyer, which was certainly a new one for me. I supposed I better get used to it with the new threat level surrounding me.

I waved my hand in front of his face. "Hello? Did you hear me?"

"We need groceries," he mumbled.

Huh. So, he was one of those men who actually did hear you when he didn't appear to be paying attention.

Digging in my purse, I pulled out my phone. "Why don't I find the closest store while you go scope out the rest of the apartment?"

With a nod, Ty headed off to the right to disappear into the kitchen. It wouldn't take him long since the place wasn't very big.

"Looks like there's a Piggly Wiggly just down the road," I announced as he dipped into one of the bedrooms.

He poked his head back out the door. "What the hell is a 'Piggly Wiggly'?"

"It's a grocery store—or I guess I should say a 'grocers' for you British Americans."

"Sounds like some sort of loony butcher if you ask me."

I laughed. "I can see where someone across the pond might make that assumption."

"Speaking of across the pond, I appreciate you translating for me, but I have been stateside for five years now. Hardly an ex-pat, but I get most of the slang."

"You didn't get Piggly Wiggly," I countered.

He rolled his eyes. "That was a longshot. I mean, who names a grocery store after wiggling pigs?"

"Good question."

"I'll tell Stuart."

I wrinkled my nose. "I'm going to have to take a whole contingent just to the grocery store?"

"Stuart will drive, and he will remain in the car in case we need a getaway."

"A getaway?"

"We have to prepare for every scenario."

"Such as an ambush at the Piggly Wiggly?"

Ty crossed his arms over his chest. "Must I remind you of the hair?"

"Right. Point taken." I felt a shudder down my spine at the mention of it. *God, how did he get so close to me?*

As Ty went next door to get Stuart, I stood in the foyer alone. Although I'd never needed a code word before with my agents, it was apparent that "hair" could now be mine. Apparently, it was the word that needed to be said for me to consider the reality of the situation every time I wasn't taking things seriously.

As I fingered the strands of my hair, I still wondered how I hadn't noticed the loss, but with the layers cut into my long mane, it made sense that it wasn't so noticeable. In fact, even now, it took a few moments to find.

When Ty returned with Stuart, I grabbed my purse and followed them out into the hallway. Ty held the car door open for me and then made sure I was buckled up before he closed the door. With Stuart behind the wheel, I handed him my phone to use for directions. Instead of sliding into the passenger seat, Ty sat in the back with me. "Another part of the plan?"

"Yes and no. I kinda like feeling like I'm being chauffeured and Stuart's my bitch," Ty teased.

I snickered as Stuart rolled his eyes in the rearview mirror. "Dream on, limey."

Ty only chuckled at the somewhat archaic insult for a British person. I once again turned my attention out the window to the scenery flying by. When Stuart pulled into the parking lot, Ty snickered. "What?" I asked.

"The sign." He rolled his eyes. "How can anyone actually shop somewhere with a psychotic-looking pig smiling on the sign?"

"Now I know what to get you for Christmas," I mused with a grin.

"Jesus, they actually have merchandise?" Ty questioned somewhat incredulously.

"Oh yes, everything from shirts to toys of the 'psychotic-looking pig' as you call it."

"Please refrain from getting me anything for Christmas, least of all something from here."

"While I sincerely hope you're not still working for me by Christmas, I am *so* getting you some Piggly Wiggly stuff."

"You're just as impossible as Barrett."

I laughed. "Why thank you."

With a frustrated grunt, Ty helped me out of the car. After strolling through the mechanized doors, he said, "Here, I'll grab us a trolley."

"We're not in the UK anymore, Batman. We can't call them trolleys—they're carts."

"Yeah, yeah. A cart."

I giggled. Said with a British accent, it sounded more like kite. I thought perhaps I should teach him another name for the object. "Back home in Virginia, some people called them buggies."

Ty eyed the cart curiously. "I'm not sure I get the correlation between this and a horse and buggy."

"Me either." When Ty didn't start pushing the cart, I tilted my head at him. "Aren't you going to be a gentleman and push?"

He shook his head. "I need to keep alert."

"Right," I muttered before I placed my hands on the metal bar and eased the cart over to the produce section.

"Look, it's not like I'm choosing to be an unchivalrous dick by not taking the trolley—er, *cart*. I really do have to remain alert."

With a laugh, I replied, "It's okay. I really do get it."

"I know a way I can make it up to you."

Even though it shouldn't have, my mind dove deep into the gutter at his statement. *Get a grip, Caroline. Remember Perry? Your boyfriend? You shouldn't be having any type of R-rated thoughts involving Ty.*

I screeched the cart to a halt in front of the display of potatoes. "Uh, what did you have in mind?"

"I'll cook dinner for us tonight."

I tore my gaze away from the spuds to stare wide-eyed at Ty. "You cook?"

He grinned. "Why does that seem so shocking to you?"

I shrugged. "I guess it's because you don't impress me as the type of man who cooks."

"And just what does a man who cooks look like?"

"I don't know if there's a *specific* look." I focused my attention back on the potato display. "You just don't seem like the type."

"My mother would disagree with you."

"Is that who taught you?"

Ty nodded. "Not only were my brothers and I expected to know how to cook for ourselves, we also had to help our mom prepare meals."

"She sounds like my kind of woman."

"I'm sure the two of you would get along beautifully considering how you both love to give me grief," he noted.

"Har, har."

After surmising a few potatoes, Ty asked, "What about Perry? Is he the cooking type?"

With a snort, I replied, "Please. Perry can barely order takeout without help, let alone cook."

Ty's reaction shocked me greatly. Where I fully expected him to make some derogatory remark about Perry's shortcomings, he merely said, "I find that sad."

"Why is that?"

"Growing up, I was taught cooking for someone was a way to show your love. Regardless of how simplistic the meal was, it was the preparation that showed you cared. After my mom had spent the entire day on her feet engaged in bringing life into the world, it meant something to her for us to have prepared her favorite meal. Or when she was dead tired and wanted nothing more than to sleep, she would make my father's favorite food or our favorite dessert."

Oh dear God. Not only could the man cook, he was also deep and thoughtful. I wasn't sure I'd ever heard Perry talk so reverently about his family or make food sound like it was on a spiritual level. Talk about being an international man of mystery with all the many layers of his personality.

I cleared what felt like a lump of sawdust from my throat. "When you say it like that, it does sound sad."

"You could also say it's a little sexist to leave the meal preparation up to you, not to mention elitist that he expects someone else to cater to his wants and needs."

And just like that, the record playing my admiration for Ty screeched to a halt. "Did you just call my boyfriend sexist and elitist?"

Ty tossed a few russet potatoes into a clear produce bag. "I believe you heard me."

"I was hoping I heard you wrong."

"Nope. You heard me correctly."

I snatched a produce bag off the dispenser. "And you're not going to apologize?"

"For speaking the truth?"

Pushing myself in front of him, I countered, "For being a dick."

Ty chuckled. "Don't get your knickers in a twist."

"I'm not. I just don't appreciate you talking derogatorily about Perry, especially when he isn't here to defend himself."

"You're right. I shouldn't have said that." He gave me a pointed look. "I apologize for calling him sexist and elitist."

Although he vocalized the words, it was apparent Ty wasn't entirely sincere. Deep down, I knew he wasn't terribly off the mark with the sexist comment. As a modern woman with a career, it was only natural to expect my significant other to help out in domestic areas, and yeah, Perry was also pretty elitist since he always deferred anything domestic to the help.

Argh. I hated for Ty to be right. Huffing, I shoved the cart over to the meat department, pushing a little harder than was completely necessary. I glanced over at Ty, who was suspiciously eyeballing all the patrons of the Piggly Wiggly as if he was waiting for someone to try to assault me with their cart or attempt to knock me out with a pork loin. "What are you cooking for us tonight?"

"I suppose that depends on you."

"How so?"

"You aren't a vegetarian, are you?"

I grinned. "You mean that little tidbit wasn't in my file?"

"I wasn't given a file on you."

I furrowed my brows. "You weren't?"

"No. I prefer to do my own research."

Um, okay. "By *research*, do you mean creeping on my social media?"

"Somewhat. Not only does it give me the ability to get to know you, it also shows me areas where we might need to tighten up security-wise."

Crossing my arms over my chest, I leaned back against the meat counter. "What did you learn about me?"

"You prefer tea over coffee, which makes sense since you spent a year in England. You love to take photographs of any type of flowers —the more colorful the better. There was probably a week this summer where you photographed every possible flower in the Rose Garden."

"Hey, there are some of the most gorgeous roses you'll ever see in your life there."

"You won't get any arguments from me."

"Anything else?"

"You enjoy spending time with a select group of girlfriends who have a penchant for wine dinners and bad television."

I threw my head back with a laugh. "Okay, you got me on the wine dinners and bad television."

Ty eyed me curiously. "You don't post any casual pictures of you and Perry. They're all from events and taken by professional photographers."

Before I could stop myself, I blurted out, "That's because he has to give me permission before I can post anything to social media. You know, so it puts the best image forward."

Once again, Ty gave me one of those intense looks like he was staring through to my soul. "You don't mind posting casual pictures. There are lots of selfies of you."

I shrugged. "I don't mind people seeing me without makeup or with a messy bun. I like imperfections."

"It's not so much the imperfections as it is you being real. You're accessible and approachable, which is usually a wonderful attribute to have, unless it attracts a stalker."

"Lucky me," I grumbled.

"Anyway, I don't recall any posts where you voiced your undying support of PETA, so can I correctly wager you're not a vegetarian or vegan?"

"You're right. I'm a meat eater."

"Are you a fan of sausage?"

The part of me that worked with teenage boys inwardly snickered at the innuendo of his last statement. Outwardly, I remained straight-faced. "As a matter of fact, I am."

"I plan on giving you a little taste of back home—well, back home for me, that is."

"The only food I had when I visited the East End was some amazing curry."

"The East End is filled with fabulous Indian restaurants I could never do justice to with my cooking, let alone finding the right ingredients here in the backwoods."

I snickered. "We're not in the backwoods."

"It feels like it. The last time I saw so much camouflage in one place was at a sporting goods store."

"Whatever." I wheeled the cart over to the pork section of the meat department for Ty to pick out what he wanted. While he eyed the different brands, I asked, "Are you going to tell me what you're cooking, or is it a surprise?"

"Have you ever had bangers and mash?"

I nodded. "I had it few times at this pub we always hung out at. It's good."

"If you appreciated the curry of the East End, I think you'll appreciate my recipe."

"Now I'm intrigued." Truth be told, I was more than just intrigued by the prospect of Ty cooking up some exotic blend of bangers and mash, but it wasn't just about the food. He could have been cooking jellied eels—another East End food—for all I cared. It was more about the process of watching him cook. I envisioned him rolling the sleeves of his white shirt up to his elbows while he got down to business in the kitchen. What was it about a man rolling up the sleeves of his dress shirt? Not just any man, of course—one who exudes strength and power. I knew seeing him create a meal with such passion would be a thing of art.

Coupling that visual with our easy, surprisingly comfortable banter, if we had been two different people, it would have been a truly romantic moment there in the Piggly Wiggly—but we weren't, and in that moment—also surprisingly—I didn't like having to remind myself of that. *Weird.*

CHAPTER FOUR

AFTER WE SPENT a considerable amount of time perusing the aisles of the Piggly Wiggly, Caroline was finally finished, and we made our way to the checkout. In true small-town fashion, she struck up a conversation with the middle-aged cashier. While she appeared utterly charming, I probably came off as an ass because I kept looking around and narrowing my eyes at anyone who looked even slightly suspicious, especially the *male* middle-aged cashier who seemed utterly enthralled by Caroline.

At the sight of us walking out of the mechanized doors, Stuart began easing the SUV closer to our place on the curb. After popping the hatch, Caroline wheeled the cart over to the back of the SUV. Just as I was about to start helping her with the bags, I heard a shout behind me. "Hey! Come back here."

Whirling around, I saw a man waving wildly at Caroline. "Fuck! Assailant!" Stuart shouted.

I shoved myself between the man and Caroline, shielding her from him. Grabbing her by the waist, I hoisted her up and threw her in the back of the SUV. "Omph!" she cried as her body bounced on the carpeting of the hatch. After slamming the door, I stepped back just as Stuart screeched away from the curb.

Now that I knew Caroline was safe, I turned my attention back to the man. Hurling myself at him, I took him down to the curb. "What are you doing?" he demanded.

"Stay down. I'm calling the police."

"The police? But what did I do?"

"You've been harassing the president's daughter."

"I just came out to give her the coupons she forgot!"

"What?"

He nodded. "Look in my right hand."

After rocking back on my knees, I grabbed his arm and pried the contents from his fingers. Once I unraveled it, I grimaced. "Son of a bitch."

I had completely and utterly misread the situation. Speaking into my microphone, I said, "Stuart, it's a false alarm."

"Are you fucking kidding me?" he blared into my ear.

"No, I'm not."

"We're headed back."

"Roger."

I figured then it was past time for me to get off the man, and I rose to my feet before reaching down to help him up. I brushed off his white shirt, which I had accidentally dirtied when I knocked him to the ground. Upon closer inspection, I saw the nametag on his shirt. "Sheldon, I'm terribly sorry for my actions."

He narrowed his brown eyes at me. "I think it's me who needs to be calling the police."

"That won't be necessary." Reaching into my pocket, I fished out my badge. As I flashed it at him, I said, "Agent Fraser with the U.S. Secret Service."

His eyes bulged before he gasped. "Wait, that was President Callahan's daughter?"

"Yes, sir, it was. I hope you can understand that we take the safety of the president's children very seriously, and upon first reflection, it appeared you might've been preparing to harm Ms. Callahan."

"Oh, no. I would never want to do that. I voted for her dad. Never thought I'd vote for an independent, but he won me over."

"I'm happy to hear that, sir. I certainly hope this unfortunate incident won't in any way skew your views on him."

He waved a hand dismissively. "No, no. I understand. More than that, I can't wait to go home and tell my wife Caroline Callahan came into *my* store today."

For my sake, I hoped he left out the part where a Secret Service agent mowed him down because he thought Piggly Wiggly coupons were a weapon. Once the other agents found out about this, I was going to catch hell in the form of their constant ribbing. At least Stuart would be going down with me—he'd made the assumption to start with.

After he drove up, he made quick work of putting the SUV in park and opening the hatch. I hopped off the curb and went over to the back. Caroline sat with her knees pulled against her chest. When she pursed her lips at me, I held up my hands. "I'm sorry. It was a false alarm."

"That's what Stuart said."

"We can never be too careful."

An amused look twinkled in her blue eyes. "Apparently not when we find grocery cashiers to be a threat to my safety."

"He appeared to have a weapon in his hand, and he was shouting at you," I argued.

"I believe the weapon turned out to be coupons."

Man, she was really on my dick about this one. *Shit.* I should never be thinking of Caroline on my dick in any form or fashion. It was just too wrong. "Yes, the weapon turned out to be your coupons."

"Right."

I extended my hand to her. "Come on and get out so we can load the groceries up and get the hell out of here."

After I helped Caroline slide out of the back, she started helping me load the bags. "Should I go inside and offer an autograph to smooth things over? This is the closest grocery store to the apartment, so I'd hate to not ever be able to come here again because you clotheslined a guy."

"I didn't clothesline him. I merely took him down as part of protocol."

"I'd say you missed your calling in football, that's for sure."

Since I was already kicking my arse for making a mistake, the last thing I needed was for her to continue giving me a hard time. Even though Barrett and Thorn were both known to give me hell, there was something far more grating with Caroline doing it.

With a growl, I demanded, "Are you really going to make me

remind you of *that* word again?" When the smile on her lips faded, I instantly felt like an arsehole. "Sorry," I said genuinely as I shoved in two more bags with the psychotic smiling pig on them into the hatch.

She shook her head. "No, you're right. I shouldn't be giving you such a hard time, especially considering what it could have been."

"Yeah, well, it was still a cock-up." I met Stuart's gaze in the rearview mirror. "Wasn't it?"

He grimaced. "Yeah, it was."

"Look, I'm just glad the two of you were on the ball. Next time, it might not be a false alarm."

"Just rest easier knowing we won't let anything happen to you."

Caroline smiled. "I know, and it means a lot."

Since we'd finished loading the bags, I put her in the SUV before taking the cart back. I groaned when I saw Sheldon, along with several other employees, pointing and peering out the window. "Fucking fabulous," I muttered under my breath. The only potential saving grace would be if no one managed to capture the incident on camera. It wasn't so much about my personal mortification, but more that I'd be pissed if the stalker found her on the first day because some jackwad alerted him of our location. *Thank God this* is *in the backwoods.*

While Caroline and I shuttled the groceries into the apartment, Stuart kept an eye on things with SUV still running. I hoped once Caroline was in bed, I could get a briefing from him about the status of the stalker. Although all his previous contact had been through snail mail with the post office, we weren't sure if her change of location might alter his methods. Since she'd been furious after learning that the Secret Service went through her mail, we thought it best to keep it a secret that we were now screening her emails. She'd probably be just as pissed at that one, but her safety came first.

Once we had everything inside, Stuart went to park, and I got down to the business of preparing dinner. One way an outsider could tell this wasn't your average first apartment was the fact that there was a mini TV on the counter. Not only did it have a live feed of the hallway, lobby, and parking lot, it also had cable access. Since I knew Stuart would be watching the feed, I flipped it on to the BBC.

I'd started organizing the ingredients on the counter when Caroline plopped down onto one of the bar stools. "Keeping an eye on me because you don't trust me with your food?" I joked.

She grinned. "Actually, I thought I'd get a front-row seat while getting a little work done."

"Works for me." As I sliced into the package of sausage, I said, "Who knows—by the time it's all said and done, you might be cooking for me."

"I wouldn't hold my breath on that one," she replied wryly.

"Want some wine?" I suggested.

"Mmm, I'd love some."

I pulled two wineglasses out of the cabinet before grabbing a bottle of red from the pantry. "Nice vintage," I mused as I eyed the $7.99 orange price tag.

Caroline laughed. "Hey, I like to think it's a step up from boxed wine."

"That it is."

"Let me guess: you just assumed someone like me would be a diva with really expensive wine."

Okay, so she had me there, at least on the expensive wine part. Nothing I'd previously known of Caroline screamed diva, so I couldn't imagine unearthing that trait about her. "I suppose I assumed as someone who has traveled extensively, you would prefer a more quality wine."

"I won't lie that sometimes I like a really expensive bottle, but for the most part, the cheap stuff de-stresses me after a long day at work the same as an expensive one would."

"Makes sense," I replied as I poured our glasses.

After I handed one to her, she smiled. "Thank you."

"Should we toast now or wait until dinner?"

"What are we toasting? That my stalker doesn't frequent the Piggly Wiggly?" she teased.

"Har, har. I was thinking more about the fact that it's your first night in the apartment."

"Well, that's not entirely true. I did stay a couple of nights two weeks ago to unpack and put everything together."

Right. I'd forgotten about that, though of course the apartment hadn't just magically filled with furniture and décor. "Okay. Then we could toast our first night in the apartment." The moment the words left my lips, I cringed. Couples and lovers toasted first nights in apartments, not Secret Service agents and their targets. After clearing my throat, I prepared to work at digging myself out of the hole I'd gotten into. "I just thought since our situation was so unique, it might not hurt to toast it."

Caroline smiled. "Makes sense to me." She held up her glass. "To us and our crazy cohabitation."

I laughed. "To us." After we each took a sip, I said, "And to you and starting your new career."

She placed a hand over her heart. "Aw, that's so sweet. Thank you."

"You're welcome." After I set my glass on the counter, I gave her a pointed look. "From here on out, I'll be picking the wine."

With a laugh, Caroline replied, "The job is all yours, Mr. Wine Snob."

As I started working on the potatoes, I jerked my chin toward the papers Caroline had spread out in front of her. "What are you working on?"

"The final edits on *Satchel and Babe Hit the Books*."

Unable to conceal my surprise, I asked, "You have a book editor?"

Caroline giggled. "Shocking, isn't it?"

"Sorry if I sounded surprised."

She shrugged. "It's okay. Most people are somewhat perplexed that an international relations major is writing a children's book."

I really didn't know why I was surprised. The more I got to know her, the more it seemed there was nothing Caroline couldn't do, nothing she wouldn't try. She was just that gifted. "Is it one like your mum's?"

"As a matter of fact, it is. She loaned the characters to me." With a grin, she added, "She figured I would earn more money that way, and she knew how desperately Read 4 Life needs the money."

Like other First Ladies, Jane Callahan had penned a children's book about the family dogs, Satchel and Babe, and their life in the White House. It had been an instant hit, especially the summer book tour that featured Jane along with Satchel and Babe. I don't even want to imagine what it was like to be the agents assigned to the dog detail.

"What's it about?" I asked as I stole another peek at one of the pages.

"Satchel and Babe are taught how to read and a whole world opens up for them through books." After wrinkling her nose, Caroline said, "Yeah, it's a little cheesy."

"Maybe for adults, but I'm sure it'll be great for kids."

"I really wanted a tie-in that would work well with the literacy initiatives. At first, Satchel's a reluctant reader, and Babe has comprehension issues."

"Sounds relatable for kids. Hell, it's relatable for me. I struggled a lot with reading when I was a kid."

"You did?"

I nodded. "One day it finally clicked for me, but for many years, I considered being a primary school dropout."

Caroline laughed. "I can't imagine that considering how far you've come."

"To being elbow-deep in mash in the boonies?" I joked.

With a teasing roll of her eyes, she replied, "No, that's not what I meant."

"I've done pretty well considering I never finished uni." I winked at her. "I've never written any books though."

"It's only a children's book."

"Don't discredit yourself. Children's books are the gateways to teaching kids to read. You and your mum have a great angle to not only help with reading, but to let kids learn about history. I learned a lot about the White House from your mum's book."

Her brows shot up. "You read *Satchel and Babe in the White House?*"

"I certainly did. I have an autographed copy as well."

"I'm impressed."

"I sent a few copies back home to my nieces and nephews."

"How many nieces and nephews do you have?"

"Five—Ainsley, Pippa, Charlotte, Owen, and Shawn."

"How often do you get to see them?"

"Not as often as I'd like." I gave her a knowing look. "Considering I'm married to my job and they're across the pond."

"You could always take some time and visit them now," she said pointedly.

I shook my head. "Not until your psycho stalker is caught."

She sighed. "You and your honor."

"I know. It's a real pain in the arse, isn't it?"

"Yep." After taking another sip of wine, she tilted her head at me. "What about your brothers and sisters?"

"Only brothers. There were four of us."

"Bless your mom's heart," she mused.

"You don't have to worry about her. She's a tough ol' bird who kept us all in line."

"And made you all cook dinner."

I laughed. "Exactly."

"She sounds like a wonderful woman."

"She is. She just retired from forty years of midwifery. She started out just like that BBC show *Call the Midwife.*"

Her eyes bulged at the television reference. "You're kidding. I love that show. I devoured it in a bingeing storm this summer."

"Yup, that was Mum. I don't know how she managed to do it, keep the house going, and raise four unruly boys."

"What about your father?"

"He worked the docks. Well, he's still working the docks. I swear, the old man will just keel over one day right there by the water."

"He doesn't want to retire?"

"Nope. He's one of those idle hands kind of men. He likes being busy."

"Sounds like he and my dad would have a lot in common," she noted with a smile.

"At least on the work ethic. My dad has never been one for politics."

Her expression darkened. "Sometimes I wish my dad wasn't."

"Because of the stalker?"

"No. Not just because of that." She traced the mouth of her wine-glass with a manicured finger. "He's always given so much of himself for this country, from going to war to being a senator and now to being president. He barely takes time just for himself, and I know he doesn't get enough sleep. I just worry the stress of it all is finally going to catch up with him."

The extent of her worry was palpable. I abandoned peeling the potatoes so I could reach across the counter to grab her hand. "Your dad is a tough old chap. He's not only got the heart to do the job, he has the strength as well. He's got so many people rooting for him that he's going to get by just fine. If any man was ever genuinely called to the presidency, it's him."

Her somewhat astonished gaze traveled from my hand back up to my eyes. For a moment, I wondered if I'd overstepped my bounds. Perhaps I had become too comfortable in my protection of Barrett and Ty, and I needed to be less touchy-feely with Caroline. In this day and age, you can't be at all handsy with any female, least of all the daughter of the president. What surprised me most was that I wasn't generally a very tactile person, yet something about Caroline's genuine daughterly concern overrode that.

Thankfully, a beaming smile lit up her face. "That's one of the sweetest things anyone has ever said to me about my dad."

"As amazing as President Callahan is, I find that hard to believe."

"I'm serious. Sure, people say nice stuff all the time, but you can tell when it's calculated and insincere." She squeezed my hand. "I know you meant those words from the bottom of your heart."

With a wink, I replied, "Glad I'm not cutting onions, or you might mistake me for crying."

Caroline laughed. "Whatever. Go ahead and be the hard ass, ya big softie."

When I opened my mouth to challenge her, an upbeat ringtone interrupted me.

A guilty look flashed in Caroline's baby blues before she jerked her hand from mine. "It's Perry."

I nodded before picking up the peeler again. Instead of leaving the room, she went ahead and answered. "Hey you! It's so good to see you."

"Hey, sexy tits," Perry drawled over FaceTime.

What the fuck? Since Caroline's head was bent over her screen, I freely rolled my eyes at the epic wankery coming from the phone. Jesus, I was starting to loathe the guy as much as Thorn did.

Caroline shifted on her stool, and I could easily read her embarrassment from across the counter. "You know I hate when you call me that," she hissed in a low voice. At least she didn't find everything about Perry endearing. Maybe there was hope she'd wise up and drop the douchebag.

"Come on, you and I both know you have the most amazing tits around. I'm seriously missing them at the moment."

At Caroline's horrified intake of breath, I gripped the potato peeler tighter in my hand. It took everything within me to focus on the pile of potatoes in front of me. Part of me was inwardly stabbing Perry with the utensil while the other was desperately trying not to side-eye Caroline's chest to either deny or confirm Perry's statement. Sure, I would have been blind not to notice that she had a great body. With her stature and good looks, she could have easily been a model, but you didn't think sexually about the boss's daughter, not to mention your best friend's sister.

"I'm missing you, too," Caroline said. She still hadn't dared to look up to gauge my reaction to the idiot's comments.

"How's it going in the sticks? I wasn't sure you would actually have cell reception out there."

"It's not a third world country, mate," I muttered under my breath.

"Who the fuck is that?" Perry demanded.

Oh shit. I'd forgotten he was on speaker. I threw an apologetic look at Caroline.

"That's Ty, my Secret Service agent," she explained.

After she turned the phone so I could see Perry, I forced a smile to my face. With a potato in my hand, I waved. "I'm Agent Fraser. Nice to see you again."

Perry narrowed his eyes at me. "Yeah, nice seeing you, too." From his tone, I could tell he would have much rather seen dog shit on the bottom of his thousand-dollar loafers.

"Ty's making us bangers and mash like he used to eat back home," Caroline said.

"You're really putting him to work, aren't you?"

"Actually, it was his idea."

Since you could have cut the tension in the room with a machete, I tossed the potato on the counter. "Listen, mate, I'm glad I have the chance to talk to you for a minute. I just wanted to let you know you don't have to worry about me and Caroline living together. She's my target and nothing more." Glancing from the phone, I grinned at Caroline. "And I have a girlfriend," I lied.

She rolled her eyes at me. While she might not have wanted to lie to Perry, I had no qualms about it. In my opinion, it was a dick move aimed at a giant dick.

Perry chuckled. "Thanks, *mate*, but I don't need any reassuring. I'm not the least bit worried about you and Caroline. You don't date the help, do you, babe?"

It took everything within me, all my years of training not to go off on him. Back in the day, I would have mopped the floor with an elitist wanker like him. I would have started by knocking the shit-eating grin off his face so hard he would have spit out a few of his perfect veneers.

When I glanced from the phone to Caroline, mortification filled her face. After a few seconds passed, she drew her shoulders back and whirled her hand around so she could face Perry on the phone. "Ty is not the help, and you sound like an elitist prick for saying that," she snapped.

As I turned my back to her to mix up the potatoes, I couldn't help chuckling at her response. A few hours ago she'd been insulted when I'd alluded to Perry being an elitist, yet there she was calling him one.

"Easy, babe. I didn't mean anything by it."

"Yeah, you did. Ty's a veteran of the British Army, so he deserves respect, not to mention the fact that he's an esteemed agent who is giving up everything to ensure my safety."

I stopped mixing up the mash. Holy shit, Caroline didn't play when it came to putting anyone in his place. Thorn would love this. I knew it would make him feel a little better about the Perry/Caroline romance.

"Okay, okay. I'm sorry," Perry finally said.

"Did you hear that, Ty?" Caroline called.

I threw a glance at her over my shoulder. "Loud and clear."

"Good."

Perry cleared his throat. "So, tomorrow's the big day at the new job, huh?"

With a snort, I went back to preparing dinner. He was such an arse, and having spent the last twelve hours with Caroline, I could honestly say I was surprised at the attraction. They were like chalk and cheese. *Date the help.* As the conversation grew fainter, I turned around to see Caroline had gone into her bedroom. After blowing Perry's hair back in front of me, I couldn't imagine why she felt the need for privacy. I hoped she wasn't going to flash him her "sexy tits" while they had phone sex. Shuddering at the thought, I focused all my attention on frying up the sausage and seasoning the potatoes.

CHAPTER
FIVE

I WASN'T sure how long Caroline was gone. After turning up the volume on the television, I focused on some of the news from back home while I finished the meal. Just as I was serving up the portions, she reappeared. Considering her expression wasn't tense, I assumed the rest of the conversation had gone well. Obviously, Perry had to have some charm. "I hope you're hungry," I said as I motioned to one of the plates.

"I'm starving."

With a nod, I carried them over to the kitchen table. In her absence, I'd also set up linen napkins along with the cutlery we would need. At the sight of the fully prepared table, she let out a low whistle.

"What?" I demanded.

"I'm impressed," she replied with a smile.

I rolled my eyes. "Because I know how to set a wee table?"

"I'm not going to lie and say I wasn't fully expecting us to sit in front of the television."

"Don't tell me you have some of those telly trays like my mum and dad do."

She giggled. "We call them TV trays."

"Whatever."

"Now that you mention it, maybe I should get some."

"Oh no. I'm not sitting behind one of those things." I jerked my chin at the table. "Besides, what is the point of having this if you're not going to use it?"

"For decorative purposes?" she suggested.

"Whatever. Sit."

With a coy smile, she asked, "Is that a command?"

"Yes." When she gave me an exasperated look, I added, "Only because I don't want your dinner getting cold."

"Okay, I'll sit."

Since this wasn't a date, I refrained from pulling her chair out. Instead, I eased down into the seat across from her. While she reached for her fork and knife to dig in, I sat back, waiting for her response to the food. When she took a bite of the mash, her brows momentarily creased, but then her eyes rolled back. "Wow, that's amazing."

"You really like the spices?"

"I do." She grinned. "It's seriously better than any I had in England."

Having gotten a sufficient ego boost, I reached for my fork and started digging in.

"You know, you're really a triple threat kind of guy," Caroline said.

"How's that?"

"You have looks, a demanding career, *and* you can cook."

I laughed at her summation. "Why thank you. I also read."

"Once again, that's very impressive." She tilted her head at me. "How is it you're still single?"

I choked on a piece of sausage. Reaching for my glass, I quickly sucked the water down.

When I recovered, Caroline was staring at me with an amused glint twinkling in her eyes. "Sore subject?"

"No, not at all. You just took me off guard."

"I thought an agent was always on his guard."

I narrowed my eyes at her. "I am when it comes to my target. However, when said target poses a question out of the blue, I can be excused for having a reaction."

"You're still not answering the question."

With a growl, I forcefully raked the tines of my fork through my mash. "Jesus, you're as stubborn as your brothers."

Caroline laughed. "I am a Callahan through and through."

Even though she was so much like her brothers, I still didn't have the ease with her that I had with them, and it wasn't just because we didn't know each other as well. It stemmed from the fact that she was a woman. "Look, I'm not being purposely evasive. I'm just not used to talking about something so personal with someone I don't know, least of all someone who is my target."

"I'm sorry if you feel I'm being intrusive. Since you're privy to everything personal in my life, including phone calls with my boyfriend, I didn't think it was poor form to ask."

"Poor form?"

With a grin, she replied, "Sorry. I sounded like my mother then, didn't I?"

"Maybe, but that isn't a bad thing."

"Did someone break your heart?" she questioned softly.

"You really are relentless, aren't you?"

"I'm sorry. We can change the subject if you'd like."

Although she was giving me an out, I knew deep down she wouldn't be letting the subject go. While it might not happen that night, she would get me to answer come hell or high water. I decided to go ahead and put both her and myself out of our misery.

"Yes, someone broke my heart. Her name was Gemma, and we were eighteen. She was supposed to wait for me while I was away in the Army, but she didn't."

Caroline winced. "That's terrible."

"It was. It totally fucked with my head for a long time since she had been totally playing the part of the girlfriend keeping the home fires burning."

"I can only imagine." She eyed me curiously. "That was at least ten years ago—surely there's been someone since then."

"Oh, there have been many," I quipped.

Wrinkling her nose, Caroline said, "Does that mean you're a manwhore like Barrett used to be?"

I snorted at the comparison. "I wouldn't say that. I've had two long-term relationships over the years, which is more than Barrett could say before Addison."

"But none lately."

"No. Nothing serious since I came to the States."

"Are you okay with that?"

I shrugged. "It's just the way things are."

"It doesn't have to be."

I groaned. "You can go right ahead and nix any ideas about fixing me up."

"Who said anything about fixing you up?"

"You didn't have to. I could see the wheels turning in your head."

She pursed her lips at me. "That just goes to show how you don't know everything. I wouldn't dream of fixing you up right now. I need you focused on catching my stalker. Any distraction means stretching out this living arrangement."

"Good point." I chuckled.

Just when I thought I was off the hook, Caroline pointed her fork at me. "That doesn't mean when you go back to Thorn's protection, I won't try to set you up with someone then."

"Lucky me."

"Don't sell yourself short. Any woman would be very lucky to have you."

I shook my head. "You can't honestly say that."

She blinked at me. "Why can't I make that observation?"

"Because you don't really know me."

"I think I know enough of you to say that."

Clenching my jaw, I replied, "You really don't."

"You can't possibly be hiding any major skeletons or you wouldn't have been inducted into the Secret Service," she challenged.

Caroline's defense of me was both endearing and infuriating. Of course, she didn't realize her own naiveté. How could she when she was dating a prick with the emotional depth of a guppy? "I'll leave it at this: combat changed me, and I'm married to my job. On the surface, maybe I look like a catch, but once you dig deeper, I'm not."

"I think you sell yourself short," she murmured.

"That's romanticizing it."

"Just because you're fractured, it doesn't mean you're broken.

Look at Thorn—after everything he went through, love was still possible for him. He just had to find the right woman."

She was right. Thorn had been through even more in battle than I had. Not only had he been wounded, but as a commanding officer, he'd faced the loss of some of his men. He'd experienced debilitating PTSD that culminated in a therapy support dog.

I nodded. "While that's true, everyone's situation is different. We all have our own coping mechanisms."

Caroline nodded. "In case you missed it, humor is mine."

"I'd gathered you used sarcasm, and that is considered the lowest form of humor," I quipped.

My comment garnered a scowl from Caroline. "While I might be sarcastic at times, I find it's much easier to laugh about a situation than cry. How else could I possibly stay sane with a psycho out there who wants to hurt me?"

"You're very brave." When she rolled her eyes, I shook my head. "No. I really mean that."

"While I appreciate the compliment, I don't feel very brave, especially next to someone like you who has been to war."

"Once again, I think you're elevating my worth a little more than I deserve."

A small smile curved at her lips. "Once again, I think we're just going to have to agree to disagree."

"I think that's reasonable."

She took another sip of wine. "I don't think you could argue with the fact that this meal is amazing."

"I'm glad you like it."

"Does this mean you'll be my personal chef as well as my Secret Service agent?" she asked teasingly.

"No, it does not."

"Bummer. The one thing I really loved about the White House was having a chef."

"I can imagine you enjoyed the housekeeping and laundry service as well."

With a laugh, she replied, "Apparently you haven't spent a lot of time with my mother. Since I was crashing for the summer, I was expected to do my own laundry and keep my room clean."

"Really?"

"Oh yeah. Jane Callahan is hardcore."

I chuckled again. "That she is. I'm surprised she hasn't called yet, let alone your dad."

Pink tinged her cheeks. "Actually, I talked to them while I was in the bedroom."

"It's nothing to be embarrassed about."

"I'm not."

"Then the heat must be up too high because your cheeks are red."

With a roll of her eyes, she huffed, "The heat isn't too high."

"Ah, so you are embarrassed."

"Yes." She pinched her index finger and thumb together. "Just this much."

So, the douche hadn't been the reason for her relaxed mood. She shouldn't have been embarrassed, though. She had awesome parents, and her love and respect for them was one of her best qualities. I laughed as I tossed my napkin onto my empty plate. "Whatever."

Before I could stand up, Caroline shot up in her chair. "Since you cooked, I'll do the cleaning."

"You don't have to do that."

"It's okay. I want to."

"All right. If you insist." While I was fine with allowing her to wash the dishes, I could at least help her clear the table. As I took my glass and plate into the kitchen, I said, "If I keep eating like this, I'm going to have to acquaint myself with the building's gym."

"Let me guess: you can't leave me alone to go work out?"

"Not unless another agent comes in."

"Impossible." After cleaning her plate off into the garbage, she said, "I'm happy to work out at the same time, but I have signed up for some hot yoga classes downtown."

"Hot yoga?"

"Think yoga, but with the heater cranked up."

"I see."

"You're welcome to join me."

"Thanks, but I don't do downward-facing dog and that bullshit." The only dog-related position I liked was doggy style, but I refrained from adding that tidbit.

"It might be just what you need to relax and de-stress," she challenged as she filled up the sink.

"I think I can get the same thing on the treadmill and lifting weights."

"Suit yourself."

From the determined look in her eyes, I could tell Caroline wasn't going to be happy until she had me toting a mat and wearing yoga pants, which wasn't going to happen since no self-respecting man would be caught dead in them. While she worked on the dishes, I pulled out my laptop to catch up on some work emails. Once she was finished in the kitchen, she came back out and worked on her book edits. We sat together in a comfortable silence for over an hour before she yawned and stretched her arms over her head.

"I think I'm going to go ahead and go to bed."

Although it was only nine o'clock, I didn't argue with her. It'd been a crazy couple of days, not to mention the next day would be pretty stressful as well. "Okay. Good night."

"Night." Once she closed the door of her bedroom, I rose out of my chair and grabbed my phone. I dipped into the hall bathroom and closed the door. Since I wouldn't leave her alone in the apartment to get a briefing, I dialed Stuart's phone. "Hey, how's it looking?" I asked.

"Everything seems quiet on the email front, but her personal website is getting lit up with hits."

"From a single IP address?"

"No. He's too smart for that. The location pings around different sites in the metro DC area."

I rubbed the five o'clock shadow creeping its way across my chin. "He's not on the move—*yet*." Considering Caroline had only recently learned of her stalker, her social media had been vague about her new living arrangements. While she'd alluded to the fact that she would be working for Read 4 Life, she'd never come out and said in what loca-tion. Thankfully, she had a good head on her shoulders. She had listened when I'd outlined what she could and couldn't post. In fact, she'd made a humorous remark about being like *Where's Waldo*, saying she'd be so hard to find it would almost be annoying. I respected that. I respected *her*. She was a Callahan through and through, and that made watching her significantly easier.

"From her website traffic, it's just a matter of time before he figures it out." One thing that set Caroline's stalker's traffic apart from others was how many times a day he visited her site. There might be one hundred visits from one location where normally there were only two or three. Since he was smart, he would move to another location the next day.

"At least that gives us the chance to get the upper hand on him."

"That's true." After Stuart yawned, he asked, "How are you settling in?"

I eyed the minimalist level of boxes of my shit I'd brought. In my mind, I hoped to nail the stalker's psycho ass to the wall so quickly it wouldn't be necessary for me to unpack completely. "I'm settling."

"Let me guess: your shit is still in boxes while the closet has maybe three suits hanging up."

I chuckled. "Yep."

"I don't blame you, man. I'm hoping this wraps up as soon as possible too. If not, my wife will be on my ass to move her out here like I did while I was in Oxford."

"Enjoying the bachelor life a little too much?" I quipped.

"Maybe a little. If only she didn't have a job where she can work remotely," he lamented.

"Go easy on her—she's been married to you for twenty-five years."

Stuart laughed. "That's true. I guess she deserves a medal by now."

"Exhibit A of the reasons why I'm still single."

"Just wait. One day some woman is going to get her hooks into you, and then you'll end up an old married fart like me."

Can't see it happening any time soon. "Whatever, man. How about we worry about the matter at hand?"

"Fine. I'm going to watch the screens tonight, and then Arjun is on with you guys tomorrow."

"Sounds good. I'm going to go get some shut-eye. Call me if there are any updates."

"Will do."

After I hung up with Stuart, I shed my shirt and pants. While I was accustomed to sleeping in my shorts with Barrett and Thorn, I'd actually gone so far as to purchase pajama pants and paired them with white undershirts—anything to put Caroline more at ease. The last thing either of us needed was for something to go down during the night and my dick to be swinging in the wind.

Climbing into bed, I hoped for smooth sailing the next day.

When the alarm woke me a little after six, I groaned and burrowed deeper under the covers. It felt like I'd just fallen asleep, maybe because I'd tossed and turned for part of the night, my mind swarming with wild scenarios of what the stalker's next steps might be.

Since I knew Caroline planned to get up around seven, I thought I better go ahead and hit the shower. Then while she got ready, I could catch up on anything that had happened overnight.

After entering the bathroom, I found Caroline's door closed. Before I stripped off my shirt and pajama pants, I walked over and flipped the lock. While I showered, I mentally went over the schedule for the day. We needed to be at Caroline's office by nine, and it was a ten- to fifteen-minute drive depending on the morning traffic. She would remain at the downtown office building until five. The one aspect of her job that had the potential for trouble was the changes in location.

Some days she would be traveling to schools within the county while others she might be across the state, and the unknown always raised the bar for security concerns and issues. Considering the tenacity of her stalker, he wouldn't be dissuaded just because her usual daily pattern changed.

I shut the water off and then reached for the towel on the hook beside the shower. Just as my hand brushed against the cotton fabric, the bathroom door blew open, and a bleary-eyed Caroline stumbled through the door. *What the fuck?* How the hell had she gotten inside when I'd locked the door? The only answer I could come up with was the lock somehow malfunctioning.

Caroline's bleary-eyed look was fleeting. The moment she saw me standing there in all my naked glory her eyes bulged like she'd just gotten a jolt of the strongest espresso. Her mouth dropped open into the perfect O of surprise.

Fumbling for the towel, I knocked it off the hook, and it tumbled onto the bathroom tile. "Fuck," I muttered. After I bent down to snatch it up, I looked up to find Caroline staring at my junk. While I would have assumed she would avert her eyes, her gaze was zeroed in on my crotch.

While I should have immediately flung the towel in front of myself, I found myself in a stupor at Caroline's reaction. Never in a million years would I have imagined she would still be staring, but there was something more. It was almost like there was a longing in her expression, and that fucking rattled me.

After I swung the towel in front of me, Caroline seemed to snap out of the spell brought on by my cock. I inwardly groaned when she licked her lips then said, "I, uh, I'm s-sorry. I w-was half-asleep and n-needed to p-pee."

"It's okay. I'm sorry too. I could've sworn I locked the door."

"Uh, yeah, we'll have to check that."

When she still remained standing there, I cleared my throat. "If you'll let me have some privacy, I'll get dressed."

"Right. Yeah. Okay." She then whirled around and ran into the door. "Ow!"

"Shit. Are you okay?"

"Yup. I'm fine," she squeaked. I couldn't tell if the high octave of her voice was from the pain or her embarrassment.

After scrambling out of the bathroom, she slammed the door behind her. I sank back against the wall and exhaled a ragged breath, wondering what the actual fuck had just happened.

CHAPTER SIX

IT WAS OFFICIAL—I was in hell. Okay, maybe it was more of a mortification-based hell, but trust me, it was hellish. How else does one explain having a constant barrage of mental flashes of Ty's dick? I was well aware that other women would have paid good money to see Ty's junk,, but not me. My only concern was Perry's penis—or it *should* have been.

Yeah, it wouldn't take a lie detector test to confirm I was stretching the truth on that one. Sadly, Perry's penis was pretty much the *last* thing on my mind as Ty's reigned supreme. I mean, it was perfection, and I wouldn't even consider myself a "dick" girl.

The truth was, I wasn't wigging out just because I'd seen Ty's penis in all its glory; it was the fact that I'd had a physical reaction to it. I'd gotten the "tingle", if you know what I mean. My traitorous vajajay didn't care that it was all kinds of wrong since Ty was the Secret Service agent sworn to protect me *and* because I had a boyfriend back home in DC.

Nope, it had the audacity to tingle. And now, because of that tingle, I was a basket case just in time for my first day on the job. Since it was just a little after eight in the morning, it was too early to start drinking to wash away my sorrows.

Normally, I was a great believer in communication. It was essential in both personal and professional relationships. When you weren't able to speak freely, unnecessary problems arose. Even before I'd been forced to somewhat censure my social media, I was never one for passive aggressive posts. No, I would go directly to the person causing the issue and make sure I talked it out with them.

As I lathered up my hair in the shower, I was utterly clueless on how to use my mantra of speaking freely on this situation. Obviously, I had to talk to Ty about what had happened. I had to assure him that in spite of me ogling his manhood, it would not in any way undermine the professional rapport we had.

Yeah right.

Maybe I didn't have to say anything at all. In the precarious situation we found ourselves in, perhaps it would be better just to sweep this one under the rug? In the vast scheme of things, it would all be easily forgotten.

When yet another dick flashback assaulted me, I realized there would be no way to easily forget. Alas, this one would probably haunt me until I was old and grey. I'd be moseying down the hallway on my walker at the nursing home, just minding my own business, and *BAM*, there would be Ty's dick. I'd probably end up in some "I've fallen and I can't get up" situation.

Yeah, I can imagine what you're thinking at the moment: overreact much? Trust me, I get it. Although my neurotic side was kicking ass and taking names in this situation, there was a voice of reason deep within me was saying to chill out, saying I should take a step back and take a deep breath. It was just a penis—it certainly wasn't the end of the world. Ty and I would move past this, and all would be right again . . . well, at least until my stalker reared his psychotic head.

Listening to my own voice of reason, I took not one but a few deep breaths and then finished my shower. I managed to do my hair and makeup without another incident. I then slipped into the outfit I'd picked out the night before, and only when it was time to leave my bedroom did I start feeling apprehensive again. It was probably because I was about to face the music, i.e. I was about to face Ty.

When I came out of my bedroom, he was pacing around the living room. "Good morning."

"Good morning," I murmured as I averted my eyes to the floor.

"Are you planning on doing breakfast here or at the office?"

At that moment, food was the absolute last thing on my mind. I was far too focused on how not to have Ty's dick flash before my face while I was in his presence. "I'll just grab something at the office," I replied to my messenger bag rather than to him.

"I'll alert Arjun you're ready to go. He's on protective duty today."

"That'll be great." I continued fumbling around with my bag so I wouldn't have to look at Ty. After I'd rearranged the same folders for the fifth time, he received the word that Arjun had the SUV waiting for us.

I grabbed my keys and tossed them into my purse before heading out the door with Ty close on my heels. Silence hung heavy around us as we made our way downstairs on the elevator. I fiddled aimlessly with a string on the cuff of my shirt as the metal walls seemed to close in on me. Of course, I'd wedged myself into a corner to try to put as much distance between Ty and myself as possible.

When the doors dinged open, I'd never been so thankful to escape an elevator in all my life. After I broke into a full gallop, Ty had to hustle to catch up with me. I barely gave him time to hold the door open for me, least of all to do his usual situation check.

He did manage to get the SUV door open for me, and I hopped inside.

"Good morning, Ms. Callahan," Arjun called out pleasantly.

"Good morning, Arjun. How was your first night in West Virginia?"

He grinned at me in the rearview mirror. "Exceptionally quiet."

I laughed. "It's a 180 from Oxford and DC, huh?"

"Yes, ma'am, it sure is."

After Ty slid onto the seat beside me, the jovial atmosphere became strained. I would have ventured to classify it as downright tense, and it didn't escape me when Arjun furrowed his brows in confusion before turning his attention to the road.

Read 4 Life's office was located in downtown Charleston. It only consisted of a main room that was allocated for my office, a larger one we used as somewhat of a board room, and then a waiting area where my assistant and friend, Selah, was located. We tried hard to minimize our overhead so the majority of our funds went directly to books and materials for kids and educators.

After Arjun dropped us off at the curb, Ty held the building door open for me. "Thank you," I muttered. Of course, his nice gesture meant I had to brush against him to get by. You can only imagine what being so close to his body did to me.

Yep, another flash of his dick in my mind.

"Dammit!" I cried as my hand flew to my forehead.

"What's wrong?" Ty asked.

Well, you see, it's like this: I keep getting bombarded with images of your dick from this morning. "Um, just a little headache," I lied.

"Would you like me to have Arjun get you some medicine?"

Yeah, I'd love to see Arjun ask the pharmacist what he or she would suggest to wipe the image of your fabulous dick out of my mind. I'm pretty sure he'd have grounds for filing a complaint about a hostile work environment. I flashed a weak smile at him. "No, that won't be necessary. I have some Advil in my purse."

Once we got upstairs, I was desperate to escape into my office and bury myself in work. Only then might it be possible to erase the horrors of Ty's dick from my mind. When we breezed into the office, Selah rose out of her chair and came charging over from around the desk.

"Oh my God! I'm so glad to see you!" she cried as she flung herself at me.

I squeezed her back. "It's good to see you too." Glancing around the office, I said, "Looks like you've made yourself at home and have taken good care of the place."

She grinned. "I've tried. Here's hoping I don't manage to kill the two potted plants considering I've been known to have a black thumb."

Since I was somewhat of a plant and flower connoisseur, I made a mental note to make sure to check the plants' hydration levels.

Selah turned her attention from me to Ty. "Well, well, well, if it isn't the usurper."

His blond brows shot up in surprise. "Pardon?"

"You're sleeping in my bed."

He gave her an apologetic smile. "I do apologize for any inconvenience you've experienced. I do hope the other members of the team were able to make the transition as seamless as possible."

His words practically melted Selah into a puddle at his feet. "Oh, they've been wonderful." She batted her eyelashes at him. "I'm sure you're going to be a very attentive neighbor, aren't you?"

"I will certainly try, although my attention will be focused on Caroline."

I was surprised to hear him mention me considering how invisible I felt standing there. Of course, the same could be said for Selah, who only had eyes for Ty.

"I'm sure you'll have some downtime though," she practically purred.

"A little, yes." It surprised me when Ty shifted on his feet, appearing somewhat uncomfortable about her comment. It was a new experience for me since I'd never seen him even remotely nervous before, not even after DickGate, which was what I had decided to name what had happened that morning.

"I'll be happy to show you around."

"We'll see." Extending his hand, Ty said, "Since we haven't been formerly introduced, I'm Ty Fraser."

"Selah McCallister."

With a wink, Ty said, "For the record, your bed is extremely comfortable."

My mouth dropped open. Well, that was a surprising turn of events considering his previous embarrassment at her attention. Had he just used a pick-up line? Wouldn't that somehow go against the Secret Service agent code of conduct? In a way, I felt like an outright shrew for even questioning it. It wasn't like he was forsaking my safety to chat with Selah, not to mention the fact that he was a free agent with no girlfriend. Since Selah was single too, I didn't know why I should've cared, but I did.

Selah giggled as she swatted his arm playfully. "I'm glad to hear it."

I cleared my throat. "Yeah, well, now that the two of you know each other, I'm going into my office."

"I'll be here at my post."

Ty's post was designated as the sofa out in the waiting area. Before, it hadn't occurred to me to be bothered that he'd be out there with Selah, but now I was having second thoughts. Of course, I didn't necessarily want him to be up under my skin by sitting in my office.

When Selah followed, I threw a surprised look at her over my shoulder. "Was there something we needed to go over before this morning's meeting?"

"Not exactly."

I shrugged out of my coat. "Then to what do I owe the pleasure of your company?"

"Oh come on, CC. It's been a ghost town around here the last two weeks waiting on you to get here. I need a little girl talk."

"We've talked every day on the phone."

With a huff, she flopped down into one of the overstuffed chairs in front of my desk. "It's not the same."

Ty poked his head in the door. "I'm sorry, I'm having issues with the feed so I'm going to step out in the hallway for just a second."

"Okay. That's fine."

Once Ty was gone, a curious smile curved on Selah's lips. "Soooo?"

"What?"

"How's the cohabitation going? I figured it was best to ask while he was out in the hall."

Instantly, Ty's manhood once again flashed before my eyes, which in turn sent mortification coursing through me as well as heat burning between my legs. It was so intense I fought the urge to fan myself. "Uh, fine. It's going fine."

"Oh no. What happened? He seems so nice." She waggled her brows. "Not to mention hella easy on the eyes."

"He is." With a shake of my head, I quickly corrected myself. "He is nice." I plopped down into my chair. "I just said everything was fine."

"Yeah, well, you're a terrible liar. Something most definitely happened."

I didn't dare look at Selah because I knew the moment I did, I'd be spilling my guts. She had that kind of effect on me. I'd often teased her about me asking Dad to get her into working interrogations for the CIA.

"Caroline," Selah implored in a singsong voice.

I fiddled with the edge of my desk planner. "It's just different living with a man."

"How so?"

"Well, as you're well aware, there's only one full bathroom."

"Yes."

"So, it's difficult sharing a bathroom with a man who is practically a stranger."

Selah wrinkled her nose. "Ew, did he leave the toilet seat up?"

"I wish," I mumbled under my breath.

"Then what happened?"

I knew there was no way I was going to get out of telling Selah about the incident. She was going to hound me and hound me until I folded like a house of cards. Craning my neck, I surveyed whether Ty was still out in the hallway. When I didn't see him in the lobby, I sucked in a ragged breath. "I saw his junk."

Selah shrieked. "Oh. My. God!"

"Yep, those were pretty much my words." *For more than one reason.*

"How did it happen?"

"I accidentally walked in on him coming out of the shower."

"Oh shit. You got the whole enchilada!"

"I sure did." Rubbing my hand across my forehead, I prepared to relate the rest of my mortification. I hoped unburdening myself might make me feel better. "I was so shocked that I just froze. Forget seconds ticking by—I'm sure it was minutes."

"You got a good eye-full—nice." Hopping up on the side of the desk, Selah leaned forward. "Okay, I need deets."

"I just told you what happened."

She rolled her eyes. "Duh, I want to know about the particulars of his anatomy."

"Of course you do."

"Look, I've been dick deprived for weeks in this town. I need a little tease to get me through."

"I hear Pornhub is pretty good."

"Caroline," Selah warned.

"Fine. You want the details? Here it is: Ty Fraser has a monster-dick. Like, it's enormous. Industrial-sized. *The* biggest dick I've ever seen in person, in pictures, and possibly in porn."

At the sound of a throat clearing in the doorway, every molecule in my body shuddered to a stop. *Oh please, God. This can't be happening. My Secret Service agent did NOT just hear me describing his dick.* Finally, I dared myself to peer around Selah's ass on my desk. "Yes?" I squeaked.

Like any self-respecting man who was packing a super-schlong, Ty had the nerve to appear somewhat pleased by my statement. I swear, it looked like he puffed out his chest, but then the look was erased and he appeared to be his usual businesslike self. "I just wanted to let you know I got the feed working, and I'll be at my post."

"Thank you."

"Would you like me to shut the door?"

"Uh, no. That's fine." I stared pointedly at Selah. "We're just about to go to the conference room for our meeting anyway."

"That's not until ten," both Selah and Ty said in unison.

Inwardly, I throttled Selah for not blindly following my lead. Of course Ty would know the ins and outs of my schedule and be a stickler for staying on time. "Yes, so it is. I suppose if you feel it's a risk to my personal security, it would be fine to close the door."

"It's fine."

Once the door shut, I face-planted on my desk. "Oh God, kill me. *Now.*"

Selah dissolved into giggles. "Did that seriously just happen?"

"For the record, you're the worst friend ever, not to mention the least supportive employee," I muttered.

"I'm sorry, Caroline, but that's some hilarious stuff."

I pulled my head up to glare at her. "I'm so glad you can find my mortification amusing."

"I don't—I want to crawl in a hole for you—but come on. Put the shoe on the other foot. Wouldn't you find something like this pretty damn hysterical?"

Hysterical? Hell no. Ty knew what I thought about his junk, which in turn made me feel like an epic fool. "I'm going to need you to ask me that on another day."

"Okay, okay, I'll be serious. What are you going to do?"

"Ignore it? I mean, I've been ignoring what happened all morning."

"How's that been working for you?"

"Not well."

"Then I'd suggest another course of action."

"Request another agent?"

Selah crossed her arms over her chest. "I'm thinking something not quite so extreme."

"What's something I wouldn't have to give my father an explanation for?"

"Come on, CC. You and I both know what you have to do."

I groaned. "Talk to him."

"Exactly."

"Fine. I'll do it before our meeting."

"Good, 'cause if you don't clear the air, I might have to start burning some sage in here."

I snorted. "Whatever."

After she hopped down from my desk, Selah asked, "Before Ty heard your overwhelming praise for his cock, what was the real reason you were so embarrassed about seeing him naked?"

"Uh, I don't know. I think seeing the dick of the man willing to take a bullet for you is horrifying in itself—like, what if it'd been Stuart or Arjun?"

"But it wasn't. It was the very panty-melting Ty."

I furrowed my brows at her. "What's your point?"

"I'm thinking you're not so much embarrassed as you are angry with yourself."

"Yes, Dr. Phil, you're correct. I'm angry I walked into the bathroom without knocking, thus seeing Ty's dick." I pursed my lips at her. "How much do I owe you for this session?"

"I'd wager dinner and drinks that you had a very physical reaction to seeing Ty, one you didn't expect to happen considering you should be getting satisfaction from Perry's dick."

Fuck me, she was good. See what I mean about the CIA? "I am very satisfied by Perry's dick," I argued.

"I never said you weren't."

"But isn't that what it means if I was"—I lowered my voice to a whisper—"turned on by Ty's penis?"

Selah shook her head. "Lots of women are very satisfied by their men, but they still enjoy seeing a fine piece of manhood."

I shifted in my chair. "It just feels wrong, like I'm cheating on Perry or something."

"No offense, babe, but I hardly doubt Perry hasn't seen some tits or ass in your absence." When I started to protest, Selah held up a hand. "Like at a club or in porn."

"Maybe. I haven't ever thought of asking him about that." In my mind, I couldn't imagine a conversation that started with, *Hey Perry, been ogling any stray tits or pussy lately?* Even though we communicated easily, I didn't see me ever discussing anything like that with him. Part of me was afraid of what the answer might be—not that I thought he was cheating. Granted, Perry had a lot of faults, but he wasn't a cheater. Since he had future political aspirations, he was too concerned with his image to be caught up in a scandal.

"Bottom line, just don't beat yourself up. I have a feeling even Mother Teresa would have gotten a lady boner at seeing Ty's junk in all its wet and glistening glory."

I rolled my eyes. "Yeah, thanks."

"Hell, I haven't seen him naked, and I'm already turned on."

"I noticed."

Her brows shot up. "What? You don't think I should try to seduce him?"

"No. It's not like that." Oh yeah, it was exactly like that.

"Then what is it?"

"It's complicated. I mean, he's here to ensure some weirdo doesn't try to kill me. Normally, I wouldn't care about him dating"—I gave her a pointed look—"or screwing."

"You know me so well," she joked.

"Bottom line is I don't want him getting distracted."

Selah grinned. "And my pussy would be a distraction?"

Since I hated hearing that word, I wrinkled my nose. "Uh, yeah, I guess so."

"Fine. I'll restrain myself until your stalker is caught."

"How kind of you."

"I try. And let me tell you, it'll take a hell of a lot of restraint to stay away from that tasty morsel."

Oh God. I really didn't need any more of Selah's descriptions of Ty's deliciousness. I was already waging a war within myself. With a shake of my head, I knew it was time to put DickGate behind me. After checking the time, I tilted my head at her. "I think you could go ahead and get the conference room set up."

With a nod, Selah said, "I concur. Besides, we desperately need a subject change." She wagged her brows at me. "I've never had the urge to rub one out during the work day."

I rolled my eyes. "Seriously? I could have lived a lifetime without hearing that."

"Just promise me one thing."

"I'm afraid to ask."

"While I'm slaving away in the conference room, you'll talk to Ty."

With a groan, I replied, "Fine. I'll do it."

"Good."

After walking Selah to the door, I poked my head out in the lobby. "Um, Ty, can I see you in my office for a moment?" Nodding, he tossed his magazine on the table and rose out of his chair, and as he passed by me, I prayed he couldn't see how badly I was shaking. Once he was inside, I closed the door. "Please, have a seat," I said, motioning to the chairs in front of my desk.

After he sat down, I made my way to my desk on shaking legs. I didn't so much sit down in my chair as I flopped down. Once I righted myself, I glanced up at Ty. He stared curiously at me.

"I guess you're wondering why I called you in here."

"I would imagine it's to discuss some facet of our cohabitation?"

Ding, ding, ding! We have a winner. "Uh, yes, actually, it is." My tongue darted out to moisten my dry lips. "Listen, I think for us to be able to continue living and working together comfortably, we need to clear the air between us."

"Or more importantly, we need to find a way to make the air more *clothed* between us?" he asked.

A nervous giggle tumbled from my lips. "Well, yes, that too."

"I actually worked up a shower proposal on my iPad this morning."

"You did?" Damn, he really was always on top of things.

He nodded. "I felt it was the best way to ensure there were no more . . . mishaps."

"Uh, yeah, that's a good idea."

He reached into his briefcase and pulled out his iPad. "Since I seem to be more of an early riser, I thought I could go first."

"Sure. That would be great." When he offered me the iPad, I reached across the desk to grab it. As I gazed at the schedule, I noted the thoroughness of his planning. He ensured at least a fifteen-minute window between when he would be in the bathroom and when I would.

"Does that look like enough time?" he asked.

"It does." I slid the iPad back over to him. "Nice job. You've thought of everything."

"I also thought it would be a good idea if I allocated the half bathroom in the hallway as mine for everything except showering, and you could take the other."

"You don't have to do that."

"You say that now, but what happens when you walk in on me peeing?" he questioned matter-of-factly.

The mention of him peeing inevitably made me think of his dick and the actual reason for our sit-down. After crossing my legs, I said, "Okay, I suppose we can enact that."

"Good. That should take care of any future problems."

"I think so." I twisted the hem of my skirt nervously between my fingers. "There is one more thing I'd like to talk about."

"What would that be?"

"I feel I owe you some sort of apology for what you overheard between Selah and me."

"Ah, I see. *That*." For the second time that day, a flicker of apprehension filled Ty's face. I could tell he didn't want to rehash the conversation any more than I did, but I knew we couldn't move forward until we did.

"Yes, that." When Ty's gaze met mine, I said, "I just wanted to apologize for what I said. It was improper of me to be discussing your —" *Oh God, please just let the floor open up and swallow me whole.* That was the only scenario I saw that could possibly work.

With an expression as equally pained as the one I imagined was on my face, Ty held up a hand. "It's okay. I know what you're alluding to."

"Uh, okay, good."

"I accept your apology, and I assure you I will never reference it again."

"Thank you. I appreciate that." I swallowed hard. "Considering how much you're already sacrificing for this job, I don't want to do anything else to make it harder."

When Ty's eyes flared, I knew I had completely and totally used the wrong expression. While he might not have been outwardly fawning over my reaction to his dick, I got the impression that inwardly, he wouldn't be forgetting it any time soon. Somehow that seemed dangerous for both of us.

Ty held out his hand. "Here's to us starting fresh."

I nodded. "To starting fresh."

CHAPTER SEVEN

AFTER THE INITIAL cock-ups of the first few days, the next three weeks went off without issue. Caroline and I fell into a familiar rhythm together. I wouldn't say it was as easy as the one I had with Thorn, but surprisingly, it worked well. The first order of business had been adhering to our bathroom schedule, and I was proud to say no one's private bits had been on display for the other person. We did end up revising it slightly because Caroline decided she wanted to rise at seven to get in a workout in the apartment gym.

As for Perry, she began taking his calls in her bedroom, which thankfully limited my exposure to the wanker. Unfortunately, he was scheduled to spend the upcoming weekend with her.

Although I hated admitting it, he did have some game. He'd sent flowers on Caroline's first day at work and weekly bouquets of her favorite lilies. He also sent her funny emails throughout the day that of course we also saw since we were screening her personal and work emails. I supposed there was some decency within him, but I still hated the thought of her ending up with him. Somehow, I had to believe there was yet another side of him I wasn't aware of that had made her fall in love with him.

When it came to the stalker, the emails began again around the second week, their content just as vile as before. Since I'd promised Caroline to always shoot straight with her, I made sure to inform her of the dates and times we received anything. She seemed slightly relieved there were only emails so far because it meant the stalker probably wasn't aware of her location, but I knew it was only a matter of time before the letters started up again, which would mean he knew her address. Read 4 Life had been given several dummy addresses throughout West Virginia with only serious inquiries being forwarded to the right address and in turn, to Caroline.

It was a gorgeous late September day where the morning commute included a plethora of colors with the leaves changing and all the early fall decorations. Our morning routine usually consisted of a stop at Caroline's favorite local coffeehouse. Dan and Shirley, the owners, had been really nice the first time I'd performed a security sweep before Caroline entered. They usually knew what time would be arriving and always saved a chocolate croissant for me. It gave me the fortification to do a sweep of the lobby and elevator car of Read 4 Life's building before I went and got Caroline out of the car.

On this day, while I munched on my croissant, something felt off, like there was an electricity in the air that hadn't previously been there. It immediately put me on alert.

Just as we stepped off the elevator, something caught my eye. A box sat in front of the door. Although I was accustomed to many deliveries at Read 4 Life, something seemed off about this one. The fact that it had been sloppily painted blood red caused the hairs on the back of my neck to stand up.

I threw my arm out in front of Caroline. "Stop."

"What's the matter?"

Instead of answering her, I pressed my microphone to Beverly, one of the newest members of Caroline's security detail. "We have a suspicious package. Call 911 and prepare to get target out of the vicinity."

"Copy that."

I then shoved Caroline back into the elevator and smacked the button back downstairs.

"You don't seriously think that was a bomb?" she asked, her tone a mixture of frustration and fear.

"No, but I'm also not taking any chances."

"What about the other people in the building? Shouldn't they evacuate, too?"

"They'll get the word when Beverly calls 911. It'll be more as a precaution." I refrained from telling her that by having everyone evacuate the building, we could get photographic evidence of everyone who had been in the building, which we would in turn cross-check with the security tapes.

The elevator doors opened, and we hustled back out onto the street. After opening the SUV's door for Caroline, I pushed her inside. "You're not coming?" she asked, her voice wavering.

"You'll be fine. I'll be in touch with Beverly the entire time to let you know what's going on." Sitting there on the seat, she appeared so fragile. I wanted to be able to crawl up inside and gather her in my arms, to find a way to stop her trembling, but I couldn't. Part of ensuring her safety was to get her out of the area and for me to try to find the psycho.

After I helped pull the seatbelt around her, I placed my hands on her shoulders and looked her square in the eyes. "Caroline, it will be okay," I said firmly.

Although she appeared ready to cry, she bobbed her head in agreement. "Sure."

Reluctantly, I stepped back and closed the door. With the squeal of the tires, Beverly took off, and I was once again standing on a street corner watching Caroline's fading taillights. Glancing around the street, I shook my head. "You're not getting her, motherfucker."

Before I could step back into the building, two police cruisers arrived. One was from the FBI field agency in Charleston, and the other was from the local police department. I didn't have to flash my badge and introduce myself; I'd gone through those formalities at the precinct when I'd come in to survey the scene before Caroline arrived.

I followed two of the officers upstairs to Read 4 Life. Upon closer inspection, it was obvious the package wasn't an incendiary device. I'd pretty much known that from the start, but I'd wanted to involve the FBI so we could get a clean catch on fingerprints and any further DNA testing.

After an officer handed me a pair of gloves, I crouched down to take a better look. It was an average box painted red—at least I hoped it was paint. Taking a pen from my pocket, I used it rather than my fingers to flip open the lid. Hundreds of different scenarios ran through my head of what might be inside. None were good.

Lying on a bed of tissue paper was a blonde Barbie doll. A pocketknife was jammed into her chest, and a note was pinned to her clothing: *Soon.*

"Fuck. He knows."

"Knows what?" one of the officers asked.

"Her location."

The officer grimaced. "Shit. I was hoping this was just some sort of office prank and not related to the stalker."

"I wish it was just that." After using my phone to take a few pictures from different angles, I stepped back to let the FBI agent do the bagging. I thanked the officers, and then I headed back downstairs while the rest of the PD searched the building. Instinct told me they wouldn't find anyone, but it was best to follow protocol. Once he'd been alerted of the situation, Stuart had called the security company to pull the building's tapes, and we'd be reviewing those as soon as I could get Caroline secure.

Appearing somewhat thrown together, he sat in a parked SUV on the curb. I slid into the front seat beside him as he said, "Of course shit would hit the fan on my day off."

"Yeah, it sure as hell did."

"Another present like her hair?" he asked grimly.

"Yes. This one came with a warning."

Unlocking my phone, I showed him the pictures I'd taken. He knuckles whitened as he gripped the steering wheel. "Jesus Christ. James is going to go through the roof."

"I know. All the Callahan men are."

I could only imagine the next step of the plan would be to just hide Caroline out at some remote location. Of course, Barrett would probably argue how that never seemed to work out in the movies. All of them would probably initially overlook the fact that even if she was scared shitless, Caroline wouldn't hide out. It just wasn't who she was.

"How's Caroline?" I asked

"Beverly has her at a coffee shop a few blocks away."

"Take me there."

Stuart nodded. "What's the new plan?"

I raised my brows in surprise. "You're asking me?"

"I might be her protection leader, but you're the one who is truly in charge."

My head fell back against the leather headrest. "Truth is, I honestly don't know. Outside of reviewing the tapes for any leads and hoping forensics can lift some DNA, I have nothing."

"On the off chance he's staying in the area, I went ahead and pulled all the hotel records for the past few days."

"Good one," I murmured as I rubbed my eyes. As I racked my brain, another idea hit me. "I'll give my old boss in London a call." If there was anyone who could lend an objective eye, it would be Ethan Blackstone of Blackstone Security. Not only had I started my first job as a bodyguard through him, I'd also learned a hell of a lot about personal security.

"Couldn't hurt," Stuart replied.

Instead of going to All the Perks, our usual coffee shop, Beverly had spirited Caroline six blocks away to a Starbucks. After Stuart let me out, I headed inside. My eyes bounced around the room, searching her out, and I found Beverly first since she sat at a table directly in front of Caroline. I was sure she had strategically put them at the back of the store so no one was getting to Caroline. Beverly nodded her head in acknowledgment before rising out of her chair.

At her table, Caroline's laptop was open, but her vacant stare showed she wasn't paying attention. Her emotional grid was a wreck. When she saw me approaching, a relieved expression came over her face.

"Hey," I said as I sat down across from her.

"Hey," she replied.

"So, it wasn't a bomb."

She nodded. "Beverly told me."

"Good."

The last thing I wanted to do was tell her what the box had actually been, so I just sat there, fiddling with one of the napkins on the table.

"What was it?" Caroline finally questioned.

"It doesn't matter. You're safe."

Caroline grabbed hold of my arm. "You promised complete honesty, remember?"

Damn me for agreeing to that back in DC. With a resigned sigh, I pulled my phone from my pocket and unlocked the screen. Once the picture came up, I handed it to Caroline. At her horrified gasp, I cursed under my breath.

"Is that . . ." she finally questioned.

"Real blood?"

Unable to speak, she merely bobbed her head.

"We won't know until the lab tests it. Stuart's on his way to get it to the local FBI field office." Motioning to the door, I said, "Come on. Let me get you back home."

Caroline's brows shot up into her hairline. "Get me back home? Why wouldn't I go to work?"

"You've had a traumatic morning."

"Look, Ty, I have twenty cartons of books to sort through today or I don't get to make tomorrow's elementary school trips." A steely determination set into her jaw. "I've allowed this psycho to disrupt almost every facet of my life, but I won't let him disrupt the lives of these kids."

Damn her and her honor. At that moment, I would have rather her been some shrinking violet who demanded to be taken back to her apartment to go into hiding, but not Caroline Callahan.

Since I knew it was pointless arguing with her, I merely nodded. "All right. Let's get you back to work."

She opened her mouth to argue with me before closing it. "Really?"

"Yes. Really. The building has been thoroughly searched, and the FBI is currently reviewing the security tapes.

"Good. And thank you."

After getting up from the table, I helped Caroline pack up her things and gather her trash while Beverly went for the car. As we started out the door, Caroline grabbed my arm. "There's something I need you to do for me, and I want it done in the next few days."

"Okay. I'll try."

"I want you to teach me self-defense."

"I don't think that's really necessary considering the protection you're given."

"What happens if you're incapacitated as well as the others? Am I just supposed to take it like some damsel in distress?"

"It wouldn't come to that."

She cocked her brows at me. "How can you be so sure?"

The truth was, I couldn't say with absolute certainty it wouldn't. The odds were slim, but I wasn't a man who dealt in absolutes. I liked to have a backup plan for my backup plan, but I had my reasons for not wanting to teach her self-defense. It wasn't some bullshit thing about not believing in a woman's ability to protect herself—I'd fought alongside a lot kickass women when I was in service.

It stemmed more from the fact that I was slightly uncomfortable about putting my hands onto Caroline during the instruction period, and also about having her put her hands on me. Obviously, self-defense training was very physical, and after she'd had the reaction to my dick, I'd been slightly on edge about anything tactile with her. I was probably overreacting, but at the same time, I didn't think it hurt to be careful.

At my continued hesitation, Caroline crossed her arms over her chest. "Look, if you won't teach me, I'll just find someone else who will." With both Caroline's resources and determination, I didn't doubt her. She could have a first-rate instructor on the next plane in.

Huffing out a frustrated breath, I replied, "Fine, I'll teach you—but on one condition."

"What would that be?"

"After you learn a few maneuvers and become somewhat capable of defending yourself, you won't interfere with the protection your agents give."

She rolled her eyes. "Fine. I agree."

I extended my hand to her. "Shall we shake on it?"

"Sounds good to me." As we sealed the deal, a smirk curved on Caroline's lips. "I reserved some gym time for us this evening after hot yoga."

Blinking at her, I asked, "Pardon?"

"While you and the local PD were checking out the building, I was formulating my self-defense plan."

"You work fast," I remarked with awe.

"Thank you. Now if you don't mind, I'd like to get back to the office so I can make quick work of all the cartons I have to go through."

I opened the door on the SUV. "Your wish is my command." As she crawled in, I couldn't help mumbling, "Completely owned, just like with your brothers."

Of course, she heard me. Turning around, she winked. "Yep. Totally owned, Fraser."

And just like that, her confidence and strength reappeared. This woman would never cease to surprise me, and I wished I didn't like it as much as I did.

CHAPTER EIGHT

I WAS IN HELL, or at least an earthly version of it. What else would you call a room with the heat cranked up to a hundred that was populated by scantily dressed hot bodies bending themselves into outrageous positions? Did I mention Caroline was one of them? Or that her skin glowed under a sheen of sweat from her exertions?

While I was sure I looked like an epic creeper just hanging out in the back of the room, I didn't feel comfortable leaving Caroline alone, not with her stalker having made an in-town appearance that day. Although I probably would have been safe on one of the treadmills outside, I just didn't feel it afforded me enough time to get to her. The crazy fucker could be anywhere. Even though both Beverly and Stuart had made a sweep of the building before we arrived, I was still on edge. I'd made sure to explain the situation to the instructor, but I'd held back from making an announcement to the entire class as not to embarrass Caroline.

As she lithely stretched her leg over her head, a jolt went through my lower half. I shook my head, trying to get rid of the R-rated thoughts running through my mind. I tried giving myself a break for my perverted thoughts based on the fact that I was A) a man, and a man will think of sex even on his death bed, and B) I was a man who was not consistently getting laid.

The combination of A and B made for a very volatile situation. Throw in C) a very young, sexy woman with a rocking body on display in spandex, and I was doomed. Had President Callahan been so desperate to protect Caroline he had never imagined a scenario where I might be interested in banging his daughter? I was pretty sure the answer would've been no that one. He was a man of honor, while I was obviously lacking.

I ran my hand over my face. Jesus, I really needed to get to laid. Since the dating options in the area were more than limited, I wasn't sure how I was going to make that happen. Caroline's assistant, Selah, had made it pretty clear she would be up for something without me having to try too hard. I was a man, and she was a woman, so a meeting of sexual needs could be on the table, but would that get in the way of protecting Caroline? Even on my days off, I didn't feel comfortable leaving her alone for too long. Would I even dare to try securing time for a quickie? Dammit, protecting Barrett and Thorn never created these problems.

"All right, ladies. Namaste. Great class."

As the other women started talking and going for their water bottles, I stalked straight over to the thermometer and cranked the AC on. Caroline grabbed a towel out of her bag and began swiping the layer of sweat off her skin. My mind, which remained in the gutter, couldn't help wondering if she got that sweaty during sex. Grunting, I lifted up the mats we would need and took them to the center of the room. As I got set up, the other women dispersed, leaving Caroline and me alone.

"Ready to learn how to take some asshole down?" I asked.

"More than ready."

"I just wanted to make sure you weren't too tired."

With a laugh, she uncapped her water bottle. "I'm not tired, just more limbered up."

Oh yeah, you're limber, and I've unfortunately had to watch it all. "Right. Okay. Well, let's start on the mats with you facing me." Once we were squared off, I nodded. "One of the easiest areas of self-defense comes from Krav Maga."

Caroline's eyes bulged. "You're going to teach me stuff from the Israeli Army?"

I laughed. "Trust me, it's not that intense, just some basics."

"If you say so."

"First one is the easiest. It's important to remember there are only two areas on the body that cannot be made stronger through conditioning and therefore are particularly vulnerable to attack."

She tilted her head at me. "Let me guess: a good ol' kick to the groin."

"Exactly, but I'm not talking about a little kick. You want to ravage the area if you can."

"Jesus," she muttered.

"It can mean the difference in disabling your assailant for a moment and for several minutes."

"I'll keep that in mind."

"First, you're going to want to assess how high your attacker's groin is."

Sweeping her hands from her hips, Caroline demanded, "Seriously? Who has time to calculate groin ratio during an attack?"

With a roll of my eyes, I replied, "It only takes a few seconds."

"Fine, fine." Her eyes dropped from mine to eye my crotch. "Okay, I'm staring at your groin." The moment the words left her lips, pink bloomed along her cheeks. I know she had to be remembering that morning in the bathroom when she'd seen my cock in all its glory. Clearing her throat, she asked, "What now?"

"You want to make sure you have enough room to drive either your shoe or your shin into the groin, preferably the shin because the harder the hit, the more incapacitated your opponent will be."

After lifting her leg slightly, Caroline nodded. "I think I'm good."

"Okay. You're going to want to stand with your feet hip-width apart or slightly more. Make sure to place your right leg behind you." I stopped for a moment. "You are right-handed, aren't you?"

"Once again, I think the agency is doing a great disservice not having useless information like this in my file."

"Answer the question."

"Yes, I'm right-handed.

"Good. You're going to want to lead with the dominant leg, which will be your right one. Before you do that, raise your hands to your chest like you're going to block a punch."

"Um, I don't know what that means." She batted her eyelashes at me. "I'm a lover, not a fighter."

"I can see that." Stepping forward, I reached down to grasp her wrists. "You're going to keep your elbows tucked and your hands held up high." I slid my hands down her forearms, and I couldn't help noticing the shiver that went through her at my touch.

I hoped it was because she was still cooling down from hot yoga and not because she was having a reaction to me.

I then brought her forearms upright. "With the back of your hands out, you can put them in front of your face to block any hits. You can also use your hands to redirect any punches."

"I don't make fists?"

"No. It's easier to block any hits if you leave your hands open."

She nodded. "I still don't know if I could ever hit someone in that kind of situation."

"You'll be surprised what adrenaline will help you do."

"I hope so."

It was then I realized I was still holding her arms. After letting them go, I took a step back. "Okay, let's practice."

Caroline's mouth dropped open. "You want us to practice me kicking you in the balls?"

I snorted. "Not quite. You're going to practice kicking, and I'm going to deflect them." Turning away from her, I went to the corner of the room and picked up one of the weighted balls. "You're going to kick this rubber ball rather than my real balls."

"Nice one."

After I rejoined her, we got started. "Good force," I said when she kicked the first time. "You want to angle your hips a little more."

Oh Jesus, I really didn't want to be discussing her hips. Why hadn't I pawned this off on one of the other agents? I was sure it wouldn't have been half as awkward with them, especially if Beverly had done it.

We went through the drill about ten times. "Okay, I think you have that one covered."

"No offense, but I'm pretty sure I had that one covered back in fifth grade when a sixth-grade boy grabbed one of my boobs on the playground."

"You nailed a kid in the balls?"

Tightening her ponytail, Caroline said, "Yep, I sure did."

I was suitably impressed. Apparently, Caroline had been a badass since childhood. "Good for you."

"After I got dragged into the principal's office, Dad was like, 'I hope you don't expect me to punish my daughter for defending herself.'"

"Sounds like him." I tossed the ball back off to the side of the mat. "Okay, you've got the groin kick down, and another move I want to teach you is if you get attacked from behind and someone's forearm is around your throat." Motioning to her, I said, "Turn around."

After she whirled around, I closed the gap between us. When I pressed myself flush against her, Caroline immediately tensed. "I haven't done anything yet," I argued. I wondered if she was thinking the same thing I was—that we fit together pretty well. I couldn't help noticing how the perfectly the round globes of her ass molded against my groin.

"I know. I just don't like someone coming at me from behind."

Okay, so maybe she wasn't thinking anything perverted like I was. To get my mind back on track, I threw an arm around her neck. "You're going to want to put your hands on both my hands and fore-arm. Then I want you to tuck your chin to the left." After she complied, I said, "Now press your left shoulder to my chest so you can create some space between our bodies."

"Okay," she said.

"Now step your left foot between us."

"Is this when I'm going to do some weird backward kick to your groin?"

With a chuckle, I replied, "No, you're going to try to duck your head under my arm and get away from me."

"Got it." After she'd dipped out from under me, Caroline faced me in a full fighter's stance, a fierce look of determination on her face.

"Good. I like you came out ready to throw punches. You can

always disable your opponent with a few hits or a kick to the groin." When she flashed me a wicked grin, I shook my head. "That is *not* an invitation right now."

"Bummer."

"I think we should take a water break. You apparently need cooling off from the violence you'd like to inflict on me."

"Har, har."

We walked across the mats to the corner where our water bottles were. After taking a few long swigs, Caroline eyed me curiously. "Did you learn Krav Maga in the Army?"

I shook my head. "Actually, I learned it down on the docks while waiting around on my father. It was a 'this bloke had learned it from this bloke' kinda thing. With four brothers, I wanted to learn how to defend myself." With a wry smile, I added, "I learned ways to kill men with my bare hands in the Army, not just to defend myself."

She didn't appear too surprised by my declaration. I guess it came from having a father and brother in the military. "Do you ever miss military life?"

"Not really. I joined up because I knew I wanted a job where I could help people, but after doing my tour, I knew I didn't want to make a career out of it. I found there were other ways to help people."

Caroline's frustrated growl took me by surprise. "Now you're stuck in the backwoods trying to outwit my stalker. I don't know how noble that is."

"I'm helping you, aren't I?"

"Yes."

"Then I'm fulfilling my purpose, much more than when I was just a bodyguard for rich people who didn't have anyone threatening their life."

"Like Barrett?" she asked teasingly.

I laughed. "With Barrett, I like to think I was not only his bodyguard, I was also helping him keep his life somewhat in order."

"I'm sure he needed all the help he could get."

"Pretty much, but he's reformed now."

She grinned. "That's right. Addison made an honest man out of him."

"She was the best thing that could've ever happened to him."

"Ah, the old adage about the love of a good woman saving a wayward man?"

"Exactly."

Tapping her finger on her water bottle, she continued eyeing me. "Has that ever rung true in your life?"

"Who says I was ever wayward?" I teased.

"No one. I just assumed you might've been like Barrett."

"Compared to Barrett, I'm practically a virgin," I replied with a wink.

"Interesting. I always thought Army guys were manwhores."

I shrugged. "Some are, but some are married or in committed relationships. When you're deployed, all you want is someone waiting back home for you, someone who will give you a reason to keep going." When Caroline gave me a sad smile, I decided it was time to turn the tables on her. "What about you? Have you ever been wayward?"

She snorted. "Seriously? I know we don't know each other *that* well, but come on."

"Are you saying I should be able to judge by appearances? Because those can be deceiving."

"It should be pretty evident I'm not a classic, wild rich girl."

"At first glance, you're not, but it's been my personal experience that many reserved, put-together people have the tendency to throw caution to the wind."

"Like how?"

"What, you want an example?"

"Sure."

I shifted on my feet. While this was a conversation point I would have easily shared with Barrett or Thorn, I wasn't so sure about sharing it with Caroline. "Uh, yeah, so back in New York, I had a fling with a librarian at the New York Public Library. She wore pearls and glasses. She totally looked like a cat lady waiting to happen."

Caroline leaned forward. "And?"

"And she was a total freak, okay?"

Surprised laughter tumbled out of Caroline's mouth. "Um, okay then."

"Just proving a point."

"Somehow I didn't think that was the way you were going to prove your point."

With a sheepish grin, I replied, "I'm kinda wishing I hadn't."

She smacked me playfully on the arm. "You know, you're really cute when you're embarrassed."

"Whatever."

"As for me, I can safely say I've never been wayward. There have been a few moments of wildness, but for the most part, I've always stayed within the lines."

For some reason, her statement was comforting. "You and Thorn really are so much alike."

"You think so?"

"I guess after Barrett, your parents were thrilled to have another responsible, thoughtful child," I joked.

Caroline laughed. "I suppose so."

I capped my water bottle. "Okay, that's enough talking. Let's get back to work. Let's see you get away from me a few more times in that attack-from-behind move."

"Gladly." As we started back across the mats, Caroline asked, "Did you and the librarian get freaky in the reference section or in fiction?"

Pinching my eyes shut, I shook my head. "You did not just ask me that."

"I can't help it."

"Try harder."

"Does that mean you're not going to answer the question?"

"No, I'm not."

"Oh, come on. You can't unload a nugget like that and not expect some commentary on it."

"Caroline," I growled.

"Ty," she fake-growled back while grinning at me. It was both infuriating and endearing.

Falling behind her, I threw my arm around her throat. "All right, Miss Smart Arse, let's focus."

Instead of her bringing her hands to my arm and turning into me, she brought her left foot back to kick me in the shin.

"Ow! What the hell?" I cried out, and with me momentarily distracted, Caroline jacked her foot into my knee. "Oh no you don't." Using my strength, I flipped her around before pushing her down to her knees on the mat.

"Get off me."

"Make me."

After the story of her kneeing the kid in elementary school, I should have known to expect the unexpected from Caroline. The next thing I knew she was bringing her head back to crack her skull against mine.

"Jesus Christ!" As pain ricocheted through my head, I momentarily loosened my grip, which enabled her to slip away from me.

Instead of slinking away, she lunged forward, taking us both down onto the mats. We began to roll around, me deflecting the hits she was throwing. It didn't take a genius to realize she was taking her rage out on me. In her mind, I was the stalker. Finally, I stopped trying to protect myself, and I let her really get her aggression out.

"That's it, Caroline. Give it all up," I urged.

My words seemed to enrage her further, and she began slapping me.

When tears began streaming down her cheeks, I knew I needed to flip the switch. Things had gotten too serious too fast. Like her brothers, she was proud and determined. She couldn't bear appearing vulnerable to anyone, and from her anger, I could tell how much pain she had been suppressing. Only there in that room could she finally let it all go.

It was time to let her off the hook. Bringing my hands to her ribs, I began tickling her.

Her grunts and shrieks of anger turned into giggles. "W-What a-are y-you d-doing?" she huffed.

"Tickling you."

"N-No shit. B-But why?"

"You needed your switch flipped."

We rolled to another stop. This time with Caroline lounged across my body. *God, the feel of her . . .* Thank fuck she wasn't across a certain body part, or she'd have very quickly come to learn just how sexy I found her.

"My switch is perfectly fine, thank you," she protested. *In more ways than one, sweetheart.*

"Oh really."

"Yes, really."

I reached up and began tickling her again.

"Ty, stop!"

Although I should have, I couldn't bring myself to stop. Her laughter was music to my ears. It was freeing and comforting, and I wanted more than anything to bring more laughter to her life. I wanted us to be able to stay in that innocent, worry-free moment forever, which confused me. My life had never really been worry-free. My job meant I was expected to be at attention at all times when with my target, yet right then, I just wanted to hear her relax, let loose, and laugh. How could one woman seem to alter my thought processes so easily?

CHAPTER NINE

TY FRASER WAS TICKLING ME. The former British Army badass was tickling me. As laughter tumbled out of me, I couldn't help enjoying my elevated mood. Everything had gotten way too serious there for a moment. I'd really lost it. I wasn't sure why or how, but somehow Ty had a key to my moods and how to improve them. *How is that actually possible? How does he read me so easily?*

A throat cleared in the doorway, and both Ty and I jerked our gazes that way. It was Arjun. Since he was looking at the ceiling, the floor, and the walls—anywhere but us—I could tell he was completely uncomfortable.

"Uh, there's an FBI field agent on the secure line for you."

"Right. Okay."

I quickly scrambled off of Ty so he could get up. After he shot up off the mat, he nodded at Arjun. "Keep an eye on her for me."

"Will do."

After Ty left, the most painfully awkward silence filled the room. Rising up off the floor, I gave Arjun a weak smile. "Ty was kind enough to show me some Krav Maga moves."

"That's good. You should be equipped to defend yourself."

"I'm not sure how good I am it considering I had just tripped him up when you came in." Okay, so I was exaggerating the truth just a little to try to save face. I didn't need Arjun telling Stuart he'd found Ty and me in a potentially compromising position. I was sure that kind of news would make it straight to my dad.

"Don't sell yourself sort since you were able to take him down."

"It was more dumb luck than anything, especially since I fell myself."

"You'll get there."

"I hope so."

The conversation stalled, and once again, a feeling of awkwardness permeated the air around us. Keeping myself busy, I walked across the mat to get my bag and water bottle. I then joined Arjun in the doorway. "We can go on out to the car if you'd like. I'm pretty sure we're finished with tonight's lesson."

He nodded, and we'd just started toward the exit when Ty came through the door. His grim expression told me the news wasn't good. "What did they say?"

"Unfortunately, they couldn't get any DNA. This guy is better than we thought."

Anxiety tightened its way through my chest. There was something very disheartening about the news that the stalker had outsmarted the FBI. I knew I shouldn't get discouraged because we were talking about the technology and strategy of the FBI against one man, but at the same time, I felt defeated.

Once again in tune with my mood, Ty shook his head. "I know this isn't the news we were hoping for, but we will find him, Caroline."

Although I didn't feel it, I did nod my head in agreement. "You're right. I know." I spoke with conviction in my voice, but I didn't feel it.

Ty gave me a sad smile. "Come on. Let's get you home."

When he placed an arm around my shoulder, I was both surprised and touched. With the way I was feeling, I didn't shy away from him. Instead, I let him draw me against him. Somehow, next to his strength, I felt safer than I had all day. The fact that he smelled so damn good was also inviting. How he could smell so nice after exercising was beyond me.

Just as we'd started on the road home, Ty asked Arjun to take a left at the next red light. "Where are we going?"

He pointed out the window. "There's a liquor store up ahead on the corner." He winked at me. "We're out of wine, and given the day you've had, I thought you might want a fifth of Jack or tequila."

Emotions overwhelmed me. I fought the urge to both laugh and cry at his thoughtfulness. "I think wine will be good."

"Your usual vintage?"

"Nah, buy a twenty bottle one."

Ty whistled. "The lady is going big."

I grinned. "Yes, I am."

While I waited in the SUV with Arjun, Ty ran inside for the wine. "He's probably getting himself some scotch," Arjun mused.

"Seriously?" Besides the wine our first night, I'd never seen Ty drink.

Arjun nodded. "It's been a hell of a day for him too. I'm sure he'll have a glass or two before bed. Nothing to compromise him should anything happen, just enough to take the edge off."

An ache spread through my chest. I hated that the case was getting to Ty. I knew it was part of his job to protect me, but he'd already sacrificed so much. Like Arjun had predicted, Ty came out with two bottles in a bag.

"Did you get something for yourself?" I asked, throwing a look at Arjun in the mirror.

"I might have. Is that a problem?"

I shook my head. "Since today sucked epic ass, I think it's only fair to pass drinks around to everyone."

Ty and Arjun chuckled. "I would probably have to agree with that," Ty replied.

After we got back to the apartment, I trudged back inside. I couldn't help noting how different my mood had been when we'd left that morning, all because of my damn stalker.

"You want the shower first?" Ty asked.

I gave a slight shake of my head. "No. I think I'll call Mom and Dad."

"They already know about the Barbie."

"Oh, I figured. My call is more about just hearing their voices."

"I understand." He jerked his chin to the door. "Arjun will be stationed at the door while I'm in the shower."

Ordinarily, I would have rolled my eyes at the ridiculous security level, but after that day, I welcomed it. As we stood there in the foyer, Ty seemed hesitant to leave me, so I gently said, "I'll be fine. I'll nurse my bottle of wine and call Mom and Dad."

"Okay. I won't be long."

"Take your time." Inwardly, I smacked my hand against my forehead at telling him to take a long time in the shower. There was something a little illicit in the suggestion, like he'd be taking extra time to lather up his dick. *Eesh.*

He nodded. Reaching one of his hands over his shoulder, he jerked his T-shirt over his head before turning toward the bedroom. I'd only seen him shirtless a handful of times, and my eyes now homed in on the tattoo that covered most of his back. "Wow, I don't think I've ever really seen your tattoo in all its glory. It's epic."

"Thanks. It's for my Army regiment."

Taking a step forward, I got an even closer look. A St. Edward's crown sat at the top, and below it was a tusk-like horn. Underneath the picture, there were some words. When my index finger traced over the lettering, the muscles on his back undulated under my touch.

It took me a moment to find my voice. "First into the fight and the last from the fray." I peered around his shoulder at him. "That's a profound motto."

"It's what we abided by. We were the first ones sent in, and we didn't leave until the job was done."

"You still abide by that today."

He turned toward me. "I suppose I do."

"Don't be modest. It's the truth."

With a smile, he replied, "I'm glad you think so. I wouldn't have wanted to abandon the creed."

"You haven't. You live by it each and every day, and I'm very grateful—especially today."

His expression darkened. "You don't know how much I wish we'd gotten answers. As much as I hate that he tracked you down, I was hoping it might be the break we needed."

"I know. I hoped the same thing."

With a decidedly defeated energy hanging in the air, Ty gave a brief shake of his head. "Well, anyway, I'll go have a shower, and then it's yours."

"Thanks."

I watched his retreating form enter his bedroom. In spite of my former protests, I really was grateful Ty was there in Charleston with me. I understood why both Thorn and Barrett trusted his presence so implicitly. He was so . . . solid, undemanding yet relentless. If there was one thing keeping the pieces of me together, it was him.

While Ty took his shower, Mom and Dad tried everything they could to put me at ease. There words were comforting, but after the call was over, I found myself more emotionally scattered than before. After Ty gave me the green light, I slipped into the bathroom to take a shower myself. The scorching hot water felt heavenly against my aching muscles. When I reached for my shampoo bottle, I almost knocked over Ty's body wash. I started to move it aside when something overcame me. Uncapping the lid, I brought the bottle to my nose. Closing my eyes, I inhaled a whiff.

Oh yeah. Epic manly smell—or I supposed I should say epic manly *Ty* smell. I'd certainly smelled it when we'd been up close and personal at the gym. It wasn't anything like Perry's. His smell came from one of the most expensive colognes on the market, while Ty's was much more lowbrow. The differences shouldn't have been too surprising considering what total opposites they were. Of course, I probably shouldn't have been comparing my boyfriend and my agent at all.

With a sigh, I close the bottle, shoved it back onto the ledge, and went on with my shower, keeping my mind free of any more thoughts of Ty . . . at least for a little while.

After I turned off the water, I stepped out of the shower to the aroma of spices in the air. Oh man, Ty was cooking dinner for us. I could almost hear the echoes of Salt 'N' Peppa's *Whatta Man* echoing in my mind. After drying off and throwing on some pajamas, I came out of the bedroom to see Ty setting the table.

"Is that seared salmon?"

"Indian seared salmon. I finally located a lot of the spices. Well, I guess I should say Amazon located them for me."

My stomach rumbled appreciatively. "It smells delicious."

"Sit down, and I'll grab the wine."

I didn't argue with him. Instead, I slid into a chair in front of a heaping plate of salmon, steamed broccoli, and wild rice. While my mother would have chided me on my lack of manners, I snatched my fork up and dug in. I was that hungry. "Oh. My. God. This is so good."

Ty appeared with a glass of wine filled to the brim. "I'm glad you like it."

"Like it? I think I'm in love."

I swallowed hard and reached for my wine glass when Ty's eyes momentarily flared. "Really, I just threw some things together."

"You don't need to be modest. You're a seriously amazing cook."

He smiled as he sat down across from me. "Thank you. I didn't get a chance to cook for Thorn as much as I did for Barrett."

"Let me guess—you made a lot of hangover food for Barrett?" I questioned.

With a snort, Ty replied, "Good guess." He then proceeded to regale me with many stories of Barrett's antics. Laughing about my goober of a brother was just what I needed to continue lightening my dark mood.

After we finished eating, I insisted on washing the dishes and cleaning up since he had cooked. He reluctantly let me. While putting away the mess, I also managed to put away the wine—two full glasses' worth. By the time I finished with the kitchen, I had a nice buzz to head to bed on.

As I collapsed onto my mattress, I heaved a resigned sigh. *God, what a day.* From start to finish, it had been a shit show. It hadn't been enough for my stalker to rear his head by having a package show up at my work; on top of that, the evening with Ty had been completely confusing.

At the thought of Ty, I instantly saw his chiseled abs in front of me . . . that sinfully sexy V dipping into the waistband of his pants . . . the broad, muscled shoulders. His thighs had been rock hard against mine. It had been absolutely delicious lying across him. He seriously had *the* most amazing body of any man I knew.

I smacked my hand to my forehead. *Caroline Callahan, would you get a grip? You have a boyfriend, remember?*

A boyfriend who was coming for a visit that weekend. Considering my state of horniness, that was a good thing. Running my fingers across my forehead, I growled in frustration. I knew I was never going to get to sleep without taking care of business. I was just too wound up and in desperate need of a release. An orgasm was just what I needed to help me get a good night's rest.

Craning my neck, I eyed my nightstand. I knew within the top drawer was the answer to my problems: my vibrator. With a huff, I kicked off the sheets and rolled over in the bed. Leaning over, I slid the drawer open and grabbed the vibrator.

With it in one hand, I used my other hand to grip the waist of my pajama pants. I wriggled them over my hips and down my thighs. Once they were bunched at my feet, I spread my legs, brought the tip to my pussy, and turned on the vibrator. Instantly, I jumped from the sound echoing off the wall, not from the jolt of pleasure. *Shit, has it always been this loud?* I flipped it off and glanced at the bathroom door. What if Ty heard me?

Surely, I was just being paranoid, right? How could he possibly hear a little humming through the bathroom and a wall? Since my core was still aching, I turned the vibrator back on. Biting down on my lip, I worked it over my clit. "Oh fuck," I murmured as the sensations reverberated through me.

My free hand slipped inside my pajama top to cup my breast. As my fingers tweaked my hardening nipple, an image began to form in my mind. A muscled body with a chest covered in tattoos covered me in his weight. A strong hand replaced mine on my breast to tease and squeeze my nipple. Below my waist, the vibrator became a pulsing erection rocking against my clit. When I slipped the vibrator inside me, I shrieked, my toes curling into the mattress.

I began rocking my hips against the vibrator. With each thrust, I climbed higher and higher. He was taking me higher and higher with his powerful cock, and then I exploded in a convulsion of cursing and sheet grabbing and lip biting.

When I came back to myself, I realized I'd literally broken out in a sheen of sweat. I couldn't remember a time when I'd come so hard during a solo session.

Oh shit.

I hadn't been getting off to the vibrator—I had gotten off to Ty.

He'd been the image in my mind, the hands on my body, the dick inside me.

A chill went over me. How could I have just gotten off to my Secret Service agent? To Ty? Wasn't fantasy a part of emotional cheating? I'd never, ever cheated on a boyfriend before. Sure, I'd found other guys hot and had tingly moments around them, but I'd certainly never gotten off to one of them.

I groaned. This time it wasn't out of pleasure but emotional turmoil. Part of me argued I shouldn't beat myself up considering the day I'd had. Like in a dream, a moment in time had been imprinted on my subconscious. Ty was the last man I'd been around so it made sense I would have a fantasy about him.

Yeah, I know. I wasn't buying it either.

All I could hope was that Perry's arrival that weekend would push any and all inappropriate thoughts of Ty from my mind. If not, I was in big trouble, because I lived with this man. I had no illusions that he would want to pursue anything with me because he was all about professionalism. Nothing good could come from me falling for the man who was protecting me. There was too much at stake and too many people who could get hurt.

CHAPTER
TEN

AS I SAT at my desk in my bedroom, I bent my head over my laptop. For probably the hundredth time in the last half hour, I'd watched the tapes of the stalker. Well, I supposed I should say the phantom stalker. Not only had he been smart when it came to making sure there was no human DNA in his package, he'd also shorted out the security cameras for two minutes and fifteen seconds.

Apparently, two minutes and fifteen seconds was how long it had taken for him to arrive at the building, take the elevator up, deposit the package, and then get the hell out of dodge. The fucking bastard was good.

I willed myself to stop and get my arse in the bed when a noise from Caroline's room caused the hairs on my neck to stand up. Rising up out of my chair, I walked over to the bathroom door. Per our bathroom schedule, this time of night was when I was supposed to use the hall bathroom to take care of business.

At the sound of her moan, my hand flew to the doorknob. Pushing it open, I stepped into the bathroom. As light flooded the space, I saw it was empty. Thankfully, Caroline wasn't sick or hurt. In my mind, I'd dramatically imagined her passed out on the floor.

As I crept across the tile toward her bedroom door, I thought I heard a faint buzzing sound. Surely, if someone had been using a saw, it would have been picked up on the security tapes—unless the stalker had scrambled the access for a few minutes.

Just before I could yank the door open, Caroline's throaty cry caused me to freeze. "Oh fuck!"

Oh fuck was right. I knew that type of cry, and it wasn't one of panic or alarm or pain. It was one of pleasure. Just beyond the door, Caroline was getting off. From the sound of the buzzing, I knew what was giving her the pleasure.

As she continued to moan, my traitorous cock jumped in my shorts. Glancing down, I shook my head. "Stop it!" I hissed.

I could not get an erection to Caroline. It was just too wrong on too many fucking levels. For one, she didn't know I was listening to her, and creepy didn't even begin to describe the invasion of privacy. Secondly and most importantly, she was my target and the president's daughter. You just don't do that shit.

To my cock, however, she could have been a nun, and it still would have been rock hard. Whirling around, I got the hell out of there as quickly and quietly as I could. I figured putting distance between myself and Caroline getting off was the only thing that would nix my hard-on, but even after I was back in my bedroom, it throbbed between my legs. It didn't help that my mind kept replaying a soundtrack of the sounds I'd just heard.

Normally, I would have taken a cold shower to get rid of it, but I couldn't let Caroline hear me up in the bathroom. I also didn't particularly like the idea of going to the kitchen and dousing it with a cup or two of cold water.

I plopped down in my desk chair. Opening up my computer, I opened up an old standby for situations like this: Pornhub. Jerking my shorts down, I palmed my cock with one hand. With the other, I turned on a clip of two hot blondes going at it.

Fuck. Picking a blonde had been the wrong idea because instantly I saw Caroline writhing around on the bed. With my free hand, I slid my mouse over to some brunette lesbian porn instead. As the two girls passionately kissed, I began pumping my hand up and down my aching cock. I bit down on my lip to keep from making any noise. Normally, I liked to crank the volume because I loved hearing the noises the women made, but I had to keep things quiet this time.

As my hips rocked on the wooden chair, my hand's frenzied movements worked my dick. With everything within me, I focused on the two women, but then they began fading out. Instead, I saw Caroline beneath me. My hands cupped her pert breasts as I moved my erection against her panty-clad core. Just a slip of the fabric and I could be inside her.

No, no, NO! This was wrong. I grunted in disgust rather than pleasure, but I was too fucking close to stop. She had felt so right when she'd been lying on me. Her soft curves had molded into the rough angles of my body almost perfectly. At the thought of digging my hands into her perfect ass, I groaned. A few more hard pulls and I would have a release. Frantically, I worked my palm. Pinching my eyes shut, I focused on the pleasure and drove everything else out of my mind . . . except I could still hear those moans, that cry.

I couldn't escape the fantasy anymore. I spread Caroline's creamy white thighs and tore her panties off. When I plunged inside her, I came with a shout. I hadn't come inside her tight walls, though; instead, I'd come into my hand. I hoped like hell she hadn't heard me. Maybe she would think I was having a nightmare or getting a little too involved in a game of football.

Staring down at myself, I shook my head in disgust. How could I be such a bastard? She'd just been enjoying a moment, probably fantasizing about Perry, and I'd been some creep who sprung a hard-on and then jerked off.

As I cleaned up, I wondered if I needed a break. Maybe I was spending too much time with her and it was getting to my head. Maybe I needed to go off for the night or maybe let one of the other agents sleep inside the apartment—anything to try to retract her from underneath my skin. If not, I was in big trouble, because I couldn't fall for the woman I was protecting. It was too dangerous for both her and my job.

CHAPTER ELEVEN

BUTTERFLIES DID the samba in my stomach while I put the finishing touches on my makeup. The last time I'd been this nervous about seeing Perry had been our first date. Tonight, I'd even gone so far as to have a pre-game glass of wine to see if it would calm me down. I just wanted everything to go right. Being apart the last three weeks had been difficult. Even though we talked each and every day, there was a strain that hadn't been present when I'd been at Oxford. I chalked it up to the personal soap opera I currently found myself starring in. From a stalker to a new job and a live-in bodyguard, it was a lot to process.

After the Barbie in a Box incident, my stalker went radio silent for the next few days. According to Ty, there weren't even any emails that came through. I could tell this latest development worried him, like he imagined my stalker was saving up his energy for something really big. I couldn't even let my mind entertain that thought, or I would have ended up going absolutely crazy. I was already teetering on the edge as it was.

Besides my stalker driving me loony, there was also the other night's pleasure session that kept rearing its head to torment my subconscious. I kept analyzing every aspect of it. I'd come to the conclusion that while I might have been attracted to Ty, it didn't mean I didn't love Perry or wasn't devoted to him. Ty was just present all the time where Perry wasn't.

As for Perry, I'd chosen my sexiest black dress for the occasion, one with a plunging neckline and a hemline that twirled just at my knees. I'd paired it with a strappy pair of heels and would probably freeze outside in the weather, but it would be worth it.

I came out of my bedroom to find Ty was hunched over his laptop at the kitchen table. When he glanced at me, his eyes flared before he let out a low whistle. "Wow, you really pulled out all the stops tonight."

"You think so?"

He nodded. "He won't be able to take his eyes off of you."

My skin warmed under the adulation of his words and stare. "Thanks."

His eyes averted to his laptop screen. "To go over the schedule for tonight, you have reservations at eight at Laury's." He peered back up at me with a grin. "Don't worry, I made sure to ask for two tables, so you and Perry won't have to share with me."

I laughed. "Thank you for that."

"Arjun is there doing a security sweep. He'll be driving us tonight."

"Okay. Good to know."

"While you're at dinner, he can make sweeps at any other stops you'd like to make."

"I think for the moment we'll just do dinner and then come home. Tomorrow I'd like to show him around town."

"Do you have any specific places in mind?"

"Not at the moment, although I'm pretty sure we can rule out Shoney's Big Boy Museum."

Ty chuckled. "I'll mark that one off my list."

"If the weather is good, we could focus on Capitol Street and maybe one of the parks."

Rubbing his chin, Ty asked, "Perry hikes?"

Busted. Jeez, Ty really knew Perry well for someone who actually hadn't spent any time with him. "Not exactly, but we don't have to go crazy on the walking. You know, just something to get out of the apartment for."

"I'll make a note of it." From Ty's tone, I could tell he wasn't too worried about making the necessary security sweeps for Perry and me to take a romp in the great outdoors.

When my phone dinged, I saw the text was from Perry. "He's here at the gate." As an added security measure, Ty would be the one texting the gate code to Perry just in case my stalker was hacking into my cell phone. Ty picked up his phone, and I dipped into the hall bathroom to check my appearance once last time.

As I fluffed my hair, Ty called, "Skip the mirror. You can't possibly make yourself look any better."

My hand froze as I stared at my reflection. I wasn't sure why Ty's compliments had such an effect on me. You would have thought I was starved for attention the way I inwardly lit up whenever he said something nice. He made me all warm and fuzzy like back in middle school when a guy I liked told me I was pretty. Well, there was the obvious fact that I didn't like Ty like that, but I couldn't deny the feelings I experienced whenever he complimented me.

"It never hurts to make a few last-minute adjustments," I replied as I came out of the bathroom.

At the ring of the doorbell, my nerves once again kicked into overdrive. Once Ty checked the camera and gave me the go-ahead, I opened the door. With his roller bag beside him, Perry gave me a wide grin. "Hey, babe."

"Hey yourself."

After he stepped into the foyer, he pulled me into his arms. As his lips warmed mine, one of his hands dipped below my waist to cup my buttock. Since we weren't alone, I quickly ended the kiss. "It's good to see you," I panted.

"It's good to be seen. I'd say you're a hell of a sight for sore eyes."

"I'd agree."

Perry shook his head as he took in my appearance. "Fuck me, you look amazing."

I smiled. "Thanks. I wanted to get dressed up for you."

"I'm glad you did." Perry then clapped his hands together and waggled his brows. "All right, what kind of madness are we going to get into tonight?"

I giggled. "It's Charleston, not Manhattan."

"Come on. From the way you're dressed, I just assumed we were going clubbing."

Nibbling my lip, I threw a cautious glance at Ty. "I'm not sure a club is the best idea right now."

"You're fucking kidding me, right? We raved all over Oxford last year with Stanley."

"Stuart," I corrected.

Perry shrugged. "Whatever."

"The situation was different then," I protested.

"I see." Perry swept his gaze from mine and over to Ty. "Do all agents stateside have a stick up their ass or something?"

"Perry!" I admonished while Ty's jaw clenched.

"What? I was just joking."

"It's not something to joke about. I told you about the Barbie box."

"Caroline is right, and I'm merely doing my job. A darkened night-club full of strangers who haven't been vetted is far too great a security risk for Caroline."

"Okay, okay. We won't go clubbing. I'm sure there are a ton of other things to choose from out here, right?"

"Actually, I went ahead and made us dinner plans at one of Charleston's hippest restaurants."

"There are actually hip people around here?"

I rolled my eyes. "Would you stop being so cynical?"

Perry laughed. "I'll try, babe. For you."

"Good. Why don't you go get freshened up?"

"Now that I can do."

I showed Perry where he could put his things in my room and then showed him the bathroom. He glanced at the two doors. "Wait, so this is one of those Jack and Jill things?"

Uh-oh. "Yeah, the two bedrooms share the bathroom—at least they're supposed to, but Ty made a bathroom schedule to ensure we don't have any more embarrassing run-ins."

Perry's brows creased angrily. "Did he see your tits?"

"No, no. It was nothing like that."

"Then what happened?"

"I accidentally saw him getting out of the shower."

With a snort, Perry replied, "Like that's a big deal. You had me worried for a minute."

If you'd seen Ty's dick, you wouldn't just be worried. You'd be downright pissed because your dick is so much smaller. I decided it was probably best if I refrained from saying that.

"It was nothing really. I mean, you've seen one dick, you've seen them all, right?" I replied. At Perry's funny look, I wished for the floor to open up.

"Yeah, right."

"Anyway, I'll leave you to get ready."

After powerwalking to the door, I closed it behind me. When I came out of the bedroom, Ty was waiting on me. "He isn't going to be a problem this weekend, is he?"

"What do you mean?"

He crossed his arms over his chest. "When it comes to your safety, he isn't going to be a problem, right?"

"No. Of course not." At Ty's skeptical look, I added, "Yes, he might get pissy about the situation, but he won't do anything to compromise my safety."

"I hope not."

From Ty's posture and tone, I knew if Perry tried anything, Ty wouldn't hesitate to put him in his place both verbally and physically, and that worried me—for Perry's sake. I was just as frustrated with him as Ty was, especially since I saw how it impacted more than just me.

We made it to dinner without any further issues, but the momentary peace was short-lived when Perry saw where Ty would be sitting. Before my stalker, he was used to my agent being at a table in the restaurant, but not necessarily one right behind ours. While we waited on our drinks to arrive, Perry's face remained hidden behind the menu, but from time to time, his head would tilt to the side and his eyes would narrow on Ty. His growing agitation with the situation was apparent from the way he downed half of his vodka tonic when it arrived. "Go ahead and bring another," he instructed the waiter.

"Yes, sir."

Once the waiter had our order and had taken the menus, Perry no longer had the menu to hide behind. He shook his head at me. "Jesus, I feel like he's breathing down my neck."

"I'm sorry. Because of the threat this week, he needs to stay even closer to me than my other agents."

"Don't tell me he's going to be in the bed with us while I'm fucking you tonight."

I rolled my eyes. "Of course not. He'll be in his own bed."

Perry waggled his brows. "Guess we'll give him some spank-bank material."

"Ew. Gross."

"Come on, it's hot thinking someone can hear you having sex. It's like doing it in public."

"It might be alluring to have strangers hear you, but the last thing I want is for Ty to hear us going at it."

"Why do you care so much about what he thinks?"

"Because I respect him and his position. He gave up his job in New York to come out here with me. He deserves not to be subjected to a porno."

"You are pretty loud," Perry teased.

As my cheeks warmed at his words, I threw a glance over my shoulder to see if Ty could hear us. Thankfully, he appeared to be scanning the restaurant and not paying attention. "I'll make sure I work on that."

"Good luck with that. Since it's been a month for me, I might be the one screaming."

"I don't scream," I countered.

"You moan pretty loud while saying 'Oh God!'"

"Whatever."

He grinned. "Don't *whatever* me. It's sexy as hell. I love a woman who's vocal in bed. I mean, who wants someone who just lies there and takes it?"

Glancing around, I hissed, "Would you lower your voice?"

"What? Are you afraid some random hicks are going to find out you like sex?"

"Perry, please."

With a roll of his eyes, he replied, "Fine. Man, you've gotten uptight since you've been gone."

"I have not. I just don't want a bunch of strangers—least of all Ty—hearing about my sex life."

"Yeah, I'd hate for precious Ty's virginal ears to hear something naughty," he teased.

"Are you going to keep being a dick, or are you going to tell me all about what I'm missing back in New York?"

"I suppose I can regale you with a few stories of what the crew is up to."

"Good." As Perry started in on what his investment banker friends were up to, I exhaled a relieved breath that he'd taken the bait to change the conversation. I couldn't have cared less about any of the other patrons hearing about my sex life; it was Ty I was concerned with. After seeing his dick and getting off to him the other night, it was just too much to have him knowing even more intimate details about me.

Perry apparently got comfortable with tuning Ty's presence out. For the rest of dinner, he was his old self, laughing and carrying on. It warmed my heart because I'd missed him—or I'd missed this version of him. I didn't really want to think about what that meant. I just wanted to enjoy the moment.

When we got back to the apartment, I started for the couch to watch something on television, but Perry steered me into the bedroom. His mouth was on mine before the door clicked shut. "God, I've missed the taste of you," he muttered against my lips.

"I've missed you, too."

As his hands tangled in my hair, our tongues battled against each other. This part of my relationship with Perry had always been easy. We'd never had issues when it came to the physical aspect of things.

When Perry's hand cupped my breast, I suddenly froze. Apparently, it wasn't the reaction either one of us expected. Tearing his lips from mine, Perry stepped back before narrowing his eyes at me. "What the hell is going on, CC?"

"Nothing."

Perry's brows popped up. "Nothing? You just turned into a freakin' statue while we were making out."

I rubbed my arms as a chill went through me. "I'm sorry. I'm just not myself tonight."

"You can say that again. It's like being out with a totally different person."

Excuse me? Did he actually just say that? Asshole! "Have you stopped to think what it might be like for me knowing there's someone out there who wants to kill me?"

"Yeah, I'm sure it's been a little stressful, but you're safe here with Captain Hardass and the other agents. It's just you and me." He shook his head. "At least it was until you shut down."

"Look, I'm sorry, but it's been a crazy week with the Barbie thing. I just need some time."

Perry huffed out an exasperated breath. "Caroline, we haven't slept together since the night before you left for this shithole. I think I've been more than patient waiting on you."

Ass! I blinked my eyes. It was like I was seeing him completely as Ty did. Drawing my shoulders back, I countered, "More than patient waiting on me? Are you actually serious? You know, if you really loved me, you'd be understanding about giving me time, not to mention being a little more concerned about my welfare when there's some psycho out there who wants to kill me."

"I do love you, Caroline, but I don't think it's too much to ask to expect some physical elements of our relationships after almost a month."

I crossed my arms over my chest. "I'm not having sex with you tonight, and I'm not sure if I'll have sex with you tomorrow or Sunday. It might be a sexless weekend where we just hang out together and you support me after the really shitty week I've had." I jerked my chin at him. "Are you on board for that?"

Perry narrowed his eyes at me. "If I wanted a sexless weekend, I could've stayed back in DC and FaceTimed you. Hell, at least we probably would have had phone sex." He snatched his jacket off the bed. "I think it might be best if we take a little a break."

My mouth dropped open. "You want to break up over us not having sex?"

"Come on. It's about way more than the sex. It's about you always completely emasculating me by making decisions for us and never compromising."

"What are you talking about?"

"I've always catered to you in this relationship, but you've never done what I wanted. I wanted you to choose a job in DC so we could move in together. What did you do? Pick a job in Bumblefuck, West Virginia!"

"You know me being here isn't for forever and I plan to come back to DC after a year, not to mention the fact that you could have worked remotely here a couple of days a week. I would have supported you if you had wanted to take a job opportunity away from me."

"Can you honestly tell me one thing you've compromised for me?"

"You're joking, right? Besides living here, I've always tried to defer to you, from the smallest thing like where we went to dinner on Friday nights to the big ones like where we took vacations. All I've ever wanted was to make you happy, and in turn, for us to be happy."

"I'm sorry, Caroline. We made a great power couple for a while, but your life is a fucking circus. I just don't want to be a part of it anymore."

As I recoiled from his words, he grabbed his suitcase and then stormed out of the bedroom. I trailed behind him, unsure of what else to say or do. I kept expecting him to stop and have a change of heart, but he didn't. He never looked back at me.

After Perry slammed the front door, I shuttered my eyes in pain. *That's it? He's done? He didn't even look back?* What a horrible night to add to an equally shitty week. Even with my eyes closed, I knew Ty was there. Of course, he didn't need his spidey bodyguard senses today. That shouting match Perry and I had just had would have alerted him more than sufficiently.

I exhaled an agonizing breath. "Go ahead and say it."

"What?"

I flipped my eyelids open to pin him with a stare. "That you told me so."

Ty's expression became pained. "I couldn't do that to you."

"Why not? You've alluded to it before."

"It was different then."

Throwing up my hands, I countered, "How was it different then?"

"Your heart wasn't broken."

His words breached the dam that had been holding back my tears. My chest caved in, and I began sobbing uncontrollably. I realized in that moment I was mourning the loss of a relationship that never was. The Prince Charming I'd fabricated in my mind was really just a rat, and not even the good, clothes-making-friendly kind like in fairy tales. The man I'd expected to support and nurture my dreams hadn't fulfilled his end of the bargain. *He never really loved me. A great power couple? What the fuck?*

"Bloody hell," Ty muttered at my outburst.

"I-I'm s-sorry. I-I k-know it's n-not p-part of your j-job description," I sputtered.

"Not exactly." He gave me a sad smile. "But I'd be a real arse if I didn't give you a shoulder to cry on in your time of need."

I hiccupped a laugh. "I'd really appreciate it at the moment."

Ty bridged the gap between us. After he led me into the safe confines of his embrace, my cries began to subside. There was something about his quiet strength that calmed me. He was so broad, and I felt so small in his arms. Right then, that was what I needed. He was my quiet in this tempest. As long as he was with me, it felt like everything from Perry to my stalker was going to be okay.

"He's a sodding wanker."

My laugh reverberated against his broad chest. "I see your Briticisms are coming through."

"They seemed like the right words for the moment."

"If I'm honest, I'd have to agree."

After placing his hands on my shoulders, Ty gently eased me back where he could look at me. "He didn't deserve you. In time, you'll come to see that."

"Actually, I can already see that. I'm just wondering what the hell was wrong with me all these months," I mused.

Ty chuckled. "That one is easy—you were in love."

I groaned. "But why was I in love with such a wanker, as you call him?"

"While it chafes my arse to admit it, he did have some good points, like sending you flowers."

My heart ached a little in my chest. "That's true. When we first started dating, we had so much fun. We were always laughing . . ." Until we weren't.

"You'll laugh again with someone better."

"Says the single man," I countered.

"My singleness is a choice, just like your choice was to overlook Perry's faults for far too long."

"True." I rubbed my eyes. "This weekend sure didn't turn out like I expected it to. So much for a good time to take my mind off things."

Ty shifted on his feet. "Listen, if you want to call Selah for a hen's night, I can make myself scarce in the bedroom."

I smiled at his suggestion. "While that would be nice, she's actually gone back home to Virginia for the weekend for a family wedding."

"Oh. I see." He rubbed the back of his neck while appearing somewhat emotionally conflicted. "What is it you women do after a bloke breaks up with you?"

"Usually, we sit in a dark room eating ice cream and drinking wine while watching ridiculously sappy romantic movies."

He winced. "Seriously?"

"Yes. Why do you ask?" My eyes bulged. "Wait, are you volunteering yourself as tribute in Selah's absence?"

"Maybe."

"Why Ty Fraser, I had no idea you could get so in touch with your feminine side."

With a glower, he replied, "I'm not putting on any of those fruity face masks or letting you paint my fingernails."

"Bummer. I was going to suggest mani-pedis."

"Not. Happening."

I grinned. "It's okay. I'll take the bingeing on movies and ice cream."

"We don't have any ice cream in the house."

"Then I suppose we're going to have to make a run to the Psychotic Pig."

He grinned. "I guess so." Jerking his chin at me, he said, "You're probably going to want to change. I think you're slightly overdressed."

After I swept my gaze from him down to my sexy dress, the well of my emotions overflowed, and I sniffled. "Yeah. It would be a tragedy to waste this dress on the Psychotic Pig."

Although I hated myself for it, I couldn't stop the tears. Just a few hours ago, the evening had held such promise, only to go down in flames. A few hours ago, I'd been a girl in a relationship. Now I was single. Considering the security restrictions due to my stalker, it was going to be next to impossible to put myself out there for someone else.

When a strangled noise came from Ty, I jerked my head up. His hand was furiously rubbing the back of his neck. "Christ, if you want to wear the dress, wear it."

I hiccupped. "You think I'm crying about wanting to wear the dress?"

"Isn't that it?"

Using the back of my hand, I swiped at my eyes. "No wonder you're still single."

"Huh?"

Narrowing my eyes at him, I declared, "I'm not crying about the dress. I'm crying about the utter disarray of my life."

"Okay. Well, you went from talking about the dress to being hysterical—what else was I supposed to think?"

"That I'm still upset about Perry."

Ty's brows creased in confusion. "And how does that connect to me being single?"

I threw up my hands. "Because you thought I was crying about my dress."

"Apparently, I have a lot to learn."

"I would so say," I challenged.

"Perhaps you can be the Yoda to my Luke Skywalker when it comes to the psychology behind emotionally overwrought females."

I shot him an exasperated look. "Whatever. I'm going to change."

"Only if you're absolutely sure. I'll support you no matter what you decide to do. If you want to wear pajamas, I'll be happy to escort you up and down the aisles."

"You know, you're kinda weird, Fraser."

He winked at me. "Right back at ya, Callahan."

CHAPTER TWELVE

IT SEEMED SOMEWHAT surreal cruising the aisles of the Psychotic Pig with Caroline. Maybe it was because I had prepared for this weekend to be all about Perry. While I had never been a fan of his, I hated that things had ended the way they had. With everything she had on her plate with the stalker and the new job, the last thing Caroline needed was a broken heart.

When we got to the checkout, I groaned at the sight of Sheldon, the manager I'd taken out a few weeks earlier. At the sight of us, he threw up his hands. "It's just me!"

"Funny guy," I muttered.

He chuckled. "Hello again. Glad to see you guys."

"Nice seeing you again," Caroline said.

"Are you enjoying your time in Charleston?" Sheldon asked.

Caroline nodded. "Yes, I like it very much."

"We're all really excited to have you living here."

"I'm really happy to be here." As the words left her lips, her chin began to tremble.

Sheldon paused midway through scanning the groceries. "Are you okay?"

Caroline waved a hand. "I'm fine."

Sheldon glanced over at me. "Bad breakup," I replied.

His expression softened. "I'm so sorry. A pretty girl like you shouldn't have a broken heart."

His words cued the waterworks, and Caroline began crying right there in the checkout line of the Piggly Wiggly. When I dared to look over my shoulder, the lady behind me in line was shooting daggers my way, like it was somehow my fault Caroline was crying and not that wanker Perry's.

Right. We needed to get the hell out of there ASAP. Since they were short someone to bag the groceries, I swept past Caroline to go to the end of the checkout and started shoving food into the bags.

Upon surveying my bagging skills, Sheldon gave me a horrified look. "Be careful—you don't want to smoosh your bread."

At that moment, I would have dropkicked the bread out the door if it meant escaping the gawking looks and judgmental stares surrounding us.

Just as soon as I'd tossed in the last of the sugar-filled candy, I nodded at Caroline. "Okay. Go ahead and pay, and then we'll get you home." When she appeared momentarily dazed, I dug her wallet out of her purse. Once I had her debit card, I swiped it. "Can you enter the PIN?"

She gave me a slow nod before punching in the numbers. The register spit out the receipt, and Sheldon handed it to Caroline. With a sad smile, he said, "Take care, honey. Just remember, there are other fish in the sea."

"Thanks, Sheldon."

I scooped up the six bags. "Come on. Let's go."

As we stepped through the mechanized doors, Caroline began giggling. The giggling then turned into her bending over at the waist, laughing somewhat maniacally.

"Are you seriously laughing right now?"

Righting herself, she replied, "I just realized I had a breakdown in the Piggly Wiggly. That's like the equivalent of being one of the People of Walmart."

"I'm not really sure what that is, but yes, you did lose it back there."

"You've really never seen People of Walmart?"

I shook my head as I opened the door of the SUV for her. "No. Somehow it's managed to elude me."

After she climbed inside, she looked back at me. "You're not missing all that much. When I really think about it, the website is kind of disgusting for posting pictures of people without their knowledge."

"Sounds like a day in the life of you and your family."

"Sort of, but at least we're prepared to be photographed. These people aren't, or at least they don't really care if anyone takes their picture." Panic flashed across her face. "Oh God, what if someone recognized me and took a video of me freaking out?"

"I think the only one who knew you was Sheldon, and he was far too concerned with your emotional state to try to exploit you. Don't be too surprised if the next time we go in, he tries to fix you up with someone."

She laughed. "You're probably right."

I closed the door and then walked to the back of the vehicle to deposit the bags. Once I finished, I went around to get inside. As I was buckling my seatbelt, Beverly cleared her throat. "While it's none of my business, I'd just like to say that while I'm sorry to see you so upset, I can't say I'm too sad to see Mr. Van Neiss go."

At my contemptuous snort, Caroline shot me a death glare. "Thank you, Beverly. That means a lot."

"I'm here for you for any girl talk."

"I appreciate that."

As Beverly pulled out of the parking lot, I turned in my seat toward Caroline. "You know what?" I jabbed my finger at Beverly. "That should tell you something."

"And what would that be?"

"No one liked Perry except for you—well, and Perry. He certainly liked himself a lot."

"Yes, I'm starting to see that."

"So, take Sheldon's advice and start looking for other fish in the sea."

Caroline forlornly stared ahead. "I wish it were that simple."

"It can be. Mind over matter and all that bullshit."

"Ordinarily, it would be, but nothing in my life makes sense. In a weird way, Perry was something constant, a reminder of the life I had before the stalker."

Damn, that was grim. I hadn't even stopped to think about how the fucking psycho might have an effect on all this. Considering Perry's objection to the heightened security, it probably wasn't too much to imagine that the stalker had helped to bring on the demise of the relationship—well, along with the fact that Perry was an absolute wanker.

"I'm sorry, Caroline. I wish more than anything we'd already been able to catch the bastard."

She gave me a sad smile. "I know you do, but what Sheldon and you don't realize is it won't be easy finding someone else. Perry and I knew each other before Dad was elected president. Not only do I have the obstacle of men being either too intimidated or too eager to date me because of my father's position, I also have a psycho sending me a mutilated Barbie and clippings of my hair." She shrugged. "Who the hell is going to want to sign on for this crazy train?"

"The stalker will not be an issue forever. We will find him. It's just a matter of time. He's smart, but he's not smarter than the FBI."

"I hope so."

"Trust me," I said emphatically.

After staring into my eyes, she replied, "I always trust you, Ty. It's everyone else I don't trust." When Beverly cleared her throat in the front seat, Caroline laughed. "And of course, I trust my team."

Beverly glanced back at us with a smile. "Thanks. I just needed a little reminding."

Grunting, I ran my hand over my face. "Jesus, help me with all these needy females."

"You better watch it, Fraser. I'll use some of my new Krav Maga moves on you," Caroline challenged.

"Is that right?"

"Yep, especially the groin kick."

Beverly snickered at that comment. I was sure she would have loved to have front-row seats to see Caroline knee me in the balls. "Keep talking and you'll be watching your chick flicks solo."

"You still might want to sleep with one eye open tonight." She wagged her brows. "I might sneak in and put a pore treatment mask on you."

"Like I said before, no mani-pedis, and *no* spa treatments."

"You could probably use a good facial," she argued.

Considering my experience with facials were much dirtier, I kept my mouth shut and tried not to think about how she would be the one getting the facial. "The answer is no."

Beverly laughed. "If you do get him into any face masks or nail painting, please take pictures. The team would love to see them."

"So would my brothers," Caroline added.

"Don't count on it, Bev."

When we got back to the apartment, I helped Caroline out of the car before going around for the groceries. After picking up the bags loaded with ice cream and candy, I shook my head. "I still can't believe we just bought all this junk food."

"Hey now, don't be judging me. It's going to take a lot to nurse this broken heart."

"I suppose it could be worse, and you could be drowning yourself in alcohol."

"See? There's always something to be grateful for."

As Caroline punched in the key code on the door, I cocked my head at her. "Are you a mean drunk or a happy drunk?"

"Mostly happy. On the odd occasion, I've been known to get a little weepy."

"I guess that isn't too surprising. I would've been surprised if you told me you threw punches when you had one too many."

"Most of the time, I just tell everyone how pretty they are."

"Even the men?"

She laughed. "Yep."

In my mind, I pictured an inebriated Caroline throwing her arms around my neck and giving me a glassy-eyed stare while slurring that I was so pretty. "Interesting."

I set the bags down on the counter. "Now what do you do?"

"I sit in front of the TV, watch sappy movies, eat, and cry. That's in no particular order. Then rinse and repeat."

"Please tell me you're joking."

Straining to open a bag of candy, she replied, "As a matter of fact, I'm not."

At the prospect of watching chick flicks and repeatedly crying, I almost wished for Perry's return. Almost. "Fuck, that's grim."

"Pray tell what does a strong, strapping man like you do after a breakup?"

"I sure as hell don't gorge myself on bad television and gummy worms."

"Gummy bears," she corrected.

"Whatever."

"If I'm truly going to see the error of my ways and change, you're going to have to get a little more specific about your breakup behavior."

I reached across her to grab the pint of ice cream. "I get pissed."

"Like the British pissed of getting drunk or the American pissed where you get angry?"

With a snort, I replied, "That would be the British pissed."

"I see." She tossed a few more of those disgusting multicolored gummies in her mouth. After chewing thoughtfully, she asked, "So, after you get drunk, do you stay that way for days?"

I grabbed a bowl out of the cabinet and then slid open the cutlery drawer. "I've usually always had a job that didn't afford me much time for nursing my broken heart."

"Well, I've got the entire weekend before my job needs me."

"I'm not going to let you sit in this apartment all weekend wallowing over that wanker."

Her fistful of gummies paused midway to her mouth. "Excuse me?"

"You are beautiful and talented and kind. You have so much to offer the world. I'm not going to let you waste it mourning over Perry."

"But—"

I shook my head. "You get tonight, and that's it. Tomorrow you're getting ready to move on."

"What, are you just going to fill in for him on the plans I had this weekend?"

"If it means getting you out of the house, then yes, I will."

"You're going to live to regret making that offer."

"I'm pretty sure you can't throw anything at me that's worse than staying in this apartment watching chick flicks."

"Speaking of, let's go to the living room."

"Oh goody," I groaned.

Before she turned on the TV, Caroline set up a sugar buffet on the table. After grabbing the remote before I could get to it, she started searching through her Amazon Prime library. "Have you ever seen *The Greatest Showman*?"

"I don't think so."

"You're going to love it."

"I wouldn't be so sure," I muttered before collapsing down onto the couch.

"Come on, Ty. I'll make a deal with you: if you'll watch this without complaint, I'll let you chose the next movie."

I cocked my brows at her. "You're serious?"

"Absolutely."

Okay. I can work with this. "All right. I'll keep my mouth shut and my mind open."

"Good."

When the opening credits started, I realized it was familiar. "Wait, I have seen this."

"You have?"

"I went to see it when I was still with Barrett."

"Let me guess—Addison roped him into that one."

I chuckled. "You got it."

Growing up, Addison had always been involved in musical theater, and she had a killer voice. She'd been on the edge of her seat for the entire film, and the truth was, I'd actually enjoyed it.

After reaching for the popcorn, I settled in to watch it again. At times, I even found my foot tapping along to the music. Of course, I could have lived without Caroline remarking how "swoony" Hugh Jackman was.

I fully expected her to start panting when Efron made his appearance, but instead, she shocked me. "Do you know how many of my friends think Barrett looks like Zac Efron?"

"Seriously?"

Caroline nodded. "You wouldn't believe how many used to want to come over to the house just to swoon over him."

"Actually, I probably can," I replied with a laugh. Barrett was always one for drawing female attention wherever he went. He had not only the looks but the charm to go along with them.

Shockingly enough, I found myself enjoying the movie. I wasn't sure if I'd tell Caroline that tidbit or not. She might then think it was okay to barrage me with musicals, and I knew I couldn't handle that.

When the closing credits came on, Caroline rose off the couch. Stretching her arms over her head, she exclaimed, "That was amazing, yet again."

"Do I even want to know how many times you've watched it?"

She grinned. "No comment."

"What are we watching next?"

"You know what? I'm going to take one for the team and defer to you on this one."

"Really? You're not going to pick one you want?"

"Nah." I winked at her. "Just don't make me regret this sacrifice."

She smiled. "I think you might like the next choice."

After Netflix popped up on the screen, I saw the selection for *Call the Midwife*. "Now you're just going to make me homesick."

Her expression fell. "I'm sorry. You want to watch something else?"

"No. This is fine. I'll just need to call home tomorrow."

She grabbed the package of Twizzlers off the coffee table. "How often do you talk to your parents?"

"Usually every week, sometimes more if Mum has something she wants to tell me."

"It has to be hard being away from them."

"It is. We Skype and FaceTime a lot."

"When was the last time you were home?"

"Easter."

Caroline's eyes bulged. "That long?"

I shrugged. "I haven't been able to get away."

"We're just going to have to remedy that and get you back home ASAP." When I opened my mouth to protest and say I couldn't leave her with the stalker, she shook her head. "Even if I have to go with you."

Holy shit. "You would go to London with me?"

"Of course I would if it meant you getting to spend time with your family." Of course she would—Caroline didn't have a fucking selfish bone in her body. As much as I wanted to take her up on the offer, she'd only been in her new city a few weeks.

"What about your job?"

"I could work remotely for a week or two and let Selah handle things on the ground." With a flippant roll of her eyes, she added, "You seem to forget I lived in England for almost a year."

"I'm aware of that."

"Then just say when and I'm there."

The sincerity in her voice caused me to smile. I knew if I said I wanted to leave Monday, she'd be on the phone working her magic to make it happen, and that meant a hell of a lot to me. Once again, I allowed myself to momentarily entertain the idea of taking her to London. It would certainly throw a wrench in the stalker's plans. Of course, reality hit once again when I thought of the cost to the taxpayers of taking an entire Secret Service entourage across the pond.

"Why don't we get some ice cream before we start an episode?" she said with a smile.

"How are you still even remotely hungry?"

"Emotional turmoil burns more calories," she said matter-of-factly.

"I see."

After she'd scooped out enormous bowls of chocolate chip ice cream for us, we settled in to watch the show. Halfway through the first episode, I realized eating during a realistic medical drama might not be the best idea.

I must've been grimacing pretty hard at the screen because Caroline began to laugh. "Don't worry, Ty. It won't be you going through labor one day."

"No, but I'll still hate when the woman I love has to go through it. Hell, I hate the thought of *any* woman going through it." I motioned to the woman writhing and screaming on the screen. "That looks positively beastly."

Appearing curious, Caroline tapped her spoon against her bottom lip. "Does that mean you want children some day?"

"Of course."

With a bob of her head, she replied, "I can see that about you."

Swirling the spoon around in my bowl, I asked, "What? Me specifically pushing a pram or just that I will have children in general?"

She smiled. "A little of both."

"Considering your work with children, I can only imagine you want them."

"I do, but like you, I want them *someday*. I don't really see myself becoming a mom until my later twenties."

I winked at her. "You're almost twenty-five—how much later do you want it to be?"

She laughed. "Twenty-eight or twenty-nine, maybe? Of course, I'll have to find the right man first." Heaving a sigh, she placed her empty bowl on the coffee table. "That part appears to be especially troublesome at the moment."

"I hardly think it's time to worry about not finding the right man."

"You're right. I won't get paranoid until I'm at least thirty."

"Sounds like a good plan."

"What about you? I assume you're about to turn thirty soon."

"Yes," I replied warily.

"I know it's different for men, but do you feel even the slightest marriage pressure?"

Groaning, I let my head fall back against the couch. "From my mum, I'm under immense pressure. I'm the only one of my brothers who hasn't married."

"Are you the oldest?"

"Second to the youngest. Oliver is thirty-eight, Charlie is thirty-six, Alfie is thirty-one, I'm twenty-nine, and Freddie is twenty-six."

"You know, I've never even thought to ask you if Ty is short for something."

Wrinkling my nose, I replied, "Tyrell."

Caroline's eyes widened. "Like the House Tyrell in *Game of Thrones*?"

I chuckled. "No, like my mum's maiden name."

"Aw, you were named after your mom."

"In a way."

"All this time together and I didn't know your name was Tyrell." The corners of her lips quirked, and I could tell she was having a hard time not laughing. "Tyrell Fraser."

"Is it any wonder why I go by Ty?"

"I have to admit you do look more like a Ty than a Tyrell."

"Thanks . . . I think."

She laughed. "It wasn't a dig, I promise. Look at Thorn—he doesn't look like a James or a Thornton. He's just Thorn."

"That's true. I can't imagine calling him anything else." My gaze bounced from her over to the television where Netflix was asking if we were still watching. "Want to watch another episode?"

With a yawn, Caroline pulled her knees up under herself. "If you think you're up to it."

"I'm not the one who is yawning."

"I can if you can."

"Then let's watch another one."

After settling back in, I became so engrossed with the show I didn't realize Caroline had fallen asleep. It wasn't until her head slid across the back of the couch and fell against my shoulder that I realized she was out. Turning toward her, I eyed her sleeping face. She appeared so peaceful. Gone was the worry of her stalker and the sadness over the wanker.

In the flickering light from the television, I couldn't help admiring how beautiful she was. If she'd been awake, I was sure she would have told me I was crazy for thinking she could be beautiful in a pair of

137

yoga pants and a long-sleeved Oxford T-shirt with her long blonde hair swept back in a ponytail. She'd further argue she couldn't possibly be beautiful because she didn't have on any makeup since she'd washed her face before we went to the Psychotic Pig. But she didn't need anything to make herself beautiful—she was just naturally that way.

As I swept a loose strand of hair out of her face, I had to once again note what a wanker Perry was for walking away. How could he not have appreciated the absolute perfection that was standing right in front of him? And I wasn't just referencing her physical beauty; it was the person within. She had more heart in her right pinky than he had in his entire body.

My breath hitched when she turned her knees onto my thighs and burrowed her head into my chest. *Shit.* I needed to find a way to untangle myself, and fast. Having her that close was physically and emotionally dangerous. I hadn't experienced this level of intimacy with a woman in over a year. The hookups and casual dating I'd been partaking in didn't actually allow much time for couch cuddling.

In that moment, I allowed myself to imagine what it would be like if I were in a place to actually pursue her. If I wasn't her Secret Service agent and she wasn't my target, would we be interested in each other? If I'd met her under any other circumstances, I would have wanted to ask her out. Of course, I had to wonder if she would even want to date me.

I wasn't exactly from her world when it came to pedigree. I hadn't attended an Ivy league school, nor did I come from a fine family. I was just some bloke from the East End of London who'd happened into her privileged world because I had become a bodyguard. Deep down, I knew none of that really mattered to Caroline. The last thing she could ever be was superficial. None of the Callahan family was, nor were they pretentious. With them, you were more a member of the family than you were an employee. President Callahan's words echoed through my mind. Whether I was more family or employee, I wasn't sure where that put me if Caroline and I were to date.

Whoa, mate, getting a bit ahead of yourself there, aren't you?

Gently, I placed my hands on her shoulders and pushed her back away from me. Rising off the couch, I then nudged her arm. "Caroline?"

"Mm?"

"We need to get you to bed."

"Why?"

"Because you're asleep."

She burrowed deeper into the couch. "I can sleep here," she murmured drowsily.

"This couch is way more for looks than it is for sleeping." Leaning over, I slid one of my arms under knees while the other went around her back. I hoisted her off the couch and started across the living room to her bedroom.

Her eyelids fluttered a few times before snapping open. "Are you carrying me?"

"Yeah."

"Why?"

"Because I didn't want you sleeping on the couch."

She giggled. "Always the gentleman hero, aren't you?"

"If that's what you'd call this then I suppose so."

Throwing an arm around my neck, she declared, "Oh Ty, you're so swoony."

"Is that right?"

"Mmhmm."

"Good to know," I muttered. After I eased her down on the edge of her bed, she reached around her head to undo her ponytail. As she ran her fingers through her hair, she asked, "Are you going to put me in my pajamas too?"

Oh fuck. Like I needed to think about undressing her. I cleared my throat. "No. I think you can sleep just fine in the ones you're in." I then quickly jerked the covers down so she could slip inside. Once she was burrowed under the comforter like a burrito, she sighed contentedly. "Go on. Sleep off all the sugar," I instructed.

Once again, a giggle tumbled from her lips. "Yes, sir."

Only Caroline would manage to act like a drunk when she'd only had sugar and sleep deprivation. As I started across the floor, her voice stopped me. "Thank you for tonight, Ty."

"You don't need to thank me."

"Yeah, I do. You went above and beyond—like, my dad needs to give you a service medal or something."

I chuckled. "I'm not sure there's a medal for binge-watching television and gorging on junk food."

She yawned. "Maybe I'll have one commissioned."

"If you do, I'd be honored to be the first recipient." I winked at her. "Good night, Caroline."

"Good night, Ty."

CHAPTER THIRTEEN

I WOKE on Saturday morning to the alluring smell of fresh coffee, a welcome change from my usual alarm clock. As I stretched my arms over my head, I realized I was still in my clothes from the evening before.

And then it hit me: I was alone in my bed when I should have been snuggled up next to Perry. As the previous night's events washed over me, I could only mutter, "Fuck." It was the only word that seemed to adequately sum up breaking up with Perry.

Bringing my hand up, I rubbed my fingers along my forehead. As much as it hurt to remember the nasty things Perry had said, there was also a peace abiding in me just below the surface, a peace I knew came from Ty. He had been my angel. A smile curved on my lips when I thought of him eating ice cream and bingeing movies with me.

I grabbed a ponytail holder off the nightstand and swept my hair up. After picking up my phone, I headed out of the bedroom. Ty was in the kitchen with the small television set on. The strands of his hair were wet, so I must've slept through him getting his shower. He wore a black pair of sweatpants, a white T-shirt that was stretched across his muscles, and no shoes. I wasn't sure why the fact that he was barefoot stood out to me. Maybe I was starting to develop a foot fetish.

I could have stood there forever just watching him puttering around the kitchen. It wasn't just about ogling his perfect body; it was about how he made the apartment seem like a home. Even though my parents came from wealth, I'd grown up with Mom and Dad taking Saturdays and Sundays for themselves when it came to housework. Mom cooked, and Dad liked to mess around in the yard. We might've lived in what could have been perceived as a mansion, but it was those little touches that made it into a home.

"Morning," I finally said.

He turned around and smiled at me. "Good morning. Did you sleep okay?"

"Surprisingly, I did."

"I'm glad to hear it." He motioned to the griddle. "I thought I'd make waffles this morning."

I cocked my brows at him. "You just woke up and thought you'd make waffles?"

"Well, I thought we needed to change things up. Have you ever even used this waffle maker?"

"Of course I haven't. It was an impulse buy when I moved here."

Ty chuckled. "I imagined as much." Jerking a thumb at the table, he said, "Go ahead and sit down. It's almost ready."

"Let me help."

"Okay. You take the fruit and syrup to the table."

Of course he'd prepared fruit. I wouldn't have been surprised to find fresh-squeezed orange juice. When I reached over to grab the plate from him, I couldn't resist pinching his bicep.

He gave me an odd look. "What was that for?"

I grinned at him. "After making homemade waffles and cutting up fruit, I had to pinch you to see if you were real."

He threw his head back with a laugh. "Whatever. Just take those to the table."

After I set the fruit and syrup down, Ty joined me with a platter of waffles. "Shit, I forgot the whipped cream," he muttered.

At the mention of whipped cream, my mind went somewhere it shouldn't have. As I watched his retreating form, I couldn't help imagining licking whipped cream off his perfect abs . . . or his magnificent dick. "Get a grip, Caroline," I grumbled.

"I'm sorry, what did you say?"

Jesus. "I was just saying how delicious all this looks."

"I hope it is. I haven't made waffles in forever."

"I can't imagine you cooking anything that isn't perfection." Just as I reached my fork for a waffle, my phone dinged. Well, it more than dinged. I had only just turned on my phone and there were about twenty text alerts popping up. "What the hell?"

"Maybe wait until you've had breakfast."

I jerked my gaze from the phone to Ty, and his pained expression caused my stomach to tighten. "Why?"

Before he could answer, I quickly glanced at some of the text messages, many asking if I was okay because of the TMZ pics. *Oh God.*

When I unlocked my screen, I opened the alert from TMZ. "Shit," I muttered at the sight of Perry staggering out of a nightclub in DC with a leggy blonde on his arm. Well, at least he was honest. He hadn't wanted a sexless weekend, so he'd made sure to address that the moment he arrived back in DC. *Talk about moving on. Asshole.*

Tossing my phone onto the table, I shook my head. "Well, he doesn't waste time, does he? Of course, it shouldn't surprise me. After all, he was always pretty speedy when it came to sex."

My comment sent Ty choking on his waffle. He snatched his water up and chugged half of it down. "Christ," he muttered.

"Sorry. I shouldn't have gone there."

He snickered. "Actually, I quite enjoyed it."

I laughed. "I'm glad you did."

After wiping his mouth with his napkin, Ty shook his head. "All joking aside, I'm truly sorry that wanker is pulling such bullshit."

"Thanks. It's actually a little surprising since he's all about appearances. Getting photographed coming out of a club sloppy-ass drunk can only come back to haunt his political future aspirations."

"Hmm, then maybe it's a win-win situation," Ty mused.

"True."

Ty motioned his fork at my plate. "Now forget about him and eat."

I could do that. I'd deal with responding to texts later as well.

And then I saw one from my Satchel and Babe editor. "Holy shit."

"What?"

"It's nothing bad. It's actually pretty fucking amazing."

Ty's brow's show up. "Really?"

I nodded. "My editor wants to move up the release date before the holidays."

"Brilliant."

"Not only that, they want me to kick off the release with a book signing at the Barnes & Noble in DC next month." I squealed. "Oh my God, a book signing means I'm really an author!"

Ty laughed. "You're already an author."

"I know, but it won't truly feel real until I hold the final, finished book in my hand or sign my name in the front cover." I shivered with anticipation. "This is the most amazing news ever."

"I'd say, and it sure as hell came at the right time."

"I know." I flipped open the calendar on my phone so I could put the date down. When I started scanning the month of November, one event in particular made me groan.

"What's wrong now?"

"The state dinner is two weeks before my book signing."

Ty furrowed his brows. "Why is that a problem?"

"It's a problem because I'll be expected to be there. All of us children will be. Dad's hosting the Taoiseach of Ireland."

Quirking his lips at me, Ty said, "You do know you'll sound far less pretentious if you just say the prime minister."

"Trust me, I have to keep saying it that way or I'll forget how to say it. Besides, it's nice to appeal to his Gaelic side."

"Whatever."

I tossed my phone down and put my head in my hands. "Maybe I can fake an illness."

"Jesus, Caroline, they're not that bad."

"Oh really? How would you know?"

"I attended one with Thorn."

Duh. Now that I thought about it, I remembered Ty being there among the other agents. I removed my hands from my face. "Look, I'm not bemoaning it from the pomp-and-circumstance standpoint of the four-course meal or intense protocol. I'm bemoaning it because I'll be dateless."

"Going dateless to the state dinner merits your current nervous breakdown?" he questioned.

I rolled my eyes. "You're a man—you just don't get it."

"Why don't you enlighten me?"

Tenting my fingers, I said, "As the queen of social settings, my mother will not allow me to go to the state dinner single. I will need an escort. Because of that fact, she will go through her registry of potential Washington bachelors." I narrowed my eyes at Ty. "My mother is many wonderful things, but she sucks at being a matchmaker."

"Actually, I think both Barrett and Thorn have said that before."

"See? I'm not being dramatic. It's the truth."

"Surely your mother can't pair you up with someone worse than Wanker Van Neiss."

I snorted at his nickname for Perry. "Knowing my mother, it will be much, much worse, like epic wankerdom."

Ty pushed his plate away from him. "Shit, Caroline, that's grim."

"I know." Craning my neck, I stared into the kitchen. "Forget the wine—where's that bottle of Scotch you bought a few weeks ago?"

"You're not seriously going to start day drinking?" Ty questioned.

"I'm already in a weak emotional state because of the breakup. When you add this in, I'm either day drinking or doing another sugar binge."

"I wish I could do something to help."

As I stared across the table at him, an idea hit me with the force of a Mack truck. "But you can help me," I blurted out.

"How?"

"By being my date."

Ty's eyes ballooned. "You're joking?"

"No. I'm dead serious."

"Caroline, there is no possible way I can entertain attending the state dinner as your date."

"Sure you can. You'll be there anyway since I'm going in."

"I'll be there as your agent, not your date." He then shot out of his chair and grabbed his plate before hustling to the kitchen.

Huffing out a frustrated breath, I picked up my plate and followed him into the kitchen. "Come on, it's not like you'd *really* be my date. It would just be two friends going to a formal event together." *Sure, I might've gotten off to your image the other night, but on this night, you wouldn't be a fantasy, just a friend—and not one with benefits.*

Ty scrubbed the plates forcefully in the sink. "I don't think your parents would want me escorting you."

"And why not? I bet they'd actually be glad because they'd know I was safe even within the White House."

"I just don't think it's a good idea."

"Are you seriously going to make me beg?"

Ty's shoulders drooped. After switching the water off, he turned to me. "Caroline, for this agent-target relationship to work, we have to keep up certain walls up between us. We already come precariously close to overstepping the line because of living together."

I wasn't sure who Ty thought he was talking to. I was a Callahan— we were known for our tenacity. "Please, please come to the state dinner with me. I promise I'll never ask you to watch another chick flick as long as we live together." *Does he seriously think I'm going to give up?*

Ty stared into my eyes, and once again, it was like he was seeing straight through to my soul. "It really means that much to you?"

"Yes, it really does."

He sighed. "Fine. I'll accompany you to the state dinner."

Since I was prepared to continue begging, I blinked my eyes in surprise. "Did you just say yes?"

"Regretfully, I did."

With a squeal, I pounced on him. After throwing my arms around his neck, I said, "Thank you, thank you, thank you!"

He chuckled. "Out of all the men you know, you really want to go with me?"

I pulled away to smile at him. "Now don't be selling yourself short. I'm sure I'll be making lots of women jealous showing up with eye candy like you."

"You make me feel so cheap," he teased.

"I'm sorry. I do appreciate your brain and your brawn."

"Yeah, yeah."

"Listen, we'll have a great time. You can hang out with Barrett and Thorn, and I promise I won't make you dance with me more than once or twice."

A strangled noise came from Ty's throat. "Dance?"

"Yes. I know I said it would be more like friends, but I'll need someone to dance with. If you refuse, I'm sure my mom will start recruiting men for the task."

"We can't have that."

I giggled. "No, we can't."

A few moments passed with me pressed against Ty's T-shirt covered torso. *He's so warm, and this feels so good.* It felt *so* natural that I forgot to pull away. When I finally did, my body felt bereft.

Since it probably wasn't wise to dwell on that anymore, I said, "Anyway, crisis averted, and now I'm going to call Mom to tell her about the wanker and the book signing."

Ty grinned. "I see I'm having an effect on you."

You have no idea. "Thanks for the waffles. You're the best, Agent Fraser!" And with that, I turned on my heels and got the hell out of there. I just hoped he didn't hear my giggling as I did.

CHAPTER FOURTEEN

WHEN CAROLINE ASKED me to accompany her to the state dinner in a personal rather than a professional capacity, everything within me was screaming no. She was in a dangerous place post breakup where many women look for a rebound. While I was an obvious choice considering my accessibility, it was wrong on so many levels. Regardless of how horny I was and how gorgeous and sexy she was, I had to be prepared to be the strong one for the both of us, the moral compass, the ethical leader—yeah, all that bullshit.

I'd not only been warring with myself over agreeing to go, I was also stressing over the fact of the after-dinner dancing. I didn't know how to dance past what I'd done back in school, or the sweaty bumping and grinding I did at clubs. After witnessing a state dinner personally, I could attest with certainty that there was absolutely no grinding at the White House.

I knew there was no way in hell I would make it through the evening without having to dance with Caroline. So, for the last few days, I'd been consumed with making sure I didn't make an absolute ass of myself. That was why I was sitting in the lobby of Read 4 Life watching yet another waltzing tutorial.

"You look awfully serious today. There hasn't been a bad development with CC's stalker, has there?"

Glancing up from my iPad, I met Selah's inquisitive gaze. "No. It's nothing like that."

She swept her hand to her chest in relief. "Oh good. You had me worried since you seem a little more preoccupied than usual."

"Yeah, I suppose I am." Before I could bury my head in my iPad again, I eyed Selah curiously. "Can I ask you a somewhat odd question?"

She twirled her pen while shooting me a curious look. "I suppose so."

"Do you know how to waltz?"

"Okay, that is *so* not the direction I thought you were going."

"Trust me, it's not a subject I usually question people about."

Swinging in her desk chair to face me, Selah cocked her brows. "Why the sudden interest?"

"Caroline asked me to accompany her to the state dinner this weekend at the White House. After attending prior functions in an official capacity, I know there is dancing involved. I also know from Caroline's request she wants me to dance with her so she won't have to deal with any weirdos."

"I see."

"Protocol dictates there are several waltzes, and after reading about the reels and other types of dances, I think it's the only kind I could remotely do."

"Yeah, I think waltzing is your best bet."

"Does that mean you know how to do it?"

"Yeah, I've waltzed a few times."

"Would you mind letting me practice on you?"

Selah drew her bottom lip between her teeth before throwing a cautionary look at Caroline's door. "I'm not so sure that's a good idea."

"Why not?"

"Caroline made it very clear the first day you arrived she didn't want me starting anything up with you."

"She did?" Now there was an interesting development. Why would Caroline possibly care who I was dating? If it had been the day we came to West Virginia, she had even still been with Perry then.

"Oh yeah, she did."

"Surely she wouldn't think a dance is us starting up anything." When Selah still appeared conflicted, I said, "Look, I've spent the last few days watching YouTube videos in my room. I even broke down and asked Beverly if she would practice with me, but she told me the only hand-to-hand contact she'd get involved with me in was Krav Maga."

Selah whistled. "Shot down by one of your own."

"Tell me about it." Giving her my best pleading look, I said, "You're my only hope."

"Then you're pretty much screwed."

"Come on. Caroline's going to be busy for hours sorting the newest inventory. She said it herself." When Selah appeared to be wavering, I went in for the kill. "Just five minutes."

Pursing her lips, Selah said, "I doubt you ever use that line when trying to get a woman into bed."

I laughed. "Of course not." I waggled my brows. "My stamina is infinite then."

With a wistful look in her eyes, Selah smacked her palms on her desk. "Okay, fine. You wore me down." After she rose out of her chair, she came around her desk. "All right, how do you want me?"

"First things first. Unlike back in the day at school dances, I'm going to put my right hand on the follow's left shoulder blade."

"The follow?"

"Sorry, it's what they called it in the videos. I'm the lead, and you're the follow."

"That's a first. I'm usually the one leading the men around."

"Somehow that doesn't surprise me."

When I wrapped my hand around Selah's, I found myself surprised by the lack of electricity. Here was a sexy and beautiful woman who would clearly fuck me into next Tuesday if it weren't for Caroline putting the brakes on. While we appeared to have great conversational chemistry, there was nothing when I touched her.

"What is it?" she asked.

"Uh, nothing. I was just going over the steps in my head."

Just as I prepared to step forward on my right foot, the door to Caroline's office flung open. "Selah, did you not get my email about the Parks Elementary invoice?" Caroline asked.

Both Selah and I froze before snapping our gazes over to the doorway where Caroline stood peering at a clipboard. When she didn't get a response, her head popped up. At the sight of the two of us in each other's arms, the blood drained from her face. "Oh, I'm sorry. Am I interrupting something?"

In an utter prick move, I shoved myself away from Selah. "No, not at all."

Caroline shifted the clipboard to the crook of her arm. "I must've forgotten to pencil in the afternoon dance party on my calendar." She shrewdly narrowed her eyes at us. "Or did I not get an invitation?"

Selah flippantly waved a hand as she hustled around the side of her desk. "It's not a dance party. We were just stretching our legs. You know, it's not good for circulation to always be sedentary behind a desk."

"Oh, I'm sure that's the circulation you were concerned with."

Although it was a rarity, Selah actually blushed. "That's not it at all."

"If you'll please find me the Parks Elementary invoice, I'll let you two get back to what you were doing."

Selah dipped her head and began rifling through a folder on her desk. Once she'd found a particular slip of paper, she hopped out of her chair and crossed the room to give it to Caroline.

"Thank you," Caroline said. She then swiveled on her heels and headed back inside the office. When the door slammed, Selah jumped.

After running a hand over my face, I stepped forward. "Excuse me, I believe I need to go handle damage control."

Selah slid her reading glasses back up her nose. "Yes, please. I can't stand the thought of her being pissed at me."

"She won't be. I'm going to come clean with her about my lack of dancing knowledge."

"That's probably a good idea for both of us. Good luck."

"Thanks."

My knuckles rapped against Caroline's door. "Come in," she called out tersely.

When I entered the room, she was bent over a carton of books in the floor. The position afforded me an excellent view of her skirt-clad arse. How in the hell was I not supposed to look at it? She had one spectacular arse.

"Listen, about what you walked in on—"

"It's none of my business. What the two of you do on your own time is not my concern." She hoisted a box onto her desk, and the sound of the smack reverberated through the room. I had a feeling if she could have, Caroline would have loved to smack me.

"I asked Selah to help me practice waltzing."

Caroline's head snapped out of the box she had been digging around in. "What?"

"I know from attending state dinners with Thorn that there will be waltzing, which I have no fucking clue how to do. That's not exactly something they teach you in the Rifles Regiment." I stepped around one of the chairs to get closer to her. "I've spent the last few days watching YouTube videos, but I thought it would be better to try my moves out on someone before the big night. So, I roped Selah into dancing with me."

"You were learning to dance for me?" she questioned softly.

Nodding, I said, "I didn't want to embarrass you in front of the press corps, least of all your father."

"Oh," she murmured.

"In case you missed it, I'm not used to looking like a fool in front of others."

"I seriously doubt you could ever look like a fool."

I snorted. "You haven't seen me dance yet."

"I'm sure you're not that bad." When I opened my mouth to protest, Caroline shook her head. "You give a hundred percent of yourself in all you do, Ty. I'm sure you do the same when it comes to dancing."

"I'll probably give a hundred percent to stepping on your toes."

She grinned. "I'll live."

"As far as Selah goes, she was perfectly honorable. I had to practically beg her to help me. She did not want to go against what she had promised you."

Caroline widened her eyes. "She told you I asked her not to pursue you?"

"Yes, she did."

"I guess that makes me sound like a real bitch."

I shrugged. "I'm sure you had your reasons."

"I just thought it might be difficult working together if things didn't work out between the two of you, not to mention I felt you might not need to be distracted."

"Those are both perfectly good reasons."

She gave me a shy smile. "Maybe I didn't think she was good enough for you."

"Why's that?"

"She's a man-eater. She only wanted to seduce you. You need someone who wants you for more than just your good looks." Caroline's chin set determinedly. "You have so much to offer a woman, Ty."

Well, fuck me. "Thank you. That's very kind."

"I mean it. Not many men would have committed one of their days off to taking care of a girl with a broken heart, but you did, and that's on top of all the wonderful things you do for me on a daily basis."

"But those are part of my job."

"The other agents don't do them," she protested.

"They're also not living with you. I'd be a real jackass if I erected some arbitrary wall between us."

The corners of her lips quirked up in a half-smile. "You know, you're really cute when you're being modest."

I returned her smile. "I'll take modest over you thinking I'm an arsehole like earlier. We okay?"

She grinned. "We're fine. More than that, I'm sorry for overreacting about Selah."

"It's okay. For the record, she's really not my type."

A surprised look flashed in Caroline's eyes. "She's not?"

She had been—until she put her hands on me and I felt absolutely bloody nothing. *Unlike Caroline's hands on Saturday morning.* Having her pressed against my body had felt incredible, and even though I'd heard her chuckling as she ran off, it hadn't calmed my racing heart.

Being in such close proximity with her, having her arms around my neck—it had felt better than I'd imagined. So, no, Selah was not my type. I didn't want to be . . . pursued. I wanted to be *wanted.*

With a shake of my head, I replied, "Call me old-fashioned, but I prefer to do the chasing."

"Interesting. I never took you for old-fashioned."

I winked. "I'm full of surprises."

She laughed. "I look forward to seeing some of those surprises on the dance floor."

Just like that, my ego deflated. "I wouldn't get too excited about that."

"You know, if it would make you feel better, we could always practice at home."

"You wouldn't mind?"

"Of course not. You can consider it payback for you teaching me Krav Maga."

I grinned. "I'd like that."

"Then it's all settled. I'll go back to work, and you won't go back to dancing with Selah."

"Copy that," I replied.

And just like that, the problem was solved. Of course, in the back of my mind, I couldn't help thinking it had opened up a whole other box of problems. Unlike Krav Maga, instead of teaching her moves to push me away or to get away from me, I'd be moving in ways that would bring Caroline closer, and as I had already discovered, that could be dangerous . . . *for me.*

CHAPTER FIFTEEN

WHEN THE DAY of the state dinner arrived, I'd have liked to say I had all my shit together and wasn't nervous at all, but that would have been a lie. Remember what I said about not being able to relax in the White House even when I wasn't there in an official capacity? Yeah, I was definitely feeling that. Throw in the fact that I was escorting Caroline, and this was a whole other thing.

After Caroline cut out of work at three, we drove to the airport where the Callahan Corporation jet was waiting to take us to DC. We arrived at the White House a little after five due the traffic. President Callahan and the prime minister were holding a press conference in the Green Room while the first lady entertained the prime minister's wife with tea in the residence.

Caroline and I were briefly introduced before we were shown to our rooms. While most guests would be staying at Blair House for the night, my status within the family had secured me one of the guest rooms. Instead of getting ready in my room, I went in to have a drink with Barrett and Thorn while the girls were getting their hair and makeup done by the stylist.

As Thorn handed me a scotch, he asked, "Any developments with the stalker?"

I grimaced. "It's been pretty much radio silence the last week and a half."

"That could be a good thing, right?" Barrett asked.

"I'd like to think that, but my gut tells me he's keeping occupied in preparation of something big."

Thorn threw back his scotch. Shuddering, he said, "Fuck, that's grim."

"Tell me about it."

"Even though it's Fort Knox here tonight, I'm glad you're here with Caroline."

"Me too, though I was a little reluctant to come as her escort."

Barrett's brows shot up. "You're not working tonight?"

Shaking my head, I replied, "No, I'm here as Caroline's escort."

Barrett and Thorn exchanged a look. "Like her date?"

I choked on my scotch. "Of course not. I would have had to come with her anyway, so I'm just here as her escort."

With a chuckle, Thorn smacked me on the back. "Lighten up, Ty. We weren't about to kick your ass or anything."

I laughed along with them. "I'm glad to hear that."

We were interrupted by the valet arriving with our tuxes. Thankfully, the conversation shifted off of Caroline and me. Once we were ready, we went to the Yellow Room to meet up with President Callahan and the first lady, and Addison and Isabel came in as we were getting a drink. "

"Where's Caroline?" I asked them.

"She's back in her room getting her pearls."

With a nod, I said, "I'll go get her."

Addison smiled. "That's sweet of you."

"It's my job to keep track of her," I replied.

After leaving the Yellow Room, I headed to Caroline's bedroom. My knuckles rapped against her door. "Knock, knock," I called out.

"Who's there?"

I shook my head. "Seriously?"

Caroline giggled before opening the door. "You disappoint me. I thought you were going for a knock-knock joke."

She wore a red dress that was fitted through the bodice and then flared out from the waist. It looked like something Jackie Kennedy would have worn, and I was sure Caroline would inform me the dress was vintage.

"You look absolutely breathtaking," I said.

"Really?"

"Stop fishing for compliments. You know you'd look beautiful with your hair tied back and one of those face masks on.

Caroline giggled. "I highly doubt that, but thank you."

"You're welcome."

I motioned to the pearls in her hand. "Do you need some help?"

With a nod, she replied, "Yeah, I can't seem to get the clasp to work."

Taking the strand from her, I lifted it over her head. *Damn, she smells good.*

"Thanks. I'm trying a new fragrance."

Shit. I had accidentally said that out loud. Closing the clasp, I turned her around. "There. They look great."

As her fingers went to the pearls, she smiled at me. "Thanks."

I extended my arm to her. "Ready?"

"As I'll ever be."

"Don't tell me you're nervous—you're a pro at these things."

"I just dread anyone making comments about Perry or the breakup."

"Just tell them you decided you were much too good for him."

Caroline laughed. "I'll make sure to say that."

As per protocol, President Callahan and the first lady were entertaining special guests from the head table in the Yellow Room in the residence. Although Caroline and I weren't seated at the head table, we were considered VIPs since Caroline was the president's child.

When we entered the room, many eyes shifted to us. "This is only slightly awkward," I muttered under my breath.

Although I could feel her apprehension, Caroline quickly plastered a smile on her face and began nodding to those around her in greeting.

President Callahan motioned for us to come over. "Nolan and Fiona, I'd like to introduce my daughter, Caroline, and her escort, Ty Fraser."

"It's very nice to meet you," I said as I shook their hands.

With a smile, Caroline said, "Tá áthas orm bualadh lea."

Nolan's eyes lit up. "You know Gaelic?"

"I know 'pleased to meet you' in Gaelic," Caroline answered.

Laughter rang around the group. "You did a fine job of it," Fiona complimented.

"Thank you," Caroline replied.

As Barrett and Addison waited to be introduced, I leaned over to whisper in Caroline's ear. "Suck-up."

With a giggle, she replied, "I would call it being an overachiever."

"It was a nice touch."

"I'm glad you thought so."

When the White House Social Secretary appeared in the doorway, she nodded to Jane. "I believe it's time for us to go down," Jane said to James.

President Callahan winked at Nolan. "I don't know about you, but I'm getting a little hungry."

Nolan laughed. "I feel the same way. I'm looking forward to seeing how your chefs prepare our traditional Irish food."

"Fingers crossed it is agreeable to your palate," Jane said.

"I'm sure it will be delicious," Fiona replied.

Everyone left the room except for the president, prime minister, and their wives. As we started down the stairs, my skin prickled under the curious looks of the guests below. We stepped off the staircase to await the grand arrival of the heads of state. The Marine Corps band struck up *Hail to the Chief*, and the president, prime minister, and their wives descended the stairs. After the music finished playing, they started *The Soldier's Song*, Ireland's national anthem.

We were then corralled into the Blue Room where President Callahan and the first lady would form a receiving line to welcome every single guest. The Callahan children were to be part of the line, as well as Addison since she was Barrett's wife. That left me and Isabel to hang around together. After spending so much time with her while working with Thorn, it was nice having a moment to catch up.

Once every guest had been welcomed, it was time to proceed to the State Dining room for the dinner. While Caroline and I were seated at the same table, we weren't sitting next to each other. As the first course of pretentious food like goat cheese gateau and tomato jam came around, I thought how I'd have infinitely preferred being back home in Caroline's and my kitchen.

To my right was a famous Irish poet who had been living stateside for the last ten years. He didn't appear too interested in starting a conversation with me, so I turned to my left. Raymond Harrison was a prize-winning journalist who had been personally asked to accompany the prime minister on the trip. He was fascinated to find I came from the East End since his father was a limey, as he called him.

"And what is it you do, Mr. Fraser?"

"I'm a Secret Service Agent," I replied.

His gaze bounced between me and President Callahan's table. "Aren't you protecting the president tonight?"

I laughed. "Actually, I'm Ms. Callahan's agent." I motioned across the table where Caroline sat talking to the House minority leader.

"I see." As he raked his fork through his salad, he eyed me curiously. "Do Americans often bring their protective agents to formal dinners?"

"No, they do not. As for me, I'm off the clock tonight and a guest of Ms. Callahan."

"Interesting. It must be very difficult staying professional with such a beautiful target."

His response caused my goat cheese to lodge in my throat. After taking a few gulps from my water glass, I turned to him to do damage control. From his tone, I could tell he was imagining there was something illicit going on between Caroline and me. The last thing either of us needed was a salacious story slapped across the headlines in England. Mr. Harrison didn't appear to be a tabloid-type journalist, but that didn't mean he still might not write something about us.

"I came to the Secret Service because of my friendship with President Callahan's sons. I served as Thorn's agent before President Callahan asked me to keep an eye on Caroline."

He pursed his lips. "It must've been something serious for him to ask you to change posts."

I nodded. "Her safety was at grave risk."

"A personal threat?"

"I would prefer not to say."

Harrison held up his hand. "My apologies. It's often hard to turn off the journalist in me."

"No offense taken."

Thankfully, the waiters in their white coats appeared to clear the first course dishes. Veering the subject away from Caroline, I asked Raymond how he was liking his trip.

The rest of dinner passed by with idle conversation. Occasionally, I would catch Caroline looking at me. If I was sure no one else was watching us, I'd wink back at her, which would cause her to smile. Sometimes she would wink at me first.

As she sat there in her beautiful red dress, I couldn't help thinking she was the most gorgeous woman in the room. From the looks she'd drawn throughout the night, I knew I wasn't the only one thinking that. The room was crawling with both eligible and ineligible bachelors who would have loved to get up under the folds of her dress.

Once the dessert course was finished and I was officially stuffed, President Callahan and Prime Minister Rogers rose out of their chairs to begin the recession down the Cross Hall and into the East Room. The first time I'd seen this happen, I hadn't been able to help joking that it appeared to be a game of follow the leader in more ways than one.

"Aren't formal dinners the worst!" Caroline exclaimed as we started out of the dining room.

"They sure as hell are."

"Although the food is amazing, it makes my skin crawl having to make small talk with everyone." Leaning in she whispered, "Do you know how boring the minority leader is?"

I chuckled. "I can only imagine."

When we got to the East Room, a stage and chairs were set up for a concert. While performances could sometimes be more cultural with a cellist or a ballet, the last dinner I had attended, I'd gotten to see a performance by Garth Brooks. I was hoping for something along those lines again tonight.

After Caroline and I took our seats, anxiety prickled its way up my spine. I knew after the East Room performance we would be adjourning to the Entrance Hall, where my dancing skills would get put on display—or, more accurately, my *lack* of skills.

When the red curtain on stage opened up to reveal a man in a top hat, I cut my eyes over to Caroline in surprise. "*The Great Showman*?"

She grinned. "Rogers happens to be a huge fan."

Craning my neck to look at the front row, I saw the prime minister's face light up as he turned to President Callahan and started applauding wildly. Sitting in my chair, I couldn't help but be riveted by the performance, which was saying a lot since I wasn't a fan of live theater. Apparently, all the actors came from local DC theaters.

When it came time for the performance of *Never Enough*, I almost fell out of my chair when Addison stepped out onto the stage in a glittering white dress with her dark hair swept back from her beautiful face. I supposed I shouldn't have been too surprised considered she was an accomplished singer. At the memory of one of her more memorable performances, I couldn't help snorting.

After Caroline shot me a horrified look, I leaned over to whisper in her ear. "I was just thinking of the time I saw Addison perform *If I Could Turn Back Time* and *I Got You Babe* in a drag club."

She gasped. "Seriously?

I nodded. "Her brother owns Divas here in DC, and she was helping fill in for one of his singers."

Caroline slowly shook her head back and forth. "That's amazing," she whispered back.

As we listened to Addison flawlessly perform the song, I cut my eyes over to see tears in Caroline's eyes. I knew it was a mixture of her current emotions coupled with the beauty of the song. Reaching over, I brushed the back of my hand over hers. She glanced from the stage down to my hand and then over to me. At first, she appeared somewhat shocked, but then a smile curved her lips. She then took my hand in hers and squeezed.

Although it had initially been for emotional support, I had to admit I liked holding Caroline's hand. It was so tiny within mine, not to mention soft against my calloused skin. We remained holding hands until the last note of the song concluded and we needed to applaud Addison.

Standing in the Entrance Hall, I couldn't help remembering the iconic photograph of Princess Diana dancing with John Travolta in that very place. My mum had been a huge fan and had countless picture books about the princess. She was going to die if she saw any pictures of me dancing there tonight. I could hear her saying *"My son is famous!"* It sent a smile to my lips.

"Don't tell me you're smiling at the thought of dancing?" Caroline teased.

I laughed. "No. Actually, I was thinking about my mum."

"Aw, that's sweet."

We stood watching as President Callahan twirled Fiona around the floor while Jane appeared to be enjoying her dance with Nolan. Although Barrett and Thorn both started dancing, I remained standing off to the side with Caroline. Finally, when she appeared to be getting restless, I turned to face her. "Would you like to dance?"

Her face lit up. "I'd love to."

Just as I slipped my hand around her back, the music changed to a more upbeat tempo. Instantly, I recognized the song as Neil Diamond's *Sweet Caroline*. When Caroline and I looked over, we saw President Callahan grinning over by the Marine Corp Band.

"How the hell am I supposed to waltz to this?" I demanded.

With a giggle, Caroline replied, "Just go with the flow."

"Easy for you to say. You've had classical dance training."

"I'm pretty sure I've never performed to any Neil Diamond."

Taking Caroline's advice, I just went with the flow. We didn't exactly waltz, but we did make our way around the floor. Apparently, I didn't cock it up too much because when the music stopped, no one was staring at me in horror. Instead, they were smiling and nodding their heads like I was the fucking Lord of the Dance.

While basking in my ego trip, I stayed on the floor for another dance with Caroline. As we executed the steps, she smiled up at me. "I can't thank you enough for tonight, Ty."

"Really, it was nothing."

Shaking her head, she replied, "Don't sell yourself short. It was something, and I really appreciate it."

I couldn't help feeling a little touched by her sincerity. "Even though you don't need to thank me, I appreciate it. And you're welcome." With a smile, I added, "Actually, I've enjoyed myself tonight."

"You have?"

"Sure, the dinner was boring as hell, but it's been fun getting dressed up and hanging out."

"I would have to agree."

"And as much as I hate to admit it, I'm actually enjoying the dancing."

"Why, Ty Fraser, wonders never cease," Caroline teased.

"Whatever," I replied with a roll of my eyes.

"I'll be happy to find more opportunities for you to showcase your dancing skills."

"That won't be necessary."

"I bet we could totally go to the VFW in Charleston for some of the dances."

"Caroline, I'm not dancing after tonight, period."

She giggled. "Fine, fine—waste one of your talents."

"I hardly think dancing is one of my talents."

"It's not one of your best, but you're certainly taking to it."

"I'm glad I could rise to the challenge."

"You always rise to every challenge."

"Thanks."

Conversation seemed to fail us after that. Instead, we just continued going through the steps. Mainly, we stared into each other's eyes as we made our way across the floor. The longer I gazed into those sparkling baby blues, the more I knew I was falling fast. Instead of telling her how I felt, I kept my mask of indifference solidly in place.

CHAPTER SIXTEEN

TY FRASER WAS A TRIPLE THREAT. The man had looks, he knew how to cook, and he could dance. When it came down to it, he was probably more of a quadruple or quintuple threat.

I hadn't been exaggerating about the eye-candy factor. Every woman in the room had her eyes on him. Okay, maybe Mom, Addison, and Isabel didn't, but almost all of the others did. I'd even seen Fiona eyeballing him a few times.

I couldn't say I blamed them. He was like James Bond on steroids in his tux. I was used to the suit porn he sported on a daily basis, but man, there was something about the fit of the black tux that made me all warm and tingly.

As we started off the dance floor, Ty turned to me. "I'm seriously parched. I'm going to grab a drink. Want something?"

I giggled. "Did you just say you're *parched*?"

"Yes, smartarse, I did."

"I'll take a vodka cranberry, please."

Ty nodded. "I'll be back as soon as I can."

"I'll come find you. I'm going to run to the bathroom to freshen up. Well, I guess I'm going to hurry to the bathroom since there's not a lot of running in this dress or heels."

Ty laughed. "I'll see you in a little while."

As I started to the bathroom, Addison and Isabel swooped in to sandwich me between them. "We need to talk."

"Is something wrong?"

"Of course not. We just want a moment of your time," Addison replied.

"*Alone*," Isabel added.

"Um, okay." We stepped into a somewhat private corner of the hallway. "Okay, no offense, but you two are starting to creep me out."

An apologetic look flashed on their faces. "Sorry. We didn't mean to come off as creepy. We're just curious," Addison said.

I furrowed my brows at her. "About what?"

With a roll of her eyes, Addison replied, "Don't play coy. We need the deets about you and Ty."

"But there aren't any details."

"He's your date tonight, isn't he?" Isabel asked.

I waved my hand dismissively. "No, no. It's not like that. He's just my escort." Oh Jesus, had I actually just described Ty like he was a male escort? That was the last thing I needed to get around—that I was going through my agents like they were gigolos. I shook my head. "I mean, he escorted me here tonight."

Isabel grinned. "The fact that he's here with you in an official capacity and not just as your agent is what we want the deets about."

Of course they did. "Look, it's nothing romantic. I didn't want to have to go through the hassle of finding a date, least of all have Mom try to fix me up."

Addison's gaze bounced from mine to Isabel's and then back to me. Sweeping a hand to her hip, she questioned, "Wait, so you're saying there's absolutely nothing between you and Ty?"

As beads of sweat broke out along my temples under their interrogation, I tried appearing cool, calm, and collected. "Sure, there's something between us—we're friends, and he's my agent."

"Bullshit!" Isabel exclaimed.

"E-Excuse m-me?"

She wagged a finger in my face. "I watched the two of you on the dance floor and fought the urge to fan myself. You can't tell me there's nothing going on between you two."

Shit, shit, shiiiiit. Had I really been that obvious? Regardless of what I might have been feeling about Ty, the last thing on earth I needed was to make it apparent to everyone else, especially him. Panic crisscrossed its way through me when I thought about my father suspecting anything. Surely if he had, he would have been dragging me off to get the details instead of the girls. "But he's my agent," I once again argued.

Addison shrugged. "He's also an extremely good-looking man."

"With a heart of gold," Isabel added, to which Addison nodded.

I didn't know what to say. After all the chaos of the last few weeks, I hadn't actually stopped to process my escalating feelings for Ty, at least not until right then. "You guys really know how to render a girl speechless," I mused.

"Considering how we ambushed you, I would consider that a reasonable reaction to have," Addison joked.

"Just by watching us dance, you thought there was something between us?" When they both nodded, I exhaled a breath. "Wow, I still don't know what to say."

Isabel's brows crinkled. "You mean, you two really aren't a couple?"

With a gasp, I replied, "No, we aren't." Holding up my hands, I added, "I swear."

"How is that possible?" Isabel asked.

"All that chemistry," Addison said.

I shrugged. "I honestly don't know, but I can assure you there's nothing officially going on." *Liar, liar, pants on fire!* Okay, I wasn't totally lying. There wasn't anything official between us. While I might have been feeling something for Ty, I had no clue how he felt.

Snapping her fingers, Addison said, "Aha!"

"Aha what?" I countered.

"You said there was nothing *official* going on. I want to know what is *unofficially* going on."

Shit. I shouldn't have said that. "Uh, nothing that I know of."

"Caroline, it isn't nice to lie to your sisters."

"You're not actually my sisters," I countered.

Addison waved her hand. "Same difference."

While it would have been easy to unburden myself on them and get their advice as to how to proceed regarding Ty, I decided it was best to keep things under wraps. Somehow, I felt it wouldn't be right to tell them how I felt before I told Ty.

"I'm sorry, ladies, but there's really nothing to tell. I guess whatever"—I paused to make air quotes—"*chemistry* you saw was just friendship."

Addison and Isabel cut their eyes over to each other. From their expressions, I could tell they thought I was bullshitting them.

"Before I go, my brothers haven't mentioned anything to you, have they?"

"Oh God no. This was all us," Isabel replied.

I exhaled a relieved breath. "Good. I don't want them giving Ty shit for nothing."

Addison shook her head. "Somehow I don't see Barrett giving him shit. He thinks the world of Ty."

"Thinking the world of someone and having them date your little sister are two different things," I countered.

"True. At the same time, I think he would be glad it was someone he knew and trusted."

I turned to Isabel. "Do you think Thorn would feel the same?"

She nibbled on her lip. "That's a tough one. He loves Ty, but you are his little sister and he's very protective. I'm sure he would feel a little betrayed."

I gulped. "Betrayed?"

"That Ty had gone behind his back to date you. I mean, it's one thing for Thorn to fix the two of you up and an entirely different thing for him to sneak around with you."

Shiiiit. "Right. So true." I held my hands up. "Luckily for all of us, there's nothing going on, so there's nothing to be worried about."

With a defeated sigh, Isabel said, "Well shit."

"I'm sorry to disappoint you."

She waved a hand. "I just want Ty to have someone so much. He deserves the best there is. Even though I'm biased because you're Thorn's sister, I can't imagine anyone better for him than you."

Well then. "Thank you for the compliment."

She grinned. "You're welcome." Shaking her head at Addison, she said, "I guess we're just going to have to take matters into our own hands and find someone for him."

My stomach twisted at the thought of the two of them fixing Ty up. I didn't like the thought of Ty with anyone, though I felt like an absolute asshole for wanting to deny him any potential happiness because of my own jealousy. "Yeah, you'll have to do that," I lied.

Addison motioned to Isabel. "Come on, let's do a sweep of the party and see if there's any potential here."

Isabel nodded. "Bye, Caroline. Sorry for making assumptions."

"It's okay. No harm."

Addison and Isabel left me alone in the corner, and it took me a few moments to get myself together. After being put through the ringer, I suddenly wasn't feeling like staying at the party. Considering things were winding down, I decided no one would miss me if I snuck off upstairs. Once all the guests dispersed, Mom and Dad would be occupied with overseeing a night cap for the prime minister before bed.

"There you are," Ty said when I came back into the hallway.

"Sorry. I got stopped by Addison and Isabel."

"Yeah, I saw the three of you talking."

Hmm, were your ears burning because you were the subject of the conversation?

Holding out the drink to me, Ty said, "Here you go."

"Thanks. I think I'm going to take it for the road."

Concern swept over his face. "Are you feeling unwell?"

"No, no. I just think I'm done for the night."

"I'll walk you up."

"You don't have to do that. After all, you're off the clock tonight. Go and have fun with Barrett and Thorn."

Ty gave me a warm smile. "It's okay. They'll all be coming that way in just a little while."

Oh, right—he was staying the night in the residence. Him walking me up wasn't some romantic gesture on his behalf. It was just necessity.

As he took my hand in his, my brows shot up in surprise. "Ms.

Callahan, will you allow me the pleasure of escorting you back to your room?"

A nervous giggle bubbled from my lips. "Why thank you, kind sir."

As we started up the stairs, Ty said, "You're awfully quiet."

"Just tired I guess."

When I cut my eyes over at him, he cocked his head skeptically. "May I speak freely for a moment?"

Once again, my heart broke into a full gallop like it was at the Kentucky Derby. "Uh, sure. I suppose so."

"That was a pretty animated conversation you were having with Addison and Isabel."

Feeling lightheaded, I reached out to grasp the bannister. "Uh, yeah, I suppose it was."

Ty remained quiet for a moment. I could tell he was thoughtfully searching for the right words. "Did they upset you about something?" he finally asked.

As a matter of fact, now that you mention it . . . "Oh no, nothing like that."

"You should know by now you can't lie to me."

His words caused me to stumble. I would have face-planted at the top of the stairs if Ty hadn't caught me. As we started down the carpeted halls of the residence, I turned my gaze to him. "I'm not lying."

"You're not being honest."

"It's probably best for both of us if I'm not."

Ty sucked in a breath. "What do you mean?"

With my bedroom door in sight, I had two options: I could tell him good night and make a run for it, or I could be an adult and actually vocalize what I was feeling. I decided it was best if I went with the second choice.

"Am I just a target to you?"

"I beg your pardon?"

"Do you see me as just a job, or am I something more?"

Swallowing hard, Ty replied, "Something more as in *someone* more?"

"Yes."

"Caroline, this isn't the appropriate time or place to be having this conversation."

"That doesn't answer my question."

"I think it's the best response I can give you right now."

I snorted. "Are you serious? Saying it's not the time or place to talk about something isn't an answer. It's avoidance."

Ty threw a frantic gaze over his shoulder. "I can't do this."

Instead of crushing me, his reaction infuriated me. "Quit being so paranoid someone is going to see or hear you. This is between you and me. No one else matters."

"Surely you know that's a naïve thing to say considering I'm your Secret Service agent."

I threw up my hands. "Would you just answer the damn question?" With a shake of his head, Ty turned to walk away, and my eyes bulged at his retreating form. "Oh no, don't you *dare* leave before I can tell you I have feelings for you."

Ty's shoes skidded to a stop along the antique hallway runner. Slowly, he turned around to stare at me. "You have feelings for me?"

Oh God. I was really doing this. I was just about to come clean about what I'd been feeling the last few weeks. There was no going back after this moment. "Yes. I do. If I'm honest, I've probably had them for some time. All my feelings just seemed to converge tonight, and I knew I wouldn't be able to sleep until I told you."

Ty reached out his arms and placed them on my shoulders. "Caroline, I care for you very much—much more than an agent should for his target—but that is what you are to me: my target. Anything more would be inappropriate. I think it's understandable considering the company we've kept lately to perhaps get confused—"

I narrowed my eyes at him. "I'm not confused. I'm fully aware of what I'm feeling. If anything, you're the one who is confused."

His head snapped back on his shoulders. "What?"

"Do you want to know what Addison and Isabel were talking to me about? They were asking what was going on between us. From the way we were interacting, they thought we dating."

Ty blinked a few times. "They're entitled to their opinion."

"And I'm entitled to mine. Good night, Agent Fraser." Fearing I was about to really lose it by either going off on him or crying hysterically, I slammed the door in his face. "Wanker," I muttered under my breath before stalking to my bathroom to take my makeup off.

CHAPTER SEVENTEEN

CAROLINE HAD FEELINGS FOR ME—*ROMANTIC* feelings. Most likely, she was experiencing the same damn feelings I was, but I'd been too chicken-shit to truly admit it to myself, least of all to her. I feared the repercussions from her father and on my job too much to appreciate the amazing gift in front of me.

I got halfway out of the residence before it hit me what a fool I was. "What the fuck?" I muttered. A beautiful, smart woman had just told me she had feelings for me, and I'd run away like a wanker. I was no better than that fucking prick Van Neiss. She didn't deserve that. She deserved to hear the truth.

Whirling around, I jogged back down the hallway to her bedroom. After banging my fist against the wood, it was only a moment before the door swung open. Caroline's mouth dropped open, and I shook my head at her. "That was a dick move to lie to you like that."

"You lied?"

"Yes. I should've been honest and told you how I really feel."

"And how do you feel?"

Instead of trying to find the right words, I just launched myself at her. Grabbing her face, I covered her lips with mine. *Oh God.* She felt like home. Her lips were so fucking soft—almost too soft considering how I was ravaging them. At her gasp of surprise, I pushed full steam ahead by thrusting my tongue into her mouth. The sweetness of her taste overwhelmed me, a mixture of the champagne and strawberries from dessert.

This time I was rewarded with a moan of pleasure. With my mouth still fused to hers, I swung my leg back to kick the bedroom door closed. Caroline's hands came to my hair, tugging me closer against her. I wasn't quite so gentlemanly because one of my hands went to cup her ass, or at least I tried to cup her ass through the folds of the dress.

When she started to rub herself against my crotch, I realized things were progressing a little too fast. I finally pulled my lips from hers, and we both fought to catch our breath. "Shouldn't we talk about this?" I panted.

With a grin, she replied, "I thought we were communicating about our feelings very well."

"While I have no complaints, I do think we should verbalize what's going on."

She licked her swollen lips. "And what is that?"

"I think I'm falling for you."

"You are?"

"Actually, I don't *think* I am. I *know* I am."

Her blue eyes flared at my declaration. "You feel the same way I do?"

"Hell yeah."

Apparently, my declaration satisfied Caroline enough to postpone any further discussions. Grabbing me by the lapels, she jerked me toward her, planting her mouth on mine. My fingers slid from the base of her neck down her spine, stopping at the top of her zipper. Taking it between my thumb and forefinger, I slid it down until it stopped at her waist. With my other hand, I gripped one of the straps of her dress. After pulling it down, I dipped my head, bringing my lips to her collarbone. I kissed a trail over to her shoulder. My other hand left her waist to tug at her other strap, and the top of the dress gaped open to reveal a lacy red bustier.

Caroline's breasts strained within the fabric. At the sight of the tempting globes, I licked my lips in anticipation. "God, you're so beautiful."

She peered shyly up at me through her lashes. "Really?"

"Hell yes." Dropping my head, I kissed the top of each of her breasts.

"Mm, Ty," she murmured.

Guiding her over to the bed, I pushed her down onto the mattress. Caroline opened her legs, and I slid between them. Pushing the bustier down, I cupped one of her breasts in my hand. I then swirled my tongue around the hardening nipple before sucking it deep into my mouth.

Caroline moaned as her fingers tangled through my hair again. I continued alternating between light and heavy suction as my hand slid up under her dress to bunch the extensive fabric up over Caroline's waist.

Rocking back on my knees, I slid my tongue up her right thigh, stopping just before I reached her pussy. Caroline gasped as her legs trembled. "Please, Ty."

"Patience."

With my index and forefinger, I rubbed her over her panties, seeking out her clit to swirl my fingers over. As she became wetter, I slid the fabric to the left before plunging two fingers inside. She shrieked and arched her hips. At first, I slowly pumped them in and out, stretching her each time I entered her. Then I sped up the pace, furiously driving my fingers into her pussy.

Caroline's head swiveled back and forth on the pillow as tiny cries of pleasure came from her. Just when I felt her walls began to tighten, I withdrew my fingers. A frustrated huff escaped her lips as she propped on her elbows to stare daggers down at me.

"I want to taste you as you come," I stated.

Her mouth made a perfect O of surprise. "Um, okay." After pulling her panties down her hips and off her legs, I pressed her thighs wide apart. At the sight of her pussy all glistening and swollen with desire, I once again couldn't help saying, "Fuck, you're beautiful."

One of her hands encircled her breast. "You make me feel beautiful."

"I bet you taste just as beautiful."

"Why don't you go ahead and see?"

Dipping my head, I slicked my tongue over her sex, which caused her to shudder. I then began teasing her with my lips and tongue. I lightly swept my tongue along her folds before grazing her clit with my teeth. Caroline pumped her hips against my mouth, moaning my name. As I sucked her between my lips, I slid my hand up her ribcage to cup her full breast. I squeezed it as I alternated between harsh and soft tugs on her clit. When I plunged my tongue deep inside her, she shrieked and clawed at the strands of my hair. "Oh God, Ty! I'm coming!"

I swirled my tongue around within her as she came hard, her arousal coating my mouth. As she rode out her orgasm, I couldn't help the feeling of pride that it had been me to make her body tremble with pleasure. I couldn't wait to bury myself deep inside her. Covering her body with mine, I prepared to shed the rest of my clothes and plunge my dick into her warm, inviting pussy—but then it hit me like a ton of bricks where we were and who she was. Any plans for ravishing her were suddenly derailed.

CHAPTER EIGHTEEN

TY FRASER HAD the mouth of a god. Okay, maybe it was more the mouth of a Hoover with extreme power suction. It seemed to be everywhere: my mouth, my breasts, my clit—wherever it was, it inflamed me. It delivered an orgasm that caused me to moan and cry out and writhe on the bed like I was undergoing an exorcism.

As his suit-clad bulge pressed against my slickened core, I bit down on my lip, mentally preparing myself to take all of him within me. It'd been one thing to see his non-aroused cock; it was quite another thing to see it in all its glory, and yet another to imagine it buried to the hilt inside me. I couldn't lie—I had one of those cliché romance novel moments where I wondered if it would actually fit.

But, instead of tearing off his pants and underwear, Ty rocked back to sit on his knees between my legs.

"Wait, what's happening?" It took a few breathless seconds for me to collect myself. The loss of his body, his lips, his fingers . . . it was that intense. "Why did you stop?" I panted.

Ty raked a hand over his face, his expression grim. "I can't do this."

"Um, I'm pretty sure you can." To prove my point, I rolled my hips into his erection.

He groaned. "That's not what I meant," he choked out.

"Then what's the problem?"

"This room."

I furrowed my brows in confusion. "You want us to go somewhere else?"

After glancing down at me, Ty once again groaned. He was starting to sound like a caveman. "I can't think when we're like this." He then pushed himself away from me and hopped off the bed.

As he proceeded to pace, I tucked the sheet under me before propping myself up on my elbows. "I don't understand."

Ty motioned his hand around the room. "I can't—"

"Yeah, I get that part. My question is why."

"Because we're in the White House, and I can't be disrespectful."

"You're afraid of disrespecting the White House?" I repeated.

A nervous chuckle erupted from Ty. "When you say it that way, it makes me sound crazy."

Pinching my thumb and forefinger together, I replied, "Maybe just a little."

"Here's the thing: it's not so much about the White House itself. It's more about the fact that we're under your father's roof." Ty shook his head. "I can't disrespect him like that."

Part of me was deeply touched by his honor. The other sexed-up and incredibly turned on part of me was seriously disappointed Ty wasn't a horndog who would bone me whenever and wherever. "Damn you for being noble," I mused.

He grinned. "I'm sorry. It's just who I am."

I sat up on the bed. "And I like that part of you, very much." When Ty dropped down on the bed beside me, I batted my eyelids at him. "So, I know you can't sleep with me under my father's roof, but does that include any and all third base action?"

With a frustrated grunt, Ty threw his head back. "You're killing me, Caroline."

"I'm sorry. I'm just trying to understand all the parameters."

He cut his eyes over to me. "You're just trying to get me to compromise my honor."

I giggled. "You're making it sound like I'm some fiend trying to take your virginity."

"Trust me, I've never said no like this before." He licked his lips, which sent heat burning between my legs. "And never to someone so beautiful and sexy who I wanted so very much."

Oh God. His words lit me on fire with the same equivalent of his hands and mouth. Knowing I was going to ravage him if I didn't get away, I scooted down to the far end of the bed. "I do have one other question."

"I think I'm afraid to hear it."

"Is your honor only tied to the White House? I mean, when we go back home tomorrow, are you going to keep me at arm's length?"

An agonized look flashed in his eyes. "I should."

FUCK ME!! FUCK MY LIFE! "Um, okay. Great."

When Ty closed the gap between us, the heat of his bare thighs scorched against mine. He was really testing my resolve. "Don't get all pissy. I wasn't finished."

"I wasn't pissy."

"Oh yes you were."

"While I will agree I was disappointed and frustrated, I wasn't *pissy*," I countered.

"Will you let me finish?"

"Fine." I crossed my arms over my bustier-covered chest and waited for him to speak.

"The right thing would be for me to keep my distance from you until I'm no longer in charge of your protection." Ty reached over and took one of my hands into his. "But I'm willing to sacrifice a little of my honor to be able to kiss you every day and sleep with you every night."

"You are?"

He nodded. "As long as it's behind closed doors."

With a wrinkle of my nose, I replied, "Wow, that sounds totally cheapening."

"How is that cheapening?"

"You're hiding me away like . . ." I shuddered. "I'm a mistress or something."

Ty's eyes widened. "Of course I'm not. I could never think of you like that."

"Then what will we be?"

"Together, just privately."

"I wish I could say that doesn't bother me, but it does."

"Caroline, surely I don't have to remind you again of the precarious situation we're in."

Deep down, I knew he was right. He was my agent. Nothing good could come of us being found out, especially not for him. He'd already given up so much for his job. I couldn't have him lose it over me. "No. You're right."

"I swear to you that as soon as your stalker is found and I'm transferred off your detail, we'll come out as a couple."

I jabbed my finger at him. "The very instant, right?"

He took my finger and brought it to his lips. "The very second."

As his breath warmed against my skin, I shivered. I snatched my hand away and shook my head. "Okay, that's enough of that. In fact, we probably need to set up some parameters for the way we'll act in public."

"You aren't serious?"

"I totally am. I don't think you grasp how completely on fire I am for you right now." I jerked my head back and forth. "You just can't go touching me like that."

The corners of Ty's lips quirked up. "What if I promise to put your fire out tomorrow night? Many, many times."

My mouth ran dry at his words. "I like the sound of that idea very, very much."

"Will you be able to resist ripping my clothes off until then?"

"I can try. Of course, it'll probably help if you put your clothes back on."

"You're right. I should do that." He leaned over to bestow a tender, almost chaste kiss on my forehead. Once again, I lamented his honor.

While Ty jumped back into his tux pants and went to work tucking his shirt in, I dug a pair of pajamas out of my suitcase and started getting undressed. After slipping the bustier off, I reached for my pajama top, but the heat of Ty's gaze stopped me. He had frozen midway through buttoning up his shirt and was just staring at me with hooded eyes.

"Like what you see?" I teasingly asked.

"Fuck yes I do."

While I normally didn't shed my underwear before bed, I couldn't help shimming it down my thighs. When I stepped out of them, Ty made a guttural sound in the back of his throat. Standing before him in all my naked glory, I asked, "Having second thoughts?"

"I'm having many thoughts, some of which involve you on your back, others on your knees with my cock in your mouth. Others have you on all fours."

His words coupled with the visual had wetness pooling between my thighs. "Why don't you show me those thoughts instead of telling me about them?"

A wolfish grin stretched across his face. "Not while we're in the White House."

With a huff, I snatched my pajama top. "Ty Fraser, you are nothing but a pussy tease!"

He roared with laughter. "I'm the tease? At least you came tonight. I'm going to have to go back to my room and jerk one out."

"Will you be thinking of me?"

"Of course. I can still taste you on my lips."

I threw my hand over my eyes and groaned. "You really have to leave."

"I'm going. I'm just trying not to look so disheveled."

"I don't think anything but a shower is going to help that, especially considering what I did to your hair."

Appearing thoughtful, Ty paused in retying his bowtie. "I think it's best if I pretend I'm drunk."

"Your grand plan is to pretend you've been in here drinking with me?"

"None of the agents are in the residence. If I run into anyone, I'll just pretend I've been hitting one of the bottles from the private reserve."

"I guess it could work."

"Trust me, I can sell it."

"For your sake, I hope so."

As Ty pulled his tux jacket on, I hopped into my pajama pants. I then walked him over to the door. "Tomorrow we pretend like none of this happened, right?" he said.

Rolling my eyes, I replied, "Wow, Ty, you really know how to charm a girl."

"You know what I mean."

"Yeah, yeah. Mum's the word. We're just friends, blah, blah."

"Just try not to make any longing faces at me over breakfast."

"Like I would really do that." Okay, so maybe I might have been tempted to throw a thirsty look or two at him over my pancakes and eggs, but I was pretty sure sitting at the table with my parents would curb any and all desire to do that.

Smiling, Ty reached for the door. "Night, Caroline."

"Good night, Ty."

And then he slipped outside into the hallway. I stood there for a few minutes just staring at the door, wondering if he made it back to his room without being questioned about what he was doing. Like a goofy teenage girl with a first crush, I half swayed, half walked back to my bed. Once I collapsed onto the mattress, I pulled the covers over me. Instead of counting sheep, I started counting down the hours until Ty and I would be alone together.

CHAPTER NINETEEN

IN THE MORNING, I woke up to a feeling of peace I hadn't experienced in a long, long time. At first, I mistook it for everything with my stalker being a bad dream, but then I recalled that he was still out there.

The peace came from everything being revealed between Ty and me. While I would have loved waking up with him beside me, I lay there remembering what his lips felt like on mine. When I saw him before breakfast, it took everything within me not to run into his arms. Instead, we somehow managed to keep our hands off of each other.

After breakfast, we packed up and headed for the airport. On the plane, we were once again in full view of others. To keep from saying or doing something I shouldn't, I kept my head buried in my laptop for most of the flight. Occasionally, I would feel Ty's heated gaze on me. When I would look up, he would be staring at me like he was removing my clothes in his mind, which provoked heat between my legs. I was pretty sure when I got up I was going to find the seat wet.

I'd never thought I would be so grateful to be back in Charleston. The ride from the airport was equally painful as we were so close to being alone together, yet it seemed so far. It didn't help that Ty was in the seat next to me, and I could imagine dragging him into the back to screw his brains out.

When we arrived at the apartment, I exhaled a breath of relief. After saying goodbye to Arjun in the hallway, Ty and I entered the apartment. We stood silently in the foyer for a moment.

"So, we're home," I said.

"Yes."

I cut my eyes over to him. "And we're alone."

Ty's eyes flared with desire. "Oh yeah."

The next thing I knew we had thrown ourselves at each other. I grabbed the front of Ty's shirt and jerked it open, sending buttons cascading over the floor.

"Jesus, Caroline."

With a laugh, I replied, "Sorry. It's been so hard waiting for this."

"Tell me about it."

Grasping me by the ass, Ty hoisted me up to wrap my legs around his waist. He spun us around, pinning me against the foyer wall. With one hand, I jerked my hands through his hair, tugging on the strands while I began rubbing my hips against the bulge in his pants.

He groaned into my mouth, which fueled me to rub even harder. Ty pumped his hips against my pussy. "Let's get in the bedroom before I come in my pants," he murmured against my lips.

He walked us into my bedroom. After closing the door behind us, he hustled us over to the bed.

When we reached the mattress, I slid down Ty's body until I was back on my feet. I reached for his belt buckle. "If I remember correctly, you were left very unsatisfied last time."

"I wouldn't say that. It was fucking amazing watching you come."

I tilted my head at him. "Even so, I owe you a little oral attention."

"I don't think I can argue with that."

Bending my head, I circled his left nipple with my tongue until it was hard and erect. Then I kissed a trail over to the right one. Ty raised his hips, rubbing his erection against my stomach. When I pushed myself away, he groaned at the loss of friction.

After I slid his pants and shorts down his hips, Ty stepped out of them. Like that morning peepshow when I caught him coming out of the shower, I couldn't do anything but stare at his magnificent body. I would further add his magnificent *cock* since it was in its all its hardened glory this time.

"Like what you see?" he asked as he ran his hand down his chest to his waist.

"Oh yes. I like it very, very much."

Ty chuckled. "I'm glad you do."

"There isn't anything I don't like about you." I stepped forward, brought my hand to his mouth, and traced the full bottom lip with my finger. Ty's tongue darted out to suck the tip. Slowly, I began to kiss my way down Ty's stomach, causing his muscles to clench under my lips. Peeking at him through my lashes, his chest rose and fell in harsh pants of anticipation. Bending over, I raked my nails up and down the tops of his thighs as I kissed and licked the taut muscles of his abdomen. "Caroline," he grunted.

"What? I was just paying you back for how you teased me last night."

"Torturing me is more like it."

"Now you know how it feels."

"I don't think I kept you in suspense this long." He grinned. "Of course, it was probably more about me not being able to wait to touch and taste you."

"You make a good point. I'm having a hard time not touching and tasting you." When I gripped his cock in my hand, he hissed. "I'm glad I remedied that."

"Me too," he rasped.

After pumping my hand up and down his shaft, I slid down Ty's body until I was on my knees. I replaced my hand with my tongue. Circling his cock, I continued licking him like a popsicle while only letting my tongue give a teasing flick across the tip.

Ty's hips jerked up, trying to wedge himself into my mouth. "Harder, please." Deciding to end his suffering, I took only the tip of his cock in my mouth and suctioned hard. "Finally. Fuck yes!" Ty cried, his eyes rolling back. Letting him fall free from my mouth, I then blew across the sensitive head glistening with my saliva. "You're killing me," he grunted.

I gave him an evil smile. With my hand, I stroked him hard and fast for a few minutes before bringing him back to my mouth. As I bobbed up and down in a frenzied pace, his groans and curses echoed the bedroom. A sheen of sweat had broken out along his bare chest. "Fuck, I love your mouth."

Bringing my fingers to his base, I twisted my hand back and forth like I was opening a bottle. I alternated between tonguing and suctioning the very tip. The saliva that fell from my lips slid down his length, allowing my fingers to give him an even smoother swirl from my hand as I pumped up and down.

Just as I felt him tensing up, he eased me away. "As much as I'd love to come in your mouth, I want to be inside you this first time."

I couldn't argue with that. After helping me up off my knees, Ty pulled my shirt over my head. He then turned his attention to my jeans. Once I was left in my bra and panties, he nudged me down onto the bed. As his body covered mine, I exhaled a contented sigh.

Ty kissed and licked across my collarbone, leaving little love bites as he went, and his hands slid around my back to the clasps on my bra. After he popped them open one by one, my breasts sprang free of the cups and into Ty's ready and waiting mouth. He sucked hard on one of my nipples. After increasing the pressure, he pulled back to let his tongue flick across it. As it hardened beneath him, he let it fall free from his mouth before blowing across the puckered tip.

"Ty," I moaned, my legs scissoring beneath us.

"Patience."

"I think you mean payback," I countered.

He chuckled before licking a wet trail from the valley between my breasts down over my abdomen. His fingers came to grip the sides of my thong before he slid it down over my legs. I opened wide, giving him a great view of my pussy, but instead of touching me, he surprised me by rolling me over so I was on my stomach.

Starting at my feet, he kissed and licked up my calves to my thighs. Then he alternated with the other leg. Little goose bumps puckered along my skin and my fingers gripped the sheets as I couldn't help writhing on the mattress. This man was the king when it came to prolonging pleasure.

When Ty reached my ass, he pushed me up on my knees. He kissed and licked each globe of my ass before thrusting his tongue between my legs. I shrieked and clawed the sheets. When he started licking and sucking my clit, I pushed my hips back against his face. It only took a few minutes of the exquisite torture for me to come apart.

The mattress dipped as Ty went to retrieve a condom from his wallet. Spent from my orgasm, I flipped over on my back. After sliding the condom on, Ty returned to the bed. I widened my legs for him. He fit perfectly between them. Taking his cock in his hand, he brought it to my slick folds. Sliding the head against my clit, we both groaned.

Ty didn't prolong it anymore. Staring into my eyes, he eased slowly inside. I couldn't help shuddering under the intensity of gaze, not to mention the feel of him stretching and filling me so completely. Once he was satisfied he wasn't going to rip me in two, he pulled out and then thrust back inside. We both gasped this time. "Fuck me," he grunted.

"Mm, please."

After initially setting up a slow, tantalizing rhythm, Ty switched the pace. He began to pound into me. I gripped his biceps for dear life while raising my hips to meet his thrusts. He brought my legs up to rest on his shoulders, and the angle caused him to go even deeper. My nails raked into his skin with the pleasure.

I began building to another orgasm. When Ty reached between us to rub my clit with his thumb, I cried out as I came hard around his dick. He continued pumping into me until he came with a shout and collapsed onto me.

CHAPTER TWENTY

AS CAROLINE and I lay in a tangle of arms and legs in my bed, we desperately tried catching our breath. Once we finally stilled our erratic breathing, I brushed the sweat-stained strands of hair out of her face. "Are you okay?"

"Oh, I'm more than okay. I'm . . . wow."

"I would second that."

Propping her chin on my chest, she smiled up at me. "I'm not being trite when I say that. It really was amazing, and I don't always get to say that."

Her words had my inner King Kong pounding on his chest and roaring with satisfaction. Outwardly, I tried appearing a little humbler. "I'm glad you enjoyed it."

Her finger traced the smattering of hair on my chest. If she didn't stop touching me, I was going to be ready for round two pronto. "You know, this is when you stroke my fragile ego by elaborating on how good it was for you."

I chuckled. "What else would you like me to say?"

"I wouldn't want to put words in your mouth."

"Sure you wouldn't."

"I'm sure this is all terribly unsexy to a man of the world like you, but for me, it does matter."

Fuck. The last thing in the world I wanted was for Caroline to doubt her sexual prowess and appeal, especially after the epic fucking we'd just experienced. I reached one of my hands out to cup her chin. "You were everything I fantasized about and more."

She raised her brows in surprise. "You fantasized about me?"

"I told you Saturday night I'd be getting off to burying myself inside you. I did many, many times."

Pink bloomed in her cheeks. "I fantasized about you, too . . . but before DC."

My brows shot up. "You did?"

"Yeah. That night after our self-defense class, I was so turned on I had to break out my vibrator."

"I know."

Her eyes bulged. "Wait, what?"

"I heard you."

"How?"

"I heard a noise, and then when I investigated it, I realized it was your vibrator."

"Did you . . . watch me?"

Fuck me, that would've been hot. "No. I just heard you through the wall—the vibrator and your moans and cries."

"Oh," she murmured.

"I thought you were thinking of Perry. I had no idea you were masturbating to me."

"Well, I was. I felt horrible considering he and I were still together, but I just couldn't get you out of my mind. The feel of your hands on me, your body against me . . ."

"If I'm being really honest, I jerked off that night, too."

"You did?"

"I knew I was a dirty bastard for doing it, but there was something about the sounds you were making and then the way you'd felt against me that night."

She drew her bottom lip between her teeth. "I should be offended by your invasion of my privacy."

"I know. You should."

"But I'm not."

"Really?"

She shook her head. "No, it just really turns me on."

"I should take care of that for you."

"Yes, please."

After sliding her the rest of the way up my body, I flipped her over to where her back rested against my abdomen. She threw a glance at me over her shoulder. "Hmm, are you thinking of a little reverse cowgirl?"

"Actually, I had something different in mind."

"Oh?"

"Where's your vibrator?"

Her eyes flared. "In the top drawer of my nightstand."

Leaning over on the mattress, I then used one hand to slide open the drawer. "Purple?" I questioned as I picked it up.

"What can I say? I like a good girly color."

I snorted. "I sure as hell wasn't picturing you using a purple one."

"What did you imagine?"

"I didn't really imagine the vibrator. It was more me thinking of you."

"Mm, I see."

"Lie back." Once her head rested against my chest, I widened my thighs for her to rest between them. "Spread your legs." She once again obeyed me.

After turning the vibrator on, I slid it down her breast bone and over one of her breasts. She gasped as it zinged one of her nipples. As I circled the hardening nub, Caroline began scissoring her legs back in forth, desperate for friction from the building tension. "Do you like that?"

"Oh yes."

"Do you want me to keep going?"

"Yes . . . please."

Her breath hitched as the vibrator trailed down her abdomen. When it reached the top of her pussy, she bit down on her lip in the anticipation of what was to come. As I pressed it against her throbbing clit, she cried out. Raising her hips, she worked herself against the masterful vibrations. With my free hand, I squeezed one of her breasts, stopping from time to time to pinch one of the nipples. Just as she was getting close to coming, I plunged the vibrator inside Caroline. Pressing the tip forward toward her public bone, I let it rest against her g-spot. "Oh God! Oh Ty, yes!" she cried.

Her thighs began trembling, and her head rocked from side to side. She continued moaning with pleasure. My cock was growing hard against her ass. I debated between letting her come on the vibrator or making her wait until I plunged deep inside her. But then I figured it wouldn't hurt to make her come yet again once I was inside her.

"Ty!" she shrieked as her hips seized up and she began convulsing in her orgasm. I hated that I couldn't see her face to see the pleasure reflecting in it. She'd looked so sexy and beautiful before. After pulling the vibrator out of her, I tossed it onto the bed. With my free hand, I grabbed one of the condoms off the top of the nightstand and brought it to my teeth to open it. After ripping it open, I slid it down my length.

"Are you ready?"

"For sleep or sex?" she asked teasingly.

With a growl, I gripped her hips and flipped her around. I wanted to be able to look into her eyes when I was inside her. "You'd really be so selfish as to leave me with a raging hard-on after I got you off?"

She ran her finger over my bottom lip. "You could always rub one out—I hear you're good at that." Tilting her head, she asked, "Wait, or would it be me who was good at that since you were the one listening?"

I threw my head back and chuckled. "I think we both are." I guided my erection to her core. Rubbing my cock against her entrance, I said, "At least we were. I think once we fuck each other's brains out, we won't have the time or energy for masturbation."

"Sounds good to me." She then sat up on her knees, and her hand helped mine to glide me inside her slickened core. When she eased down on me, our eyes locked, and we both sucked in a harsh breath.

"Fuck, you're so tight," I said as I panted against her breasts.

Placing her hands on my shoulders, Caroline then began riding me. She alternated between swiveling her hips clockwise and counterclock-wise, and she'd rise up to where I almost fell free of her body and then she'd slam back down on me. After letting her set the pace, my hands came to the globes of her ass. I squeezed them as she bounced on and off of my dick. I could have stayed inside her all night, feeling her soft skin rubbing against mine, the silky strands of her hair falling in my face, and her pert breasts just within reach.

When I felt her walls tightening around me, I flipped her over onto her back. Sitting up on my knees, I began relentlessly pounding into her. "Ty!" Caroline cried as she came. I continued thrusting into her as her convulsing walls milked my dick. With a shout, I lost myself to the overwhelming pleasure of being buried inside Caroline. After my dick had stopped pulsing, I eased out of her, slid the condom off, and then got off the bed to toss it in the trash.

"I'm not sure I'm going to be able to walk tomorrow," Caroline remarked with a lazy smile.

I winced. I'd probably gotten a little too carried away after changing positions. "Sorry. Was I a bit rough there at the end?"

"No. I loved every minute of it."

The mattress dipped under my weight as I came back to bed. "You know I'd rather die than hurt you."

She grinned at me as her hand came up to caress my cheek. "Don't be so dramatic. It's a sore vagina, not a broken heart."

"I'm not being dramatic. I meant every word."

"I hardly think it's very serious if I can joke about waddling into work tomorrow or putting an ice pack on my vagina," she countered.

"I just don't ever want to get carried away and hurt you."

"With your huge cock?" she asked.

"Those are your words, not mine."

"Ha, you know you were thinking them," she teased.

With a wink, I replied, "Maybe."

She shook her head at me. "You know, it's actually endearing how modest you are about being well-endowed."

"Ah, that's just me being a gentleman around you. I tend to milk it around the lads, let them know who is cock of the walk."

She snorted. "I can only imagine what you were like in the Army, probably whipping it out for measuring contests."

"I can neither confirm nor deny that."

"Oh God," she moaned as she smacked her hand to her forehead.

"What can I say? Men are pigs."

"That's the truth." Pursing her lips at me, she said, "But somehow you managed not to get as many pig genes as other men."

"I wouldn't be so sure about that."

"Trust me, I can speak pretty knowledgeably from personal experience, not to mention the fact that Barrett is my brother."

I chuckled at the mention of Barrett. "He's a reformed pig."

"That's true." She jerked her chin at me. "Enough talking. I've got to get some sleep or I'm going to be a zombie at work tomorrow." When I started to get out of bed, her hand reached out to stop me. "Wait, what are you doing?"

"Going back to my bed."

"You aren't going to sleep with me?"

I shrugged. "I wasn't sure what to do. This is the point where, if we weren't living together, one of us would go home."

"So, in your case, it would be next door?"

"Exactly."

"Or this would also be the point where one of us stayed the night."

"Would you like me to stay?"

She gave me a shy smile. "I don't think I've had a guy leave after sex since undergrad."

Although I could have lived a lifetime without that information, I nodded. "Okay. I'll stay."

"Good."

Caroline held up the covers, and I quickly slid inside. After crossing over to her side of the bed, I decided if I was going to spend the night, I was going to be all in. That meant spooning. Caroline gave a contented sigh when I pressed myself against her. While it normally took some television or mindless reading to get me to sleep, I was dreaming almost from the time my head hit the pillow. I had to chalk it up to the Caroline effect.

CHAPTER TWENTY-ONE

THE NEXT TWO weeks flew by in a blur of work and sex. I guess you could say the two were often combined, except we never actually got it on Read 4 Life. We weren't letting anyone in on our secret, not even Selah. Our days were spent at the office or out on school visits while our evenings were spent at home in the apartment. While that hadn't changed much from before, the fact that we spent the nights together was a development.

It was harder than I imagined keeping things hidden. It wasn't just about holding back on kissing or intimately touching Caroline in front of the others. I had to temper the looks I gave her as well as the things I said. I felt wound up all day until we finally swept the apartment door closed.

It was the day of *Satchel and Babe Learn to Read*'s book signing. Thankfully, it had dawned sunny and bright, or at least I perceived it to be that way since I could see the sun streaking through the drawn blinds in the bedroom. I'd become accustomed to waking up with Caroline wrapped in my arms. This morning, my arms were conspicuously empty.

When I rolled over, she was already awake, sitting straight up in the bed. "Babe?" I questioned.

"Hmm."

"Are you okay?"

"Oh yeah, I'm fine."

I rose up to sit next to her. "Nervous about today?"

"Yeah. Just a little."

"How much sleep did you get last night?"

"Um, maybe an hour."

Pulling her against me, I kissed the side of her head. "Why didn't you wake me up?"

"You were sleeping so peacefully I couldn't bring myself to disturb you."

"Does that mean you watched me sleep?"

She grinned. "Yes, I pulled a total Edward Cullen and watched you sleep."

"Did you just call yourself a sparkly vampire?"

"I did." Her finger trailed the stubble along my chin. "Don't knock him. It's because of Robert Pattinson I have a thing for British men."

I dipped my head to nuzzle her neck. "So, I owe something to the *Twilight* franchise?"

"Yes. Yes, you do."

My hand came to her breast. "Would a morning quickie help your nerves?"

She laughed. "While I think it would get my mind off things, I'm not sure it would actually help my anxiety."

"Surely an orgasm or two would put you at ease."

Tilting her head to the side, she mused, tapping her chin. "I don't know . . . I guess all we can do is try."

"Mm, my pleasure."

Just as I started to push her back down in the bed for a morning ravishing, my phone dinged on the nightstand. Although I would have loved to ignore it, our present security issues made that impossible. Reluctantly, I pulled away from Caroline to grab my phone. "Fuck."

"What is it?"

"Stuart's on his way over."

"Which means it's time for you to leave me in my hour of need." With a pointed look, she added, "And I mean my emotional need, not physical."

"Ha, whatever. You should be disappointed I don't get to be a Dr. Feelgood and fuck your nerves away."

"Sorry, but I am disappointed you can't stay with me."

"Don't worry. It'll just be for a little while. After we get ready for the flight to DC, you won't be able to get rid of me for the rest of the day."

With a smile, she replied, "My hero."

After giving her one last kiss, I pulled myself out of the bed. I hustled out of Caroline's bedroom just in time to meet Stuart in the foyer. He eyed me suspiciously. "I thought you would already be up by now."

"I'm getting a late start. Couldn't fall asleep last night," I lied.

Stuart nodded. "I know what you mean. I've been restless the last few nights." *Try nineteen days.* The problem of this stalker was not being able to predict any of his moves, but nineteen days with zero contact hadn't meant we'd let our guard down. We were both feeling more than antsy at the moment. *What is the bastard up to?*

While I wanted to believe the stalker had eventually lost interest, the answer seemed to be that he was preparing to make another appearance, and this time he wouldn't just be leaving a box behind. I still hadn't forgotten his threat to me either. It was why the security detail had been working extra strenuously to ensure Caroline's safety at the book signing.

Caroline poked her head out of the bedroom door. "Is it okay if I take the shower, Ty?"

"Sure thing. I'll run down to Stuart's and grab mine." My gaze bounced from hers to Stuart's. "Can you man the fort while I do that?"

He nodded. "Of course."

After dipping into my bedroom, I grabbed my suit and tie out of the closet. Since I knew Caroline hated for me to be too far away from her, I made quick work taking my shower. When I returned to the apartment, Stuart was on a video call with some of the extra agents who were going to be helping us out that day with Caroline's book signing. Because of the stalker, we were taking a few of the agents from President Callahan's detail.

When Caroline came out of her bedroom, I fought the urge to draw her into my arms to lay one on her. God, she looked gorgeous in a long-sleeved red dress that hit just at her knees and a very inviting pair of come-fuck-me black heels. Once again, if Stuart hadn't been in the room, I would have been tempted to take her on the kitchen table.

Tempering my response in front of Stuart, I said, "You look beautiful."

She smiled. "Do I look like a children's book author?"

"Very much so."

Her expression darkened. "I hate that Mom and Dad couldn't be with me today."

Because of security concerns, the idea of having the first lady or president in the audience was quickly nixed by the Secret Service. "They'll be there with you in spirit. I know they're immensely proud of you, as we all are."

"Thank you, Ty. That means a lot."

When my gaze flickered to Stuart, he eyed us with a curious expression. I wondered if he was putting two and two together about something potentially going on between us. I hoped for his sake he would keep his trap shut.

After clearing my throat, I asked, "Ready to go?"

Caroline nodded. "Selah is going to meet us downstairs."

Since Selah was Caroline's PA at Read 4 Life, she was attending the signing to do all the assistant things Caroline would need. In the end, I thought it was more about moral support than anything.

Stuart trailed us out the door to get the elevator. "Did you eat?" I asked as I punched the down button.

She shook her head. "I'm too afraid I'll throw up."

"Nope. You have to eat. Do you want to pass out in the middle of the signing?"

"I think it would be better to pass out than throw up on someone," she countered.

"Neither of those are great choices." As we got onto the elevator, I turned to Stuart. "We need to stop to get something for Caroline to eat on the away to the airport."

"Copy that," he replied with a shit-eating grin on his face. *Oh hell.* He was onto us for sure. Sometime that day I was going to have to get him aside to have a talk with him about keeping it to himself.

When we got outside, Beverly was waiting with the SUV on the curb. Selah came out front looking sleek and elegant in a black pantsuit. At the sight of Caroline and me staring at her, she twirled around in her heels. "Do I look like a New York City PA rather than a backwoods PA?"

"Is that the look you're going for?" I asked.

She rolled her eyes. "Of course it is."

"Then you totally look the part."

"What else do I look like?"

"Maybe a coach in the WBNA?" I suggested.

Caroline smacked my arm. "She does not."

"Hey, it's a compliment. I happen to love watching the WNBA."

Stuart motioned to us. "Load up. It's time we got to the airport."

After I held the door open for Caroline and helped her inside, I offered my hand to Selah. As she started up into the SUV, she elbowed me in the ribs. At my grunt, she turned around and flashed me a smile. "My bad."

"Right," I muttered before closing the door. I then hopped up in the front with Stuart, and we began the trek to the airport.

———

We touched down in DC a little before eleven. A motorcade of black SUVs with tinted and bulletproof windows was waiting for us on the tarmac at Dulles. We then drove straight to the Barnes & Noble location where the signing was set to start at noon.

When our entourage swept through the door, we were met by two managers. One escorted Caroline and Selah to the back of the store so Caroline could put the final touches on her hair and makeup. While Stuart and Beverly went back with her, I stood at the front door, watching the readers file in and line up for the metal detector. The managers of the Barnes & Noble had gone above and beyond to work with our security needs. Of course, it was a first for them having a TSA-level metal detector. Previously, their only concern had been to nab shoplifters. Our concern was finding a weapon of any kind.

Bomb-sniffing dogs had been sent around the previous night at closing as well as that morning after the store opened. They'd also made their way through the crowds that had begun lining up before the signing time. We weren't taking any chances with Caroline's safety.

Arjun was manning the machine while I was eyeballing anyone who appeared remotely suspicious. Since the crowed was mostly comprised of parents and their children, no one really stood out. Arjun was manning the machine while I was eyeballing anyone who appeared remotely suspicious. The crowd was mostly comprised of parents and their children. For the most part, no one really stood out. Except for one guy.

He fit the description the FBI profiler had come up with. Late twenties to early thirties. Clean cut and clean shaven. Moderately well dressed. The moment he walked through the door the hairs on the back of my neck pricked. Besides the physical attributes, it was probably the large backpack he had slung across his shoulder that set me on edge. At the sight of the metal detector, his eyes had bulged.

As he started to walk through, my breath hitched. Inching toward him, I prepared myself to take him down. But no alarms went off. In spite of that fact, I held my hand up to him. "Excuse me, but I need to check your bag."

"Is that really necessary?"

I narrowed my eyes at him. "Yes. It is."

With a huff, he shoved the bag at me. While I unzipped it, I didn't take my eyes from his. Once I had it open, I averted my gaze to look inside. Instead of any sort of weaponry, I found Satchel and Babe books. Although I felt somewhat defeated, I knew there was still something about him I didn't trust.

After glancing at my watch, I saw it was about ten minutes before Caroline was to be announced. Since I knew she was a nervous wreck, I wanted to be there to hold her hand before she went out. "I'm going to go back to Caroline," I told Arjun.

He nodded. Just as I started to the back, the alarm on the metal detector went off. Since it had only done that twice all morning, I turned around. A thirty-something looking guy wore a sheepish expression. "Sorry. My metal always makes me go off."

"Metal?" I demanded. Bending over, he jerked up the leg on his jeans. At the sight of a prosthetic leg, my brows shot up. "Did you lose it in service?"

"Yeah. Two years ago, I stepped on an old landmine outside of Fallujah."

I grimaced as my stomach lurched. Ten years earlier, I'd witnessed the very same thing happen to a guy in my unit. Monty hadn't been so fortunate as to just lose a leg. He'd been blown completely apart and was sent home to his family in a flag-draped coffin.

Holding up a hand, he said, "Listen, if you're worried, I could always go in the back with you and take it off. Then you could check it thoroughly."

Jesus Christ. I couldn't believe he was offering to do something so invasive. "That won't be necessary. I can just pat you down here."

"Are you sure?"

I nodded. "I don't think I could do that to a fellow veteran." I motioned to his arms. "Hold your arms out from your body."

As I started patting him down, he asked, "You were service? What unit?"

"Rifles Regiment in the British Army."

He smiled. "I was infantry, too."

"Tough work being on the ground."

"You can say that again." He jerked his chin at the stage that had been set up for Caroline. "It's my niece's birthday next week back in Virginia. She's a huge fan of Satchel and Babe, but she couldn't make it to the signing, so I want to get her a book as a gift."

"That's nice of you. Maybe I can see about getting her some of the extra stuff like the bookmarks and maybe Satchel and Babe stuffed animals."

His eyes lit up. "That would rock. Thanks."

"You're welcome." Motioning to the back of the store, I said, "Excuse me while I go see about the lady of the hour."

"Sure thing."

I took the long way around the crowd to get to the back. At the doorway, Stuart stood outside, and I assumed Beverly was inside with Caroline and Selah. My knuckles rapped on the door. "It's me, Ty."

"Come in," Caroline called.

When I opened the door, Caroline sat in a chair in front of a lighted mirror. Apparently, Jane had dispatched her stylist, because a familiar-looking man stood working on Caroline's hair. Although I couldn't remember his name, I recognized him from when I was on the campaign trail with Barrett and Addison.

I walked up to her. "How are you holding up?"

"I'm okay."

"You know you can't lie to me."

With a roll of her eyes, she replied, "Fine, I'm still a nervous wreck."

Selah snickered. "She's been talking ninety miles a minute since we've been back here. It's pretty hilarious."

"I can imagine," I replied with a smile.

"I'm glad you two can see the humor in my breakdown."

"You're not going to break down. You're going to go out there, read the book like a champ, and then sign a shit-ton of books."

"How can you be so sure I'm not going to walk out there and trip or choke up while I'm trying to read?" she countered.

I winked at her. "Because I know you. Caroline Callahan doesn't trip or choke. She kicks arse."

The corners of her lips quirked up. "I suppose you're right."

"Oh, I know I am. So, you just get out there and be yourself.

She nodded. "Okay, I will."

Holding my hand out to her, I said, "Let's do it."

Before she could take my hand, I became both blinded and strangled by a cloud of hairspray. Once I regained my sight and stopped coughing, Caroline had risen out of her chair and was standing in front of me. "Right. Let's do this."

Stuart would be walking in front of Caroline as she started in while I would be taking her from behind. *Shit*—I would be following behind her. Beverly was waiting at the stage while Arjun would remain at the metal detector. Three other agents who belonged to President Callahan's detail would be filling in to walk around the store during the signing, and there were two other plainclothes agents within the crowd.

When Caroline came out of the back, applause rang out among the parents and grandparents while the children shrieked and shouted as they jumped up and down. Under the positive reception, Caroline's body language changed. I felt the confidence coming back to her as she ascended the stairs of the makeshift stage.

Once she sat down in the overstuffed chair, a beaming smile lit up her face. After picking up the microphone, she spoke confidently to the crowd. Her voice never wavered, nor did she choke as she had feared she would. She answered questions from the audience with ease and humor. After reading *Satchel and Babe Learn to Read* aloud to the crowd, a table was brought up on the stage for her to do the signing.

I moved to stand next to the right side of the desk where I was in close distance to Caroline. As the signing stretched on, everything seemed to go off without a hitch. Caroline took pictures with some of the children along with signing their books. I kept my eye on the guy with the backpack. I also informed the team over my mic to keep an eye on him. Before the signing started, he moved to the back of the line. He didn't speak to anyone else around him. Instead, he kept his gaze locked on Caroline. When she told a joke or smiled with the children, his expression never changed. There was definitely something up with him.

Then something came over my microphone that sent apprehension prickling up my spine. "A suspicious package has been reported outside. Calling in FBI."

"Fuck," I muttered.

"Brown, Tierney, and Nadeen, head outside to survey the situation to make a call on evacuation. Fraser, stand by to get target out of the store."

"Copy that."

At that moment, my attention was averted from the crisis outside as the soldier I'd met before climbed the stairs and walked onto the stage. I nodded a hello at him. When he smiled at me, icy fear cascaded over me. It reverberated from my head down to my toes. It wasn't the same smile he'd given me earlier. This one was one an almost psychotic look of triumph. While Caroline's attention was occupied by talking to a silver-haired woman, I took a step toward him.

As the elderly woman walked away from Caroline, the young man stood staring at Caroline. The Barnes & Noble manager motioned him on, but he remained standing there, his chest heaving. It was then I saw something shiny underneath his copy of *Satchel and Babe*.

"Jesus Christ!" I cried as I lunged forward. Time then slowed to a crawl. When he raised his arm with the gun, screams broke out around me. The elderly woman jumped in front me, blocking my direct access to the shooter. Instead of taking him down, I had to get Caroline.

Just as I launched myself in front of the table, the crack of gunfire went off. Fire exploded into my side, choking off my breath and causing my vision to blur. I refocused my eyes as my body skidded across the top of the table. I plowed into Caroline, toppling her and the chair. Once we collapsed onto the ground, I whirled the chair around as a shield to protect Caroline from any more bullets before covering her with my body.

Chaos reigned around me with people stampeding and screaming.

Was that another gunshot?

Fuck. Has anyone taken down the shooter?

I glanced down at Caroline, who blinked up at me in shock. The only thing that mattered was she was safe.

CHAPTER TWENTY-TWO: CAROLINE

BLINKING MY EYES, I desperately tried to get my vision to focus. My lungs burned in agony, and I fought the urge to claw at my chest. While the world around me was a colorful blur of activity, I couldn't for the life of me make it out as my ears were assaulted with a chilling soundtrack of high-pitched screams and shouts.

When my vision cleared, I stared up at the multiple levels of the bookstore. Above me, people scrambled through the aisles in a panic. *Wait, why are they so terrified? And how did I end up on the ground?*

Then my mind was bombarded by a flashback so vivid, I shuddered. A sweet grandmother was talking to me about her grandchildren's love of books then a young man stood in front of me . . . the silver gleam of a gun . . . Ty knocking me violently to the ground.

It was then I realized Ty was lying halfway across my body. He whipped his head around and pinned me with a stare. "Are you okay?" he demanded.

With my lungs compressing like an accordion, I fought desperately to breathe.

"Caroline, are you okay?" Ty repeated, his voice suddenly sounding off.

Staring into his panicked blue eyes, I bobbed my head emphatically. "Wind . . . knocked . . . out," I wheezed.

Instead of acknowledging what I'd said, confusion filled Ty's expression. Time slowed down to a crawl when he held up a blood-stained hand. We both stared at it, unblinking and unmoving. Finally, Ty broke the silence. "Wait, are you bleeding?"

As he began furiously patting my body down for bullet wounds, a chill went down my spine like I'd been doused with ice water. Although his face contorted with what could only be agonizing pain, Ty didn't seem to register it. Like always, his only focus was on me, even when he'd been *shot*.

I knew he wasn't going to find anything. I hadn't taken a hit. The only pain I was experiencing was from him knocking me to the ground. Tears stung my eyes. "N-No. I-It's you."

Ty's brows creased in confusion before his gaze dropped to the front of his suit jacket. At the sight of the sticky wetness oozing from his shirt, his eyes widened. "Oh fuck." He peered up at me. "I was hit."

In that moment, there was only one thing to do, only one thing I could do to help the man I loved. Somehow in that manic moment, I found my voice, threw my head back, and screamed, "HELP! SOME-BODY HELP ME!"

Within seconds, Stuart appeared like Superman, diving over the table to land beside us. His eyes bulged at the sight of Ty. "MAN DOWN!" he shouted over his shoulder. He then began furiously talking into his mic.

As Ty's face became the color of modeling clay, he pitched

forward, his hand landing against my chest. "Hang on, Ty. You're going to be just fine," I said.

He jabbed a bloody finger at Stuart. "Get . . . her . . . out," he rasped.

Panic ricocheted through me at the thought of leaving him. I gripped his shoulders tighter. "No! I'm staying here with you."

Ty gave a quick shake of his head. "Not safe. Go."

When Stuart reached for me, I shoved his hands away before turning back to Ty. "I'm *not* leaving you."

"Now," he commanded.

At the wail of an ambulance in the distance, Stuart once again reached for me. The combination of his size and strength quickly overcame my struggles. After he had a firm grasp on my waist, he threw me over his shoulder like I was a sack of potatoes. Once his forearm braced me under my knees, he whirled around and started into the crowd.

"Put me down!" I screamed.

"Not on your fucking life."

I smacked my palms against his back like a petulant toddler throwing a tantrum. "But I need to be with Ty. He could . . ." I couldn't bring myself to utter the words. *He could be dying.* "I need to be with him."

"You can see Agent Fraser when I know with absolute certainty this is a one-man job and your life is no longer in danger," Stuart huffed.

As Ty's crumpled form began to fade in the distance, I screamed, "I love you, Ty!" I didn't know if he was still conscious or not, but I knew I had to say it. I didn't care who heard me. The only one that mattered was Ty.

Once Stuart got to the exit, we breezed through it. One of the vehicles was waiting on the curb, the back door flung open at our arrival. After I was unceremoniously dumped onto the seat, Stuart's body came over mine. A sob tore through my chest because it reminded me of what Ty had done only minutes earlier.

"Go!" Stuart shouted.

The car's tires squealed as we peeled away from the bookstore. Although I didn't think anyone could possibly shoot me through the impenetrable windows of the SUV, I didn't yell at Stuart to get off me. Instead, I welcomed the comforting feel of him. I felt like I would have fractured apart into a million pieces without the warm protection of Stuart's body against mine.

He moved one of his arms off me to put his hand to his earpiece. "Copy that. Shooter's down."

I gasped. "They killed him?"

"No. He's being taken into custody."

For some reason, I would've felt more relief if he had been killed. It was then it hit me who else I was missing. "Where's Selah?"

"Beverly got her into one of the cars. She's fine." I exhaled a relieved breath. "Where are you taking me?"

"To the hospital."

"Oh good. I want to be with Ty."

Stuart shook his head. "You're going to the ER to get checked out."

"What? No! There's nothing wrong with me. It's Ty who was shot."

"We don't know if there's anything wrong with you. Fraser took you down pretty hard, and you could have a concussion or fractured ribs."

With all the strength I had, I shoved Stuart away. Jabbing a finger into his chest, I said, "Let's get one thing straight: I'm not getting shoved in any MRIs or CT scans, nor am I getting poked and prodded while wearing a barely there gown. The only place I plan to be in the hospital is outside his room!"

Stuart squared his jaw before glaring at me. "Jesus, you're stubborn."

"Yes. I am."

"Don't you think Fraser would want you to make sure you're okay? You're not going to be any good to him if you go into shock."

"While I appreciate your tactical maneuver there, I'm not buying it. I'm not thinking about me until I know with absolute certainty that Ty's going to pull through."

Stuart momentarily ignored me. From the look on his face, I knew he was paying attention to the feed in his ear. "Suspect says he acted alone, but it hasn't been confirmed. ATF is in route to suspect's domicile. DNA testing is under way."

"What about Ty?" I demanded.

"EMTs confirm two bullet wounds. One appears lodged in his ass and the other in his ribcage. He'll be going straight into surgery when he gets to the hospital."

"Then I'm going straight to the surgical waiting room."

With a roll of his eyes, Stuart replied, "Of course you are."

When we wheeled up at the hospital's entrance, three more Secret Service vehicles had joined our entourage. The agents swarmed the car so they could help escort me inside. At the sight of an ashen-faced Selah, I threw myself at her. Stuart gave us a few moments to hug before he urged us inside. Our group overflowed the elevator, and several agents stepped off to take the next one.

Once we got upstairs, the surgical waiting room had already been emptied and the families escorted to another location. The Secret Service contingency wasted no time ensuring my safety. None of them appeared to be entirely convinced the shooter had acted alone.

As I paced around the waiting room, I wrung my hands to keep from pulling my hair out. From time to time, flashbacks of that moment would assault me. The first time I experienced one, I almost passed out. After flailing, I pitched forward into one of the chairs, and it was then Stuart insisted a doctor come and check me out.

Thankfully, it appeared I hadn't suffered any physical damage.

Emotionally, on the other hand, I was a wreck. At the head of the ER's insistence, I was given a shot of Valium to keep me calm. A few moments later, the head of the psychiatric ward was called in to evaluate me.

With the calming effects of the Valium coursing through me, I stopped wringing my hands, but I couldn't for the life of me stop my manic pacing. Stuart appeared with a pair of blue medical scrubs in his hands. "You should probably change."

When I reached out for the scrubs, I saw my arms stained with Ty's blood. Looking down, I saw dark splotches covered my red dress, and the sight of it caused me to start crying again.

Stuart drew me into his arms for a hug. "Selah?" he called, and she appeared in an instant. "Will you help her change and get cleaned up?"

"Of course."

"Thanks," I squeaked.

At the sound of commotion behind me, I whirled around. Time slowed to a crawl as my somewhat disheveled father strode into the room with my mother close on his heels. With Dad's brows creased in worry, his gaze bounced around the room. When he finally made eye contact with me, his body almost deflated in relief. As he approached, the frayed strand holding my sanity intact came apart, sending my knees buckling. I would've melted into the floor if Dad hadn't caught me.

"Oh, CC," he murmured, his warm breath tickling my earlobe.

In spite of the medication, the thread holding together my emotions unraveled. As tears streaked down my cheeks, my chest rose and fell with harsh sobs. The soft touch of my mother's hand came to the top of my head, and she stroked my hair as my father held me tight.

"Thank God you're all right," Dad said as he squeezed me tighter in his embrace.

"Only because of Ty," I mumbled as I wept.

"I know. He's getting a medal for this one."

Placing my palms on Dad's chest, I pushed myself out of his arms. "A posthumous medal?" I couldn't help questioning in a whisper.

"Hell no. I plan on pinning it to his chest myself."

"Wait . . . he's going to be okay?"

Dad nodded. "We've been in direct contact with the doctors since Ty arrived."

Once again, my knees gave out, and I fought to keep myself upright. Dad's grip on my shoulders kept me up. Pinching my eyes shut, I murmured, "Thank you, God."

"We've notified Ty's parents, and they're on the next flight out," Dad informed me.

"Good," I murmured.

"Can I please hold my baby?" Mom choked out. Tears streamed down her ashen cheeks, and I quickly pried myself out of Dad's embrace to dive into her waiting arms. "Oh CC, we could have lost you today."

Swallowing hard, I croaked, "I know." In a way, though, the severity of what'd happened hadn't fully hit me. I could have been killed. I could have been taken away from everyone I loved. Most of all, I could have never had a future with Ty, and even though I'd only known him for a short time, the thought terrified me. *He is my future. He has to be okay.*

Mom's body trembled almost more than mine. "I don't want to let you go, not for a minute."

Shuttering my eyes, I rested my head in the crook of her neck. I was no longer a twenty-four-year-old independent woman. I was a little girl who just wanted the comfort of her mother. "I know, Mom. I don't want to either."

Dad steered us over to the couch. "Come on, you two. Take a load off."

Mom and I sat down in unison. Ever the lady, she handed me a handkerchief. As I swiped the soft cotton under my eyes, Mom wrapped an arm around my shoulder. Once I finished cleaning my face, I leaned my head against her chest. In Ty's arms, I felt unrivaled physical strength and safety, yet in my mom's arms, I felt emotionally shielded. I was so lucky to have her. *God, I'm so lucky to be alive.*

Instead of taking a seat, Dad stood in front of us. "Is there something you'd like to tell us?"

"About the—" I swallowed hard. I couldn't bring myself to utter the word: *shooting*. Of course, there were so many other ways to describe what had happened: attack, incident, violence. The word that had really been bouncing around in my mind was *why*. Why me? Why him? What tied us together to have created so much hatred toward me in his mind? Twisting the handkerchief in my hands, I asked, "You want me to tell you about today?"

"Yes and no."

I furrowed my brows. "I don't think I understand."

"We've been briefed by the Secret Service and the FBI about the shooting. I think your mother and I are both far more concerned with a certain development from today."

"Development?" I questioned.

"James, do we really need to do this right now?" Mom protested.

Dad shook his head. "I would think we would want to get on top of this considering the media already is. Do you really think it would be that emotionally taxing for her?"

I glanced between my parents. "Um, hello? I'm sitting right here."

"Sorry, sweetheart," Mom replied.

With a smile, Dad said, "Sometimes we forget you're not our little girl anymore. You're a grown woman."

It was then it hit me what he'd meant about a development. I sucked in a harsh breath. "You know about Ty and me?"

While Dad nodded, Mom said, "We saw a clip of the video on the car ride over."

Scrunching my brows in confusion, I asked, "The video?"

"Of you not wanting to leave Ty."

An embarrassed warmth flooded my cheeks. Although I couldn't remember exactly what I'd said or did, I could only imagine the worst had come out of my mouth. Because of technology, a painful and private moment was making its way around the internet.

"I really hate that you had to find out that way. Believe me, I wanted to tell you myself. I came close so many times, but I just couldn't."

"I thought we were the type of parents you could tell anything?" Mom questioned softly.

"Usually, you are, but this was bigger than just a family matter." At Dad's wounded expression, I rose off the couch. "Please don't be upset with Ty. It's obvious neither one of us expected this to happen, but after being in such close quarters with him these past two months, I started to like him—I started to like him as more than just my agent and my brother's friend. He really is one of the best men I have ever met."

"I should have anticipated this. Instead of looking at Ty from just a skills standpoint, I should have taken into account the fact that he is young and good-looking," Dad lamented.

"Yeah, Ty is gorgeous, but trust me, it wasn't his looks." *His body —well, hello, yes.* With a shake of my head, I said, "It was his heart I was attracted to, his honesty and thoughtfulness, his dry sense of humor, the way he gently pushed and challenged me, always wanting me to be the best version of myself."

The thought of losing Ty, in any shape or form, caused a hole in my heart that I didn't think I'd ever fill. I had never known the type of terror I'd felt when he held his hand up with so much blood on it. I shuddered. *How did one man become so vital to me in such a short period of time?*

"In the end, we thought it better to wait to discuss our relationship after the stalker was caught, and then he would request to be reassigned."

"We're not upset with you or with Ty. We're just a little hurt that you didn't come to us," Mom replied.

When Dad remained silent, I cocked my head at him. "Are you sure about that?"

After fiddling with his cufflinks, Dad sighed. "I can't completely agree with your mother."

"And why not?"

"Trust me when I say if we weren't having this conversation in a hospital waiting room after your attempted assassination, my reaction would be far less tempered. Ty's relationship with you goes against protocol, CC."

"Excuse me? Were you not just talking about awarding him a medal? Now you sound like you're going to fire him because we fell in love."

"Of course I still believe he deserves a medal—he saved my only daughter's life—but that doesn't negate the fact that he also did something wrong."

Seconds ticked by, agonizing moments as I processed that I'd just admitted to being in love in front of my parents. Squaring my shoulders, I decided to make a much-needed subject change. "Are you going to make him resign?"

"No, of course not. When he's recovered, we'll transfer him somewhere else."

I swallowed hard. "Away from me?"

A small smile played on Dad's lips. "In spite of the fact that I'm the leader of the free world, I don't think even *I* could keep the two of you away from each other. You are a grown woman free to make her own choices in life." He cut his eyes over to my mom. "In the vast scheme of things, you couldn't have chosen anyone more deserving of you."

My heart leapt into my throat. "You really mean that?"

Mom nodded. "Ty is everything we would want for you in a man."

I gave her a pointed look. "Even though he isn't from a society family and didn't graduate from an Ivy League school like Perry?"

Waving a dismissive hand, Mom replied, "What does all of that really matter in the end? I mean, the man took a bullet for you—two, in fact."

"Besides, Perry was a real prick," Dad chimed in.

My mouth gaped open. "Seriously, Dad?"

"Yes. I was never so grateful than when the two of you broke up."

With a roll of my eyes, I replied, "Glad you let me know."

"It would've been hard for me to give him my blessing, but I'll be happy to give it to Ty," Dad said.

Overcome with the roller coaster of emotions I'd been riding that day, I lunged at Dad. As I squeezed him tight, I murmured, "Thank you."

"You're welcome, CC."

After pulling away, I kissed his cheek, and he gave me a knowing look. "But just because I give him my blessing, that doesn't mean I'm not going to give him hell for going behind my back."

"Fine. Whatever you have to do to be the big bad president."

Dad chuckled. "It's good being the president."

At that moment, a doctor appeared in the doorway. After the Secret Service parted to allow him entry, he stepped into the waiting room. "He's starting to come around. I thought you might like to come back and wait with him."

I bolted out of my seat. "Yes. I would like that very much." Turning back to Mom and Dad, I said, "I'm sorry, but I have to go."

Mom's eyes got a little watery as she smiled. "I can't imagine anything better for him to wake up to than your face."

Swallowing the rising lump in my throat, I merely nodded. When my gaze bounced over to Dad, he jerked his chin at me. "Go take care of Ty. He sure as hell deserves a little TLC."

"Trust me, I'm going to give it to him!"

CHAPTER TWENTY-THREE

AS I DRIFTED in the shadowy world of unconsciousness, an incessant beeping slowly brought me awake. It was a mechanical noise, much like ones on alarms. Panic ricocheted through me that the beeping might be from a bomb. My eyes jolted open to survey my surroundings, but they were too blurry to focus. When I tried jerking my arms into a defensive stance, I realized they were tethered by something. *Holy shit. Have I been taken prisoner?* Blinking my eyes, I warily glanced around the room.

Oh shit. I wasn't a prisoner of a hostile foreign power, nor was there a bomb ticking down to detonation. No, I was stretched out in a hospital bed while a symphony of beeping machines echoed around me.

Although my mind swirled with questions about the hows and whys of me coming to be here, I could only focus on one thing—or I suppose I should say one *person.*

"Caroline?" I questioned.

A scuffling noise came from the right side of the bed. When I swiveled my head on the pillow, she scrambled out of the chair to come to my side. With a somewhat forced smile, she said, "Hey there."

I stared into her tear-stained face with her eyes radiating love. "You're so beautiful."

She hiccupped a laugh as tears overtook her cheeks. "You always say the sweetest things, even when you're laid up in the hospital."

"It doesn't matter where I am. It's the truth."

Bending over, she planted a tender kiss on my lips. "I love hearing it. Most of all, I love you."

In the shadowy realms of my mind, I vaguely remembered her calling out those words to me. It had somehow broken through the levels of pain and the loss of blood. As my eyes locked on hers, I said, "I love you, too." When her sapphire eyes flared at hearing the sentiment, I added, "It didn't take me getting shot to know that. I think I've loved you for a very long time."

"I feel the same way." Her brows furrowed. "How are you feeling? Are you in any pain?"

I shifted in the bed to survey my body's reactions, and an achiness radiating from my right ass cheek took me by surprise. "Is there any reason for my ass to be hurting?"

Caroline grinned. "You took a bullet there."

"I did?"

She nodded. "You were also hit in the side."

"How long have I been in here?"

"You were in surgery for just over two hours and then in recovery for the last three or so hours."

And she'd waited there for me. *Selfless. Beautiful. Lovely.*

Vaguely, I could remember the burning sensation on my ride side when I hurled myself in front of Caroline. "I'm so sorry."

"For what?"

"For the shooting."

Caroline's blue eyes bulged in horror. "You have nothing to be sorry about. If anyone should be sorry, it's me. You took a bullet for me —two bullets in fact."

I tried running one of my hands over my face but only managed to get the IV tubing tangled up. "But it was my fault in the first place."

"What are you talking about?"

"I didn't insist on a thorough security check of the shooter." A mixture of fury and regret rolled through my chest. "He was my age with a titanium leg. I didn't want to embarrass a fellow veteran by making him take off the leg, so after he was patted down, I waved him on through." An agonized sob tore through my chest when I thought of what could have happened because of my negligence. "He had to have used the leg to get the gun inside the bookstore."

Caroline reached out to tenderly cup my cheek. "It's not your fault, Ty. I'm sure he had planned on using his disability for sympathy all along."

After angrily swiping the tears from my cheeks, I said, "I plan to give my resignation to your father just as soon as I have the chance to see him."

"No. I won't let you do that," Caroline argued.

"It's not up to you. I'm not fit to protect anyone."

"But you protected me. Your actions *saved* my life."

"Yeah, and what if I'm not that lucky the next time?" I shook my head. "I won't risk anyone else's life."

Caroline placed both of her hands on my face. "You listen to me, Ty Fraser: you are *not* resigning from the Secret Service. You saved my life, and that can't be disputed by anyone. You weren't the only agent at the security checkpoint. The others could have easily asked the shooter to take off the leg. They aren't any more negligent than you are." When I opened my mouth to argue, she pressed her index finger over my lips. "Even though we don't have all the answers yet, you've said all along that the shooter was exceptionally smart to have eluded the Secret Service and FBI for so long. He momentarily outsmarted you all, but you still saved the day."

"There's going to be a firestorm when what went down hits the media."

She shrugged. "So let there be a firestorm."

With a groan, I rubbed my eyes. "It's not that simple, babe. There will be an investigation. I could be asked to resign."

"If that happens, you can just resign. Until then, you're not slinking off like you did something wrong. You're going to ride it all out. Got it?"

Jesus, she was relentless. Deep down, I knew she had a point. I needed to wait things out before I went off half-cocked, needed to follow the proper protocol and let the chips fall where they may. "Okay, I'll wait it out."

"Good. I'm glad you can finally see reason."

I grinned. "You drive a hard bargain."

"Oh, there is one more thing you should probably know."

"What's that?"

"My parents know about us."

"Fuck," I muttered. Although it should have been the least of my worries, my stomach churned at the news. In the last month since Caroline and I had started "dating", I'd probably written and rewritten the speech I planned to give him a million times. Since I wasn't known for my writing skills, it involved a lot of groveling.

"What did they say?"

"Mom was slightly pissed because we didn't come to her earlier, but she's rooting for us. Dad was—"

The door to my room blew open and all three of the Callahan men came storming through. "Fuck," I muttered again.

While Thorn and Barrett hovered by the bathroom, President Callahan marched right up to my bed. When I tried pushing myself up to face him, I winced and sucked in a breath from the pain.

"Don't be a hero, son. Press the pain button."

After huffing out a few breaths, I asked, "That's what you have to say to me after finding out I've been dating your daughter behind your back?"

President Callahan chuckled. "Of course that's not what I have to say. If you weren't lying there in a hospital bed wounded from protecting my daughter, I'd call you far worse than a sorry son of a bitch."

"Dad," Caroline warned.

"It's okay. I would have to agree with him," I replied.

She shook her head. "No, it's not okay. This is not the time or the place to do this."

"We're just talking," President Callahan countered.

Thorn nodded. "Dad's right. It's not like we're going to rough him up." He wagged his brows. "Yet."

"Exactly. What would be the point of beating the hell out of him when he is on pain medicine?" Barrett chimed in.

When I laughed, pain once again ricocheted through my ribcage. I knew it was time to take President Callahan's advice and press the button for more drugs. Before I could search for it in the bed, Caroline reached over and handed it to me. "Thanks."

"No problem."

After clicking the depressor, I waited for the liquid comfort to begin pumping through my IV. Once I had some relief, I looked at President Callahan. "As you were saying? I believe it was something about me being a sorry son of a bitch."

"I'll get back to all of that. I wanted to brief you on the shooter."

I nodded. "Yes, sir."

"His name is Vance Henderson, and he did two tours in the 6th Infantry Division."

"So he was telling the truth about his service and being wounded," I said, more for myself than for the others.

"Yes, he was. It appears after he lost his leg and was discharged, he started technical school to earn an IT degree."

"Which accounts for his use of technology." Furrowing my brows, I added, "But I would have pegged him as someone with a background in forensics."

"Apparently, his main hobby was watching crime shows. His computer search history shows countless hours of research on how to mask DNA and hide fingerprints."

"Now it makes sense. What about his work history? Had they noticed anything?"

"He worked as a driver for one of those ride-share companies, which enabled the flexibility in his schedule to travel as well as some anonymity."

Caroline glanced between her father and me. "While it sounds like the FBI has been putting the puzzle pieces together as to how he did it, do they have any idea about the why?"

"Yes, two of the top FBI profilers already sat down with him."

"And?"

President Callahan ran a hand over his face. "Apparently, you reminded him of an ex-girlfriend—a woman he wanted to marry, but who left him after he was injured."

Caroline gasped. "That's horrible."

James nodded. "He told the FBI he saw you at the grocery store here in DC, and at first, he thought you were his ex-girlfriend. Then when he found out who you were, he started following you. Then his hatred transformed because he felt you represented the unattainable female, the one he could never have because he was maimed."

Although we had the answers, it certainly did little to help my feelings. From the anguished look on Caroline's face, it didn't help her either. "It's okay, babe. They caught him. He cannot hurt you ever again."

"I know. It's just hard to hear."

"You're right. It is." I jerked my chin at her to come closer. "But I'm here."

Thorn snorted. "Seriously? You're lying in a hospital bed with gunshot wounds."

"No shit, Sherlock," I fired back.

Barrett chuckled. "You haven't lost your fire, huh?"

"Hell no, especially not when it comes to Caroline."

A strangled noise came from President Callahan's throat. "I think now would be a good time to get back to the sorry son of a bitch line."

"Yes, sir."

President Callahan narrowed his eyes at me. "You broke an oath, Ty. You swore it not just to me, but to this country."

"I know that, sir. I'm willing to take any and all the repercussions from the agency for my actions. Most of all, I'm willing to take them from all of you." I sucked in a breath as I shifted in the bed. "I never meant to fall in love with Caroline. It came on so gradually until one day it just hit me like eighteen-wheeler. I didn't want to disrespect any of you, but most of all, I couldn't disrespect myself by denying my feelings." I shifted my gaze over to Caroline. "Nor could I deny her. I don't think there's anything I could ever deny her. I love her too much."

Proving she had the biggest balls in the room, Caroline bent over my bed to kiss me square on the lips. Both Barrett and Thorn groaned while President Callahan merely shook his head.

"And I love you," Caroline said.

After she pulled away, she shot her father and brothers a triumphant look. Oh yeah, she had brass balls all right. Mine, on the other hand, were still shrunken from the arrival of the Callahan men, although looking at Barrett and Thorn, I didn't see censure. We'd all been through hell together in various forms, and I knew they'd felt confident with me by her side. With all this, though, it was hard to say.

James shoved his hands into the pockets of his pants. "Obviously, my daughter has a mind of her own when it comes to this matter. However, I would like to speak my piece."

"Yes, sir. Please do."

"It has to be acknowledged that my reaction is tempered considering the events that transpired today."

"That's completely understandable, sir."

"On the way over here, all I could think of was how close I came to losing my only daughter today. From time to time, I would focus on the video I saw of her shouting that she loved you. At times, I would get furious with you for what I perceived as overstepping your position, but then I thought of how hard I pushed you into the position to start with. Perhaps I was allowing the fates to align in a way I hadn't previously foreseen." James pulled a hand out of his pocket to point a finger at me. "I know you're a man of honor, and you would never, ever take advantage of my daughter. I further know you wouldn't do anything to hurt her. That is very evident in the fact that you took two bullets to save her."

"I would hope to never do anything to hurt Caroline, sir. However, I would point out that as a man, I'm sure I'll make mistakes. I'll do things that infuriate her. I'll get exasperated with her, but I'll never willingly hurt her, nor will I allow anyone else to hurt her."

President Callahan nodded. "You're a good man, Ty, one I'm more than happy to have dating my daughter."

My brows shot up. "So, we're good?"

"Of course we are."

I glanced around him to peer at Barrett and Thorn. "What about you two knuckleheads? Are we good?"

Barrett took a step closer to the bed. "Look, I'm still mad as hell you were sneaking around and didn't think you could tell me. After all, you've guarded my most important secrets."

"I'll take them to my grave," I replied with a smile.

"I appreciate that." He chuckled. "Now that I've had some time to cool down, I guess I understand your reasons. In the end, I can't imagine anyone I'd rather have dating my sister than you."

"Thanks. That means a lot." My gaze bounced over to Thorn's. "What about you?"

"Considering we all know how much I loathed Perry, I would have to say you are a welcome improvement," he said.

"High praise indeed," I mused while Caroline rolled her eyes.

Thorn laughed. "Truth is, man, you're already my family. Like Barrett said, I couldn't imagine anyone I'd else I'd want for Caroline than the man who willingly took a bullet for her."

Although I was touched by his words, I couldn't help teasingly adding, "Two—I took two bullets for her."

Barrett shook his head. "We haven't forgotten. We're just trying to let you save face since you took one in the ass."

"Hey, taking a bullet in the ass doesn't demean my heroics," I protested.

"Maybe a little?" Thorn suggested.

"Whatever."

"All right, you two. That's enough. I think we should probably let Ty get some rest."

It was as if President Callahan had a key into my psyche because I was starting to feel a little woozy from the drugs.

"You take it easy, man," Barrett said as we did a bro handshake.

"I'm going to try."

"Anything you need, just let us know," Thorn added as he gently touched my shoulder.

"I'm good, but thanks for the offer."

James turned from his sons to Caroline. "I suppose I couldn't convince you to come back to the White House with me to rest?"

She shook her head vehemently from side to side. "I'm staying right here with him."

President Callahan sighed. "I expected as much. I'll instruct them to have a rollaway bed brought up as soon as possible." He pointed a finger at Caroline. "I expect you to get some rest, young lady."

I nodded. "I want you to lie down for a while as well."

Caroline held up her hands. "Okay, okay. There's no need to double-team me. I'll lie down."

"Good. There will be a member of both my security team and yours stationed at the door."

"Is that really necessary?"

"From all that we know, Henderson acted alone, but I'm not taking any chances. They will remain as a precaution," President Callahan replied.

In a way, I was grateful for that. I knew in spite of my drugged state, I would remain on edge if I felt Caroline was in any danger. This way I knew she was well taken care of.

After Caroline exchanged hugs with her father and brothers, we were once again alone. "That was . . . intense," I remarked.

She grinned. "At least it had a happy ending."

"That's true. It could have gone a completely different way."

Caroline eased down on the side of the bed. "You should get some sleep."

"I'm not that tired," I replied, but the giant yawn I emitted betrayed me.

"Just close your eyes. I'll be right here. I'm safe, and you're safe."

"You don't know how grateful I am to hear you say that."

Dipping her head, she brought her lips to mine. "I love you," she murmured against my mouth.

"I love you more."

The sweet sound of her laughter was the last thing I heard as I drifted off to sleep.

TY

Eighteen months later

As I stood at the altar of St. Patrick's cathedral, I fiddled with my brand-new pair of gold cufflinks. I wasn't exactly the cufflink type of guy, but they'd been a gift from Caroline. She'd even had them engraved with my initials. It didn't escape my notice that her father and brothers each had a similar pair, and it appeared to be her way of symbolically saying I was officially part of the Callahan family.

Shifting on my feet, I fought the urge to dab the sweat beading along my forehead. To say I was nervous would have been an under-statement. When I glanced beside me at Caroline, her beautiful face spread into a reassuring smile. "I love you," she mouthed.

"I love you, too," I whispered back.

When the priest cleared his throat, my attention snapped from Caroline to him. "Today is a momentous day of joy in the Callahan family. We come together to dedicate the life of its newest member and child of God." He nodded at Thorn and Isabel. "Parents, what name do you give this child?"

While Thorn was too choked up to speak, Isabel said, "James Thornton Callahan IV." With a grin, she added, "or JT."

I really had you going there for a minute, didn't I? You thought I was about to tie the knot with Caroline. I know, I'm a cheeky bastard for leading you on like that. While a year had passed since I'd been shot, I hadn't popped the question yet.

Yet being the operative word.

At first, I had wanted to give both of us time for our emotional wounds to heal. I didn't want an engagement born of tragedy or immersed in PTSD. I wanted to be physically and emotionally healed, and I wanted the same for Caroline as well. We both continued with our private therapists, and then we entered couples counseling as a precautionary measure.

There was also the fact that I didn't want to steal the thunder around the time of Thorn and Isabel's wedding. After seeing how precarious life could be with the shooting, they'd pulled together an East Room wedding in less than three months. With two White House weddings within a year and a half, the country was completely enamored with the Callahan brides and grooms. Naturally, the attention then shifted to Caroline and me.

To say we'd become an instant media obsession would be an understatement. When Susan Ford had fallen in love with one of her father's Secret Service agents, Charles Vance, the internet hadn't existed. We, however, became a stateside version of Harry and Megan. We'd given our official story to *People Magazine* while other tabloids had spun their own tales. I enjoyed the one that claimed President Callahan had to be restrained by his Secret Service team so he wouldn't fight me for dating his daughter in secret.

For a few months, everywhere we went, there were cameras snapping photos of our every move. Our relationship was coined a modern day fairy tale. I was the heroic knight who had saved the damsel in distress—the media's words, not mine. I sure as hell would never have described myself as a knight, least of all Caroline as a damsel in distress. They would have retracted that description if they'd ever seen her Krav Maga moves.

Eventually, things started looking on track for a proposal. Sure, we hadn't been dating that long, but after you've gone through what we had, time isn't the marker you go by to measure the depth of your feelings. Of course, one could argue we'd already passed one of the tests of a relationship—we'd lived together. After the shooting, we just kept on living together. It made both of us feel safer, made it feel real. We were a couple, not an agent and target.

While we had won over the Callahan family, there was still my family to contend with. Taking Read 4 Life abroad for a month, Caroline and I stayed in the East End with my parents. I had to give her credit for how well she acclimated to my crazy family. She didn't even seem remotely overwhelmed when all my brothers and their families came over. They instantly fell in love with my "Yank girlfriend", as they teasingly called her. I knew I had their blessing to propose, but my concern was with President Callahan.

When we returned to the States, I bought a ring and made an appointment to see President Callahan. I know most men are nervous to ask their future father-in-law for their daughter's hand, but it was even more nerve-racking when you had to be fit in during security briefings on the Middle East.

In true James Callahan style, the moment I walked through the door, a megawatt smile lit up his face. "Yes, you have my permission to marry Caroline."

"Forgive me, sir, but you don't know what I came to ask you."

He rolled his eyes at me. "Ty, you made an appointment to see me. I'm pretty sure most of the West Wing knows you came to ask me to marry Caroline."

With a grimace, I replied, "Do you think they'll let on?"

James winked. "It's the White House—I'm pretty sure they can keep a secret."

What the two of us didn't know was there were two other Callahans harboring a secret, ones that would change my plan yet again. When Thorn and Isabel announced they were having a baby, I was so chuffed for my buddy I couldn't do anything to steal his thunder.

Just when the fates aligned yet again, Vance Henderson's trial began. Once again, we were thrust back into the nightmare of the shooting. Instead of going through the agony of facing Vance in court, Caroline was thankfully given the option to testify via video-taped deposition. I refused the option. I wanted to face down the mother-fucker in court. If I'd had my way, I would've thrown myself across the witness table and beat the hell out of him. Considering the security in the courtroom was Fort Knox level, I knew I wouldn't have the option.

He was found guilty of Caroline's attempted murder and would be reprimanded to a state mental health facility for at least fifteen years before he would be eligible for release. While we would have preferred life, Caroline wasn't actually a sitting president like with Reagan and Ford's assassination attempts. Hopefully, Henderson's state of mind would be in an entirely different place once he got adequate help.

It took a few months to get over the mental anguish of the trial. With JT's birth, I felt the time was finally right. I'd decided barring everything but Armageddon, I was proposing. I was done trying to find the perfect or right time. I was wanted Caroline to be my fiancée.

The priest turned his attention to Caroline and me. "Godparents, are you willing and able to fulfill your duties to bring up this child in the Christian faith?"

Nodding emphatically, Caroline said, "I am."

Of course, she would be completely at ease with being a godmother. Her ability to lead and give to others were two of the traits I admired most about her. After JT's birth, she insisted on flying to New York every other weekend so she could get in adequate snuggle time with him. Of course, that also meant my ass was in the seat next to her.

Glancing from Caroline to me, the priest shifted his glasses back up his nose as he waited for my response. "I am," I replied as determinedly as possible.

Although I wasn't as confident in my ability to be of spiritual guidance for JT, I was honored that Thorn and Isabel wanted me to be his godfather, especially considering I wasn't his brother and Barrett was. I soon learned that, always the peacemaker, Thorn had found a way to give everyone a role in his son's life: Barrett and Addison would be JT's guardians if God forbid anything happened to Thorn and Isabel.

I'd never imagined the course my life would take over the last year, and that didn't include me getting shot. There really was no place for me in the Secret Service after the world learned of Caroline's and my relationship. Regardless of who I was reassigned to protect, it seemed like a conflict of interest, not to mention if I went back to working for Thorn, Caroline and I would be conducting a long-distance relationship with her in Charleston and me in New York.

In the end, I realized it was time to leave the agency, so I reluctantly resigned and began working as a consultant for security companies. Then a side job came along that I never could have imagined before I met Caroline. With her encouragement and co-writing skills, I penned a series about Thorn's PTSD dog, Conan. In *Conan Joins the Army* and *Conan Goes to War*, I worked through a lot of my own issues as well as some of those shared with me.

With Conan in tow, I then started doing speaking engagements at local elementary and middle and high schools around West Virginia. In the last month, I'd had requests from schools all over the country. I couldn't help but joke that they really just wanted to hear my British accent.

Once again, my calling to help others had found its place. I'd been a soldier, bodyguard, and Secret Service Agent. Now it was time to try out the role of nurturer, and hopefully husband followed by father.

Which brings me back to the moment at the baptism. A snoozing JT had been passed into Caroline's arms for the celebration of the sacrament. I placed my hand on his tiny shoulder as the priest poured the water over his head three times. Startled, he popped an eye open to stare at the priest, but instead of wailing about his disrupted sleep, he merely flicked his tongue out and looked around.

With the baptism over, Caroline handed JT back to Isabel. The rest of the Callahan family, along with Isabel's parents and sister from Georgia, left their seats in the first pew to come to the altar. As I stood there with her along with her family, I couldn't help feeling slightly reborn by knowing them. I'd certainly found a happiness I hadn't known existed, both personally and professionally. I knew they would always be there for me through thick and thin—they'd certainly already proved that when I'd gotten shot.

I'd grown up thinking family meant blood and blood alone. Then serving in the British Army, I discovered that the definition of family could be stretched to include brothers in arms. Men and women who fought alongside you in battle very quickly became important people you would stand by forever. My life hadn't been bereft of family or defined by a sense of not belonging prior to meeting Caroline. In fact, even though my brothers had married women I adored, I hadn't realized I lacked that connection, that . . . completion, but now I got it. With her, I had the whole world.

After we got back to the White House, a lunch in JT's honor was served in the Family Dining Room. Isabel had stripped JT out of the lacy Callahan baptism gown and put him in a red onesie that said First Grandson. We raised a glass of celebratory champagne in his honor before digging into a three-course meal.

Once dessert was finished and we were about to adjourn upstairs to the residence, I once again took Caroline's hand. "Come on, let's get some fresh air."

She gave me a funny look. "Um, okay."

I led her out of the room. Nearly two years earlier, I'd followed the same path after she'd fled from the family meeting about me taking over as her agent. That night she'd escaped the dining room and gone out to the balcony of the South Portico.

As we stared out at the Washington Monument, Caroline leaned her elbows on the railing, and I tried hard not to have a nervous breakdown. With a dreamy smile, she said, "What a perfect day for a baptism."

"It sure is."

"JT was such a good boy. Isabel was so afraid he was going to scream and act like a spawn of Satan."

I laughed. Actually, I laughed a little maniacally because of my nerves.

Caroline cut her eyes over to me. "Are you okay?"

"Uh, I'm fine."

"You're acting weird."

Shit. My nerves were ruining everything. So much for waiting for the perfect time considering I was going to blow it all there at the finishing line. "Okay, I'm just going to go ahead and say it before I do something really stupid like run down the stairs screaming."

Caroline blinked at me. "What?" As I began dipping down onto one knee, her hands flew to her mouth. "Oh. My. God!" she shrieked.

"Apparently, you know where this is going," I teased.

"I hope I do." She frantically shook her head. "I swear, if you've led me on and you're just tying your shoe, I'm going to pull out some old Krav Maga moves on you."

With a chuckle, I replied, "That won't be necessary." After I pulled the ring out of my coat pocket, I held it up to her. "Caroline Callahan, would you make me the happiest man both here and across the pond by marrying me?"

Tears pooled in her eyes. "Yes, Ty, I would *love* to marry you."

Before I could get back up, Caroline launched herself at me. "Oomph," I muttered before the two of us went over in a pile of arms and legs onto the marble floor. "Fuck!" I shouted when my old arse wound reared its head.

"I'm sorry. Did I hurt your ass?"

I rolled my eyes. "I can't believe we're talking about my arse at a moment like this."

She giggled. "I can. This is us, babe—the good, the bad, and the ass wound."

Before I could protest that I didn't want my wound ruining my proposal, Caroline brought her gorgeous mouth to mine. I never grew tired of the feel of her smooth, velvet lips, and I was sure I would live a lifetime without it ever growing old.

When she finally pulled away, we panted to catch our breath. "You can't imagine how long I've waited to ask you that question," I said.

"Probably as long as I've been waiting for you to ask me."

"Every time I thought I'd found the perfect moment, something happened to derail it."

Her lips quirked up. "So, you decided JT's baptism was the perfect moment?"

"Not exactly. I've thought of a million different ways in which I could ask you this, hundreds of ways to be flashy, like taking you to exotic locations, but none of those felt right. Maybe it's because we're not flashy people."

Her chest heaved. "No, we're not."

"In the end, I kept coming back to the White House. Without it, we would have never truly come together. Without your father becoming president, I would have just remained Barrett's bodyguard. Thorn would have never needed a Secret Service agent, so we would have continued to revolve in each other's orbit, but it wouldn't have been the same."

Tears shimmered in her eyes. "Oh Ty, this is the perfect place."

"I know you're young, and in a way, it's wrong of me to want to tie you down in marriage."

"There's no one I would rather tie me down than you." She bent over to kiss me again. "Besides, we've been living together the last eighteen months—what could be so much different about marriage?"

I grinned at her. "Call me a selfish bastard, because I do want you to wear my ring and have my name—unless you want to keep yours, which I would totally be fine with."

Caroline smiled. "I'd be honored to take your name."

"I don't want to be a caveman, but that makes me so fucking happy."

To show her just how happy she made me, I cupped her head in my hands and brought her in for a kiss. Before my lips could meet hers, a throat cleared behind us. "Are you two okay?"

While I fully expected it to be a Secret Service agent posing the question, shock flooded me at the sight of President Callahan standing in the doorway. *SHIT* flashed like neon in my mind. I gripped Caroline's hips and prepared to push her off me, but she wasn't having any of it.

With a beaming grin, she flashed her hand at her father. "I'm engaged."

President Callahan smiled. "I can see that. I can also say it's about time."

Caroline dropped her gaze from her father to me. "He knew about this?"

I nodded. "I went to him to ask for your hand."

James chuckled. "Yeah, that was forever ago. Has it been a year?"

"Almost. Thorn and Isabel were just about to announce they were three months pregnant."

Gasping, Caroline asked, "You've known all this time you wanted to marry me?"

"I think I've known since the movie night when that wanker broke up with you." Tilting my head, I added, "Maybe even when I saw your Krav Maga skills."

She laughed. "If I really think about it, it's probably been that long for me as well—at least since I knew I loved you."

Before we kissed again, President Callahan coughed. "Why don't you two come on upstairs and share the happy news with everyone else?"

"It won't take away from JT's day?" I asked.

"Considering he's sleeping off a milk coma in one of the guest bedrooms, I don't think he'll mind." With a wink, James added, "Besides, it would be a pity to let the champagne I just ordered go to waste."

"You ordered champagne for us?"

He grinned. "Let's just say I had a hunch when you two disappeared."

"What if we had been sneaking off to have some alone time together?" Caroline suggested, which caused both her father and me to groan.

James shook his head. "Sometimes when you open your mouth, it's Barrett coming out and not you."

"You're so right," I agreed.

Caroline only giggled. "Sorry, I couldn't resist."

"Come on, Miss Inappropriate, let's get up," I suggested.

After I helped Caroline off of me, I rose to my feet. When we followed James through the door, a chorus of "CONGRATULA-TIONS!" rang out in the hallway. Standing in front of us were all of the Callahan family members, along with Stuart.

"Wait, I thought you said you ordered champagne upstairs," I said to James.

"Actually, we all stayed down here except Isabel, who went to get JT to sleep."

My eyes bulged. "You mean you were all creeping at the windows?"

"I wouldn't call it creeping. It was more selective watching," Barrett replied with a grin.

Tears sparkled in Jane's eyes. "That was the sweetest thing I've ever seen."

Addison bobbed her head in agreement. "So romantic."

"I'm not a romantic, but I have to admit you did good, man. You could tell it was all from the heart," Thorn stated.

"Thank you, guys."

President Callahan took a champagne flute off one of the trays. "If everyone would take some bubbly, I'd like to raise a toast to Ty and Caroline." Once everyone had their glasses, he nodded. "In my wildest dreams, I never would have imagined a romance blossoming when I asked Ty to protect Caroline. Very few fathers find a man they deem worthy of their daughters. All these years there has never been one to come along who I thought was even halfway good enough for my sweet Caroline." His got a bit choked up, causing Caroline to begin to sniffle. "But sometimes life throws you a curveball and sends hope in the form of someone unexpected. Many men will tell their future father-in-law-they would die for their daughters. I have the mixed blessing of knowing that is the truth. Ty, I couldn't imagine any man being worthier of my daughter's hand than you are."

Now it was my turn to get choked up. "Thank you, sir."

Barrett held his phone out to me. "Speech time, buddy. We've got your parents on Skype."

"Seriously?" I peered at the screen to see my parents' grinning faces.

"Make a speech, son!" Dad called.

"Um, wow. Okay, this is all very unexpected. I only imagined saying things in front of Caroline." I winked at the phone. "But I can't be outdone by a Yank, right, Pop?"

"Exactly."

As the others chuckled around me, I smiled at Caroline. "It's me who is honored to be loved by Caroline. Since I've been stateside, the Callahan family has been a part of my life. You've employed me and treated me like I was one of your own. I never intended to fall in love with Caroline, but there's no one else I'd rather spend the rest of my life with or take a bullet for."

Swiping her eyes, Caroline replied, "*Two* bullets. You took two for me."

I laughed. "That's right. Now even I'm forgetting."

"Don't worry, we won't let you," Thorn replied with a smile.

"Thanks, bro." I peered at the phone again. "How'd I do, Mum?"

With her handkerchief in front of her face, she blubbered, "Beautiful, my love."

President Callahan thrust his arm into the air. "To Ty and Caroline!" he proclaimed.

"To Ty and Caroline," the others echoed around the room.

After clinking our flutes together, Caroline and I sealed the toast with a kiss rather than a sip of bubbly. As applause rang out around us, I couldn't keep the cheesy smile off my face. Who would have thought taking the job as Caroline's temporary roommate would have resulted in a roommate for life?

ABOUT THE AUTHOR

CONNECT WITH KATIE

→ NEWSLETTER: https://bit.ly/2BHeOyI.

→ FACEBOOK READER GROUP (ASHLEY'S ANGELS): face-book.com/groups/ashleyangels

→ WEBSITE: www.katieashleybooks.com

→INSTAGRAM: Instagram.com/katieashleyluv

→ TWITTER: twitter.com/katieashleyluv

→ PINTEREST: pinterest.com/katieashleyluv

→ Amazon: https://amzn.to/2ExxoLf

Katie Ashley is a New York Times, USA Today, and Amazon Top Five Best-Selling author of both Indie and Traditionally published books. She's written rockers, bikers, manwhores with hearts of gold, New Adult, and Young Adult. She lives outside of Atlanta, Georgia with her daughter, Olivia, her Heeler-Mix, Belle, her Black Lab mix, Elsa, her cat, Harry Potter, and a Betta fish, Blue. She has a slight obsession with Pinterest, The Golden Girls, Shakespeare, Harry Potter, and Star Wars.

With a BA in English, a BS in Secondary English Education, and a Masters in Adolescent English Education, she spent eleven years teaching both middle and high school English, as well as a few adjunct college English classes. As of January 2013, she became a full-time writer.

Although she is a life-long Georgia peach, she loves traveling the country and world meeting readers. Most days, you can find her being a hermit, styling leggings, and binging on Netflix whenever her tdaughter isn't monopolizing the TV with Paw Patrol or Frozen.

Made in the USA
San Bernardino, CA
23 January 2019